A COWBOY'S FIRST LOVE

"Chase came up with it," Ry said. "He even created some kind of shared document where we can all upload our opinions about each horse, and then add to it when we get feedback from the guests."

"He's a smart guy."

"Chase? Supersmart and super rich."

Avery looked up at him, the horse forgotten. "Do you wish you'd gone to college like he did?"

"Nope. Not my thing." He smiled down at her. "How about you?"

"I had a rodeo scholarship to a place in Texas, but obviously I couldn't go."

"That sucks." He kissed her nose and then, more gently, her mouth.

She gave a quivery sigh and he kissed her again, licking the seam of her lips until she opened her mouth to him. He dove in, seeking her warmth, pressing her closer to him as he explored and luxuriated in her unique taste.

His hat fell off as she shoved a hand into his hair, scraping her nails against his scalp, making him arch his back and purr . . .

Books by Kate Pearce

The House of Pleasure Series
SIMPLY SEXUAL
SIMPLY SINFUL
SIMPLY SHAMELESS
SIMPLY WICKED
SIMPLY INSATIABLE
SIMPLY FORBIDDEN
SIMPLY CARNAL
SIMPLY VORACIOUS
SIMPLY SCANDALOUS
SIMPLY PLEASURE (e-novella)
SIMPLY IRRESISTIBLE (e-novella)

The Sinners Club Series
THE SINNERS CLUB
TEMPTING A SINNER
MASTERING A SINNER
THE FIRST SINNERS (e-novella)

Single Titles
RAW DESIRE

The Morgan Brothers Ranch
THE RELUCTANT COWBOY
THE MAVERICK COWBOY
THE LAST GOOD COWBOY

Anthologies
SOME LIKE IT ROUGH
LORDS OF PASSION
HAPPY IS THE BRIDE

Published by Kensington Publishing Corporation

THE
LAST GOOD
COWBOY

KATE
PEARCE

ZEBRA BOOKS
KENSINGTON PUBLISHING CORP.
http://www.kensingtonbooks.com

ZEBRA BOOKS are published by

Kensington Publishing Corp.
119 West 40th Street
New York, NY 10018

Copyright © 2017 by Kate Pearce

All Kensington titles, imprints, and distributed lines are available at special quantity discounts for bulk purchases for sales promotion, premiums, fund-raising, educational, or institutional use.

Special book excerpts or customized printings can also be created to fit specific needs. For details, write or phone the office of the Kensington Sales Manager: Attn.: Sales Department. Kensington Publishing Corp., 119 West 40th Street, New York, NY 10018. Phone: 1-800-221-2647.

Zebra and the Z logo Reg. U.S. Pat. & TM Off.

First Printing: May 2017
ISBN-13: 978-1-4201-4004-0
ISBN-10: 1-4201-4004-3

eISBN-13: 978-1-4201-4005-7
eISBN-10: 1-4201-4005-1

10 9 8 7 6 5 4 3 2 1

Printed in the United States of America

Chapter One

Sacramento, California

Before he even left the parking lot Ry Morgan heard the bass booming through the walls, and the sound of heavy partying from the third-floor apartment. When he turned the corner, he almost walked into a squad car flashing blue lights, and a small crowd of agitated neighbors gathered around the door.

"Hell, not again," he breathed as one of the helpful neighbors pointed him out to the cop.

He held his ground as she came toward him and the noise from above suddenly shut off.

"Can I help you, Officer?"

She jabbed her thumb in the direction of the apartment block. "You live here?"

"I used to. I just stopped by to pick up my stuff."

"Are you HW Morgan?"

"Nope, I'm his brother Ry."

"You sure about that?"

Used to being mistaken for his identical twin, he

cautiously reached inside his jacket, took out his wallet, and handed over his driver's license.

"Thanks." She studied it, made the usual face at his given name, and then handed it back. "Have you seen your brother recently?"

"Not for about three weeks. What's up?"

He asked even though it was obvious. The last time HW had thrown a party the police had been called. Maybe HW had learned something by not sticking around long enough to get caught in the aftermath. Ry's gut tightened.

"Is it okay to go up there? I just want to get my stuff and head out again in the morning."

"Wise decision." The officer looked at him steadily. "Maybe you can make sure the party doesn't start again."

"I'll do my best." He tipped his Stetson to her. "Thanks."

"And tell your brother that if he keeps this up, he'll be spending the rest of his evening with the Sacramento Police Department."

Ry nodded as he turned away and headed for the front entrance of the building. A police officer was escorting a group of partygoers down the stairs. There were others emerging from the two elevators, still complaining loudly about the abrupt end to their evening. Ry ignored them all. They weren't his kind of people. They stunk of booze, cheap perfume, and other substances he hoped the police hadn't noticed.

Wearily, he climbed the stairs, spoke to the building security guy who had lingered on the landing to make sure everyone had left, and went inside.

The place was a mess. He shut the door and leaned against it, letting his backpack slide to the floor.

"Well, look who's turned up."

He raised his head to see Lally Goldstein glaring at him from his brother's bedroom doorway. She wore a halter top, which had silver spangled bits on it, and tiny blue shorts. Her blond hair was piled up on top of her head in a messy ponytail.

"You still here?" Ry asked. "I thought the cops cleared everyone out."

"I live here now."

"First I've heard about it."

She tossed her head. "You left. Someone had to look after your brother."

"HW knew where I was." He glanced around the wrecked apartment. "Where is he, by the way?"

"What's it to you?"

Ry didn't even bother to answer that, and stared her down. Eventually she gave an elaborate sigh. "He should be back soon. Paul and Araz took him down the stairs when the cops turned up."

"Protecting their assets, right?"

She crossed her arms over her chest, making her fake boobs jut out. "They've done more for him than you ever did—bringing him down, making him feel bad about himself—having to hold himself back for *years* because he felt sorry for you not being as good a rider as he was."

"Yeah?" Ry wanted to turn around and walk away from all the shit that was coming out of her mouth, but he refused to leave first. He hoisted his backpack onto his shoulder. "I'm going to bed."

"You can't—"

He spun around so fast she took a step back. "HW

and I rent this place. Until I hear differently, I'm going to bed."

He unlocked the padlock he'd installed on his bedroom door, and went inside. Nothing looked as if it had been touched, which made a change. His twin tended to think that what was Ry's was his, but not vice versa. Not that Ry wanted anything his brother had.

With a groan he placed his hat on the desk and shoved a hand through his short blond hair. His stomach growled, but he wasn't going out there again to face Lally. If HW came back he could knock on the door, and be polite. Maybe Ry would talk to him.

Maybe.

He stripped off his shirt and jeans, and took a quick shower in the tiny bathroom attached to his bedroom. There was no more partying, but whether HW would come back Ry no longer knew. Sometimes his twin would stay away for days and return so shit-faced he'd sleep for a week and be as grumpy as hell if Ry tried to talk to him about anything.

He wasn't sure he cared anymore. Hunkering down on the rug beside his bed, he delved into his backpack, where his grandma Ruth had deposited enough food to feed an army. Just the thought of her lightened Ry's dark mood and gave him strength. He pictured his family at the ranch—his older brothers, Chase and Blue, and his father, Billy. They liked him for who he was. They *loved* him.

A knock on the door made him go still.

"Ry? You in there?"

He took out the bundle of food and placed it on the desk before slowly turning to the door and opening it. His twin stood there grinning like a loon and swaying slightly in his fancy cowboy boots. They were identical, so it was like looking at a drunk version of himself.

"Dude! You're back!"

Ry stepped aside and let HW in.

"Something smells good. Did you bring stuff back from the ranch?" HW wandered over to the desk and went to grab the container of food. Ry, who was stone cold sober, moved faster and blocked his twin's hand.

"What do you want, HW?"

His brother blinked big golden eyes at him. "That's harsh, Ry. What the hell is wrong with you?"

Ry leaned against the edge of the desk, folded his arms over his chest, and repeated, "What do you want?"

HW retreated to the bed and sank down on it, his expression disgruntled. "Some of Ruth's good cooking, but it looks like you've decided to hog it all for yourself."

"I'll gladly share the food with you after you've told me what's going on."

"You mean about the party?" HW hiccuped a laugh. "That was so sick, man. Those cops have no sense of humor."

"Those cops told me to tell you that if you host a party again they'll be taking you in and charging you."

"Not unless they catch me first."

"I think they'll manage it, especially if you keep drinking."

HW sighed. "Gawd, when did you become such a

boring Dudley Do-Right, bro? I'm just having some fun."

"Yeah." Ry studied his twin. HW's pupils were too wide, his eyes were bloodshot, and his whole body was shaking. "You should go to bed. I'll talk to you in the morning, okay?"

"What's wrong with talking now?"

"Because you're too drunk, or high, or whatever the stimulant of the day is, to talk much sense."

HW rose unsteadily to his feet. "Don't preach at me."

Ry set his jaw. "I'm tired. I've got a lot to do tomorrow."

His twin took three lurching steps forward that brought him right in Ry's face. "Screw you. Talk to me about wussing out on me."

Ry straightened, almost overbalancing his twin. "I am not talking to a belligerent drunk! Get out of my space, or I'll be the one calling the cops."

For one frozen second, Ry couldn't believe what he'd said, and then he realized he meant every word.

"Get out, HW. I'll speak to you in the morning."

His twin mumbled something obscene and stumbled away, slamming the bedroom door behind him. In the stillness Ry waited until he heard his brother's girlfriend start in on him, and then there was comparative silence. He slowly let out his breath.

No regrets. He'd promised himself that he'd make a clean break, so tomorrow he'd tell HW what was happening, and leave. His hand clenched into a fist, and he sat down heavily on the desk chair. Now all he had to do was follow through with his plan, and this time make sure he stuck the landing.

It was almost eleven in the morning, and Ry had made good inroads into packing up the stuff in his bedroom. He had to fit everything in his old pickup truck, and was determined to make only one trip. He'd already decided not to take any of the furniture—most of it had come with the apartment anyway, or had been chosen by HW.

He stuffed four pairs of socks in his open duffel bag. Chase had offered him his pick of the ranch land to build his own place on, which was kind of cool. Not that he needed all that space yet, but it was good to dream.

"Ry, what the hell are you doing?"

He turned to see HW propping up the doorway wearing nothing but a pair of boxers that barely hung onto his narrow hips. He was also shading his eyes against the glare of the sun.

"I'm packing my stuff."

"What the heck for?"

Ry looked his twin right in the eye. "Because I'm leaving."

HW frowned. "We always fight, bro. You know I don't mean anything. That's just the way we are."

"No, it's the way we've become. I don't like it, HW, and I'm not going to play that game anymore."

"So, what? You're walking out on me?"

"I barely see you these days. You're either training, going to extra events, or"—Ry paused—"doing other stuff I don't enjoy."

"I've been working my ass off to qualify for the national finals, you *know* that."

"Yeah. I really hope you'll get there."

"But you're sulking because I haven't been spending enough time with you? Hell, Ry, that's half your problem. If you don't train hard and compete often, you won't qualify."

"I get that."

"So don't blame me if you haven't been dedicated enough to achieve what I have."

"I don't." Ry added another drawerful of underwear to the bag. "I'm just not cut out for this life."

HW sat on the bed, his bloodshot gaze fixed on the filled and labeled boxes. "We're identical twins. If I can do it, you can."

"But, maybe I don't want to."

"So you're going to disappear, and leave me here by myself?"

Ry faked a smile. "You're hardly by yourself. You've got Lally all moved in, a great snake of an agent, and a promotional exec hanging around to protect your ass."

"But they're not you."

Ry zipped up the bag and sat on the chair by the desk, swiveling to face his brother. "You'll be fine."

"Where are you going?"

"Back to the ranch."

"For good?" HW frowned. "You're seriously not coming back?"

"Nope."

He scratched his unshaven jaw. "We said we'd never do that."

"Things change. Chase is not as bad as BB painted

him—hell, even BB agrees he was wrong, and that's saying something."

"But we've always been together."

Ry took a deep breath. "Yeah, I know."

"You and me against the world."

"As I said, things change. You're going forward into a successful career riding saddle broncs, and I'm . . ."

"Yeah, what exactly *are* you going to do, stuck in the middle of nowhere?"

"Help Chase and Blue rebuild the ranch and make it into something special. I might not be a great rodeo guy, but I'm a damned good hand."

"Help *them*? What about me?"

"I don't think you need me at the moment, bro," Ry said as gently as he could. "You're doing great."

HW shot to his feet and took a short turn around the room. "This is because I've done better than you—isn't it? Lally said you were jealous, but I didn't believe her. But now? Maybe she was right all along."

Ry stood as well. It felt like his heart was actually trying to punch its way out of his chest. "Maybe I just want different things in my life right now."

"Because you're not good enough to have what I have?"

There was a combative note in HW's voice Ry had learned to dread. "I'm not as good a rider as you are. I never will be."

"True, but only because you won't take it seriously."

"Which is the whole point, HW. Can't you at least see that? I don't care about winning as much as you do. I just don't."

"Because you know you can't beat me." HW came closer. "Admit it."

"Sure, if it makes you happy." Ry shrugged. He really didn't need to argue about something that meant so little to him. They weren't in high school anymore. Sometimes HW seemed to forget that. "It doesn't change the fact that I'm leaving."

"Abandoning me right when I need you most."

Ry blinked. "*What*?"

"That's why you're doing it now, isn't it?" HW nodded. "Yeah, you're probably hoping I'll fail when you aren't around."

His twin was probably the only person on earth who knew Ry had a temper and exactly how to make him lose it.

"That's utter *bullshit*, and you know it. I'm leaving because you have surrounded yourself with a group of people I despise, *okay*? Is that straight enough talk for you?"

HW swung around and poked a finger way too close to Ry's face. "Those people are looking out for me, and my career. They *care* about me. You're just pulling this stunt because you're jealous."

"You've been talking to Lally too much. You're my *twin*. I've spent my whole life supporting you. Trouble is, you're not interested in what I have to say anymore, and that's fine because, trust me, I'm sick and tired of saying it."

HW took a step back and a deep, shuddering breath. "Look. At least stay until I find out whether I qualify or not."

"I can't. I promised Chase I'd be back this week."

"You promised Mom you'd always be there for me."

Ry met his twin's gaze head-on. "How about just for once, you let something be about *me*?"

HW looked down at his feet. "Do you need money? Can I pay you to stay?"

Ry marched over to the door. "Get out."

"What the hell's wrong now?"

"If that's what you've become—if that's how you think you keep a man's loyalty, then go back to that bunch of losers you surround yourself with, and see what happens when you can't pay them anymore."

"Screw you." HW walked out.

"Right back at you, bro," Ry muttered under his breath, and then turned to survey his pile of boxes.

He'd said things he hadn't meant to say out loud, and HW had . . . changed beyond recognition. His brother was still caught up in being a rising star, and the better he did, the more hangers-on he'd acquire. He didn't need Ry. That was certain, but it still hurt.

They'd never spent more than a month apart in their entire lives, and now HW would be off competing in Texas next week, and Ry would be back on the ranch working with Roy. Unless HW followed through on his promise to attend Chase and January's wedding in a couple of months, he might never see his twin again.

He couldn't let himself think like that or he'd be chasing after his brother, begging to tag along for another few months. It was up to HW to get his shit together. He was *not* Ry's responsibility.

"Yeah, right. Thanks for loading that on me, Mom."

He checked all the drawers, picked up his hat, and propped open the bedroom door with his backpack. There was no sound of HW or his girlfriend in the apartment. HW tended to storm out when he lost an argument, so there was no surprise there. He hadn't even had a chance to tell his twin that their mom and baby sister might still be alive twenty years after disappearing from the ranch.

Ry picked up a stack of boxes, set off for the front door, leaving that ajar as well, and used his elbow to call the elevator. It wasn't too busy in the complex during the day as most people worked, so he had no trouble getting the boxes and bags down to his truck.

On his last trip upstairs he paused in the kitchen to grab a couple of cold water bottles from the refrigerator, and contemplated the silence. Neither Lally nor HW had made any effort to clean up yet. They were probably too used to him doing it. Not anymore. He checked his room again, making sure he hadn't forgotten anything, and then sat at the kitchen table to write HW a note.

> *Rent is paid until the end of the lease, which is up next month. I've contacted the leasing company about taking my name off, so I'm sure you'll be hearing from them when you renegotiate.*

Ry sat back and contemplated what to say next. He wasn't going to drop the bombshell about their mom in a letter. That was something HW needed to hear in person. Ry still couldn't believe it himself.

> *Good luck in the saddle bronc events, and hope you make it to the finals in Vegas. Call me when you get a chance—you know where I am. Ry*

He anchored the note under the salt and pepper and slowly stood up. There was so much he wanted to say, and so little his twin currently wanted to hear . . . He had to remember that inside HW there was a good, kind, and amazing guy—the guy he'd grown up with and loved with all his heart. Someday that HW would resurface, Ry had to believe that.

He unhooked the front-door key from his chain, laid it on top of the letter, and walked out, his throat tight and his emotions all over the place. Part of him felt like he was abandoning his twin, but the rest of him?

Suddenly felt free.

Chapter Two

Morgantown, California

"Avery? Are you okay?"

Avery Hayes opened her eyes to find she'd finally reached the bottom of the stairs. She'd tripped over one of the darn cats on the top step and fallen awkwardly, her hands occupied with carrying a huge pile of clean towels.

"Avery!"

She smiled at her mom, Sally, who was now crouched down beside her, her face ashen and her fingers gripping hard around Avery's wrist.

"Tom!" her mom bellowed. For such a small woman she had a big voice. "Call 911! Get help!"

"I'm fine, Mom. The towels broke my fall." That was pretty much the truth, apart from a couple of minor twinges that she would prefer to investigate in the privacy of her own room rather than at the local ER.

Her mom continued calling out for her father.
"*Tom!*"

"*Mom* . . . if you'd just move out of the way, I'll get
up. There's nothing wrong, really, just chill, okay?"

She placed a hand on her mom's shoulder and
gently pushed her back before attempting to stand.
She had to clutch at the banister as her left leg decided not to cooperate, but that wasn't unusual, and
she powered through the pain.

"Avery, you are *not* fine. Now, let's find your
father, and we'll go to the hospital ourselves. It will
probably be quicker anyway."

"I'm good."

"I don't believe you."

Avery took a deep breath. "Don't do this, okay?
I'm a big girl. If I was hurt, I'd go to the ER, but I'm
not. I'm just shaken up a bit. Nothing is broken."

"How would you know?"

Avery raised her eyebrows, and her mom was the
first to look away.

"Sorry, darling." She patted Avery's arm. "How
about I call that nice Dr. Mendez? He could just pop
round, and—"

Avery turned her back on her mother and concentrated on picking up the towels. She needed time
to compose herself, and folding was always soothing.
It reminded her of being a kid and being pressed
into service to fold hundreds of linen napkins for
fancy dinners at the hotel her parents still owned.

"What's going on?"

Great. Now her dad was here as well. A wall of
parental concern surrounded Avery. She met her
dad's anxious gaze.

"I slipped on the stairs. That's all."

"You're sure you're okay?"

"I'm fine. I'm going to take these towels back to the laundry. They'll need washing again, but at least the stairs got a good dusting."

"Come and find me if you need to go to the ER or anything."

"Will do, Dad."

Her mom opened her mouth as if to protest, but luckily her dad muttered something under his breath and distracted her.

Avery concentrated on walking smoothly away, which wasn't easy seeing as she really had come down hard on her left hip. Shattered bones never worked the same again. She knew that, as did her parents, but she didn't want their concern right now. Sometimes she felt smothered.

She dropped the towels into one of the bags to be picked up by the laundry guys, and contemplated the steep back stairs. If she wanted to check for damage, she needed to get up there. She didn't want her parents seeing her struggle, because then she'd be hog-tied and taken straight to the hospital whether she wanted to go or not.

"You okay, sis?"

She turned to find her older brother, Tucker, smiling at her. He acted as the deputy manager of the hotel, and basically did all the stuff no one else wanted to do. He had the patience of a saint, and she loved him to bits.

"Can you help me with something, and not tell the parents?"

"It depends what it is."

A typical answer from her always cautious brother—which was what made him so good at his job.

"Could you help me up the stairs?"

His smile disappeared. "What's wrong?"

Avery let out an exasperated breath. "Look, I banged my hip, I just want to put an ice pack on it and sit down for an hour without Mom and Dad acting as if I'm about to die, *okay*?"

He strolled toward her and she tensed.

"Hold on, sis." He picked her up. "Let's go."

"I didn't mean—"

"This is easier for me. And good practice for when I want to rescue some damsel in distress like in all those sappy historical movies you make me watch."

He started up the stairs, puffing a little when they reached the top.

"Jeez, Avery, lay off the pastries."

"You're just a slob, bro. I'm as light as a feather." She leaned down to open her bedroom door, and he carried her inside, dumping her gently on the bed, right side first.

"Thanks." Avery sighed. "Just don't tell them, okay?"

When he reached the door he hesitated, his expression concerned. "They worry about you."

"I know. And don't tell me it's because they love me. I know that. It's just sometimes they won't let me *breathe*, or do anything without getting superanxious. It's been three years since I had a single surgery. I'm doing great."

"I know you are."

"Then tell *them* that."

He leaned against the doorframe. "They watched

that horse fall on top of you; we all did. It was a damn miracle you even survived."

"But I *did*, and now I just want to live my life like a normal person, and they just worry about me *so much*." She swallowed hard. "I'm worried that one day I'll just lose it and tell them to leave me alone forever."

"Yeah?" He contemplated her for a long moment. "I won't say anything, but I'll bring you up an ice pack. Anything else you need?"

"Nope, I'm good."

He nodded and went into the hallway, leaving the door ajar. Within a couple of minutes he was back with an industrial-size bag of ice, which he left in a bucket beside her bed, three sealed plastic bags, and a couple of towels. All the Hayes kids had competed in the rodeo at some point, so they all knew the drill.

"You got something for the pain?"

"Yup."

"Then stay put for a while."

He patted her shoulder and went to the door.

"Tucker?"

"Yeah?"

"Thanks for being the best brother in the world."

"You're welcome, best sis." He blew her a kiss and disappeared down the hallway, whistling something she identified as rap music that didn't sound right at all.

She gingerly took off her pants, and studied the line of bruises down her thigh and shin where she'd hit each and every stair on the way down. Her breath hitched when she touched her hip, but the damage was minimal. She murmured a quick prayer, placed the covered ice pack against her skin, and lay back on her bed.

The family bedrooms at the Hayes Historic Hotel in Morgantown, California, were at the rear of the large house. According to her dad, the Tom Hayes who had taken over the hotel in 1930 had also kept his family in these rooms, building out the front of the hotel into its much grander form when tourism had replaced mining as the most important industry of the day.

As a kid, Avery had shared a room with her sister, but now because she was an official hotel employee she had the space all to herself. She certainly appreciated not having to pay rent. If she wanted anything to eat there was always the hotel kitchen. Most of her friends thought she had it made.

The pain eased, and Avery relaxed a little. She'd become an expert in knowing exactly how much damage she'd done to herself, first during her short-lived career as a barrel racer and then—after the final accident—simply as a means of survival.

"Ungrateful."

She said the word out loud. That's what she was. She had parents who loved her, and who had never given up on her even in her darkest days. She had family, and a job for life at the hotel if she wanted it. Even if she chose not to work she suspected she'd be nagged to death, but would still have a roof over her head and food to eat.

So what was wrong with her?

Avery closed her eyes, listening to the familiar sounds of the hotel: the crank and groan of the original elevators—which needed replacing, but which everyone thought were so elegant—the crashes and bangs from the kitchen that worked twenty-four seven to satisfy any little whim a guest might have in the food department.

Her cell buzzed and she studied the text from her BFF Nancy, who worked both at her mother's general store and at the Red Dragon bar in town. They'd met in kindergarten and had remained best friends ever since.

U coming to BB's class tonite?

Avery texted back. Sorry, can't make it. ☹

What's up?
Nothing much. I'm just a bit tired.
Want me to come over?
Nah, go and ogle BB instead.
LOL. Will do. C U tomorrow OK? X

Avery smiled at her cell. Nancy had a terrible crush on Blue "BB" Morgan, and was still in denial that his engagement to the local vet, Jenna McDonald, was really happening. From what she'd observed, Nancy wasn't going to get lucky. Blue seemed to have eyes for no one but Jenna, who was also supernice. He was only running the women's self-defense class at the local bakery out of the goodness of his heart.

He did look pretty hot as he demonstrated the moves though . . . There was usually an undignified scramble to act as his helper. Avery never offered herself up as sacrifice. She was still wary of accidentally breaking something. Being as BB, or Blue as he liked to be called these days, had served in the Marines, he could probably hurt her quite a lot. Not that he would ever do that intentionally, but she had to be careful.

Her cell buzzed again.

1900 Hours: Blue Morgan self-defense for women class. If you are attending, please let me know.
Yvonne.

Avery groaned. If Yvonne was trying to guesstimate how many people were coming, it usually meant she was planning on handing out some new confectionary delight for them to sample and rate. Last time it had been fruit tarts . . .

Darn her hip and that stupid cat.

You're not coming?

Avery groaned at Yvonne's next text. News sure got around fast in Morgantown.

Sorry can't make it.
Will you be okay for the wedding thing tomorrow?
Sure. See you there.

She received a smiley heart from Yvonne and put her cell back beside her bed. Yvonne was coordinating the catering for January Mitchell and Chase Morgan's upcoming wedding. It was Avery's job to liaise with her about the hotel's contribution to the event. The Morgan family had founded the town around 1850 and still ran their original ranch just outside the town boundary. The wedding was a big deal for the local community.

Thinking about the wedding, Avery carefully leaned over and grabbed her tablet to run through her list of action items before the upcoming meeting. She was relieved to see she had dealt with everything. Organizing a wedding wasn't a new task for her. She did it for the hotel, but the sheer size of the Morgan event meant that January needed all the help she could get. January was also lucky that she happened to be marrying a multimillionaire.

Avery pictured Chase TC Morgan when he was a senior at high school. He'd been a nerd before nerds became cool, and had often required assistance from his younger brother Blue to keep the bullies off his back. But if you took on one Morgan brother—you pretty much had to take on all four. As a proud member of a large family herself, Avery understood that.

Chase had recently returned to manage the affairs of his family ranch and had done rather well for himself in Silicon Valley. No one was teasing him anymore. He'd grown into his gangly frame, and was now tall, dark, handsome, rich, and about to marry the local historian who had persuaded him to save the ranch.

Avery smiled as she considered the happy couple. She'd seen all kinds of brides and grooms and figured she had a pretty good idea which ones were going to make it. Chase and January were solid.

She eased the ice pack off her hip and sat up, cautiously bringing her feet down onto the rag rug. The rumor mill, aka Yvonne and the gang at the coffee shop, said Ry Morgan and his twin brother would also be back for the wedding. Ry had been at the ranch quite recently, but Avery had managed to avoid him. She'd been in the grade below the twins at school, and had mixed memories of them.

There was a knock on her door and her mother peered in. Avery hid the ice pack under her pillow.

"Oh, there you are! You're not going to that self-defense class, are you?"

"Nope. I'm prepping for the meeting tomorrow with Yvonne and January." Avery showed her the tablet. "Is there anything you'd like to add to my action list?"

Her mom's relief that she wasn't going to the class was so obvious, Avery wanted to give her a big hug. She settled for patting the bed beside her.

"Come and sit here, and let's go over everything together."

Ry pulled up his truck outside the barn and turned off the engine. Silence settled around him and he let it sink in. It was twilight. The old wooden barn was silhouetted against the smudged purple sky with the backdrop of the Sierra Nevada rising above like something from an old western movie. He half expected a posse to come sweeping around the corner seeking some badass outlaw.

Home.

The main house had been built in the 1850s by the first Morgan to purchase the land. It hadn't changed much in the last one hundred and fifty years, with its elegant turned-oak staircase, sash windows brought by train from the East Coast, and fancy spindle railings enclosing the porch. Blue liked to work with his hands, and was steadily replacing and improving the original structure, which made everyone happy, and kept the house looking the same only better.

The massive wooden barn was just as old as the house, and stood on the opposite side of the wide circular driveway down a slight slope. Since his last visit Ry could see where Chase had set the new welcome center between the two structures, where they would process the incoming guests to their new family dude ranch enterprise. There would also be cabins, but they weren't going to be built until after Chase and January's wedding.

To his relief, the new center looked just like the original house, and even had some kind of flowering creeper growing up the side, making it look as old as the rest of the buildings. Chase hadn't skimped on making the place look authentic, Ry would give him that.

Ry hadn't lived at the ranch full-time since his eighteenth birthday, when he and HW had kissed their grandma Ruth good-bye and hightailed it out of there to seek their fortune. He found himself smiling. They'd been so full of hope, and so damn *cocky*. Now he was back, and his brother was still wandering.

Eight years had passed, and Ruth hadn't changed much. But from what he could already see, the ranch was about to get the makeover of a lifetime. It was the only economical way to keep the land in their family, and make a profit. Ranching by itself was no longer financially secure. Ry was happy to go along with his brother's plans. He'd much rather keep his home, be a cowboy, and share his love of the land with guests than sell it off to some developer.

A tap on his passenger window made him jump and roll it down.

"You planning on sitting there all night?" Chase, the architect of all the change, asked.

"It depends whether Ruth's cooking dinner."

His brother grinned at him. "She's always cooking. You know what she's like. She can't wait to start feeding all the new guests." He stood back so Ry could open the door and get out. "She knew you were coming today, so she's been making all your favorites."

Ry's stomach growled.

"Good thing you're hungry because you're going to be eating all night." Chase eyeballed the amount of stuff in the truck. "Do you want to bring this in now, or can it wait until morning when Blue's back?"

"It can wait." Ry took his backpack off the passenger seat.

"No HW, then?"

"Nope."

Chase sighed. "Damn. I was hoping he'd find it in him to forgive me."

Ry hoisted his backpack. "Trust me, it's not about him forgiving you. He's just being an all-round ass."

"I'm sorry, Ry."

"Don't be. Where's BB?"

"Out teaching his class at Yvonne's in town. January's down there with him." Chase walked up the steps and held the screen door open. "Although I do have to question the idea of holding a self-defense class in a pastry chef's café. I bet for every calorie you lose you add on a hundred more."

"Is Jenna there, too?" Ry asked as he kicked off his boots in the mudroom and hung his backpack on the post at the bottom of the stairs, which would definitely annoy his grandma if she noticed.

Chase grinned. "Keeping an eye on her man while he's dealing with all those females? You bet she is."

"Ry! You're back." Ruth came toward him and gave him a big hug. She wore her usual kid-size jeans, a soft blue fleece, and collared blouse under it. Her gray hair was tucked up in a neat bun and her spectacles perched on the end of her nose. She was so short her head barely came up to his chest. "Come and sit down next to Maria. Did you bring all your things?"

Ry winked at Blue's daughter and took his seat at the big table. The kitchen hadn't changed much since he was a little kid, and brought back the best, and the worst, of memories.

"Yeah, I think I got it all. Where's Dad?"

"Granddad Billy's at an AA meeting," Maria informed him. "He's going to come back with January."

"Cool." Ry poured himself some iced tea and drank the whole thing down in one gulp. Maria refilled his glass.

"Thanks." He risked a smile and she beamed back at him. "How's school?"

"Pretty good, although there aren't many kids."

"More than when we lived here," Chase chimed in. "But then we used to have all the grades together in one place, until the classes got too small and they started bussing us down the road to Bridgeport for high school."

Ruth sighed. "I suspect the middle school will be

gone soon, as well. I just hope it lasts until Maria finishes eighth grade."

"I don't mind getting the bus," Maria said. "It's kind of fun."

"As long as it turns up and doesn't leave you hanging." Ruth placed a plate in front of Ry. "Pot roast, mashed potatoes, and green beans from the garden."

"My favorite. Thanks, Ruth."

She patted his shoulder. "Eat up. You're still too thin."

Chase snorted at that, but Ruth gave him such a look that he shut down anything else he'd intended to say.

Eventually, Maria went off to bed, and Ruth brewed more coffee, bringing her cup to sit opposite Ry.

"How did it go with your brother?"

Ry shrugged. "Not too good."

She reached across and patted his hand. "I'm sorry, darlin'."

"Yeah. Me too."

"HW will work it out." Chase cleared his throat. "In the meantime, are you still available to work here alongside Roy?"

Trust his older brother to dispense with the sentimental stuff and get straight down to business. It was just what Ry needed to hear right now. What with the news about his mother, and HW's antics, he'd had enough emotional moments recently to last him a lifetime.

"Yeah, I'm ready to start whenever you need me."

"Great. I'll wait until Blue and Billy get back, then if you're up for it, we can discuss who's going to be running each variable within the new organizational framework structure I've prepared."

"He means who will be doing what," Ruth said and rolled her eyes, making Ry snort.

"What's so funny?" Chase sat back and looked at them both. "Isn't that what I just said?"

"Nerds," Ruth muttered.

Ry grinned at his grandma, and for the first time in a while the heaviness he'd grown accustomed to around his heart lifted. HW might not be with him, but there was plenty for him to do after all, and he was wanted. Perhaps that would be enough to get him through the hard stuff and start living a different life. A life out of his twin's shadow.

Chapter Three

Avery got out of her car and stretched out the stiffness in her legs before turning to grab her bag from the rear seat. January had asked her and Yvonne if they could meet at the ranch to go over the wedding plans. It looked like she was the first one to arrive.

A door banged, and she turned to see a cowboy coming down the steps of the house. He slowed as he approached and lifted his head, making her heart stutter as she recognized his familiar golden eyes.

"Avery?"

She managed a smile, which was probably more like a grimace as she fumbled around for her cane.

"Well remembered. Now, which one are you? HW or Ry?"

"Ry."

"Are you sure?" Oh, dear God, why had she said that? He'd think she was referring to—"Ha! I'm just kidding, I knew—"

"Yeah. HW's in Sacramento." He gestured at her

bag. "Are you coming to see January? She said she was expecting her wedding committee."

"Yes, I'm liaising with her on behalf of the hotel." He picked up her bag and set off back toward the house. She followed more slowly, the effects of falling down the stairs still bugging her. "You don't have to carry—"

He was already way ahead of her. "Not a problem."

She reached the steps and slowly levered herself up onto the wraparound porch, where he was holding the screen door open for her. It took her an ice age. She was aware of his gaze and braced herself for the usual barrage of insensitive questions, but he didn't say a word. Not that he ever said much. He'd always been the quieter twin.

She managed to get through the door without falling flat on her face. "Thanks."

"You're working for your parents now?"

He carried her bag through to the kitchen, where the smell of fried bacon still lingered. To her dismay there was no one else there, so she was going to have to keep talking.

"I'm the events coordinator—you know, weddings, special dinners, dances, anniversary parties, that kind of thing."

"Cool." He placed her bag on the table. "I can see why January needs you. "

"I'm not sure she does. She seems to have everything well in hand." Whatever she really thought, that was nice and diplomatic. Her dad would be proud.

He leaned a hip against the counter and focused on her face. He wore an old tight-fitting green T-shirt under an open denim shirt, faded jeans, and muddy boots, which Ruth would probably kill him for wearing in the house. Paired with his white Stetson he looked like every woman's dream cowboy.

"I don't think she's doing that great, Avery. She looks worn-out."

It was downright disconcerting, like he could read her mind or something. But then they had grown up together, so maybe he saw more than she realized, and he'd always been a good judge of character when he bothered to pipe up—much better than the rest of his brothers, and refreshingly direct.

Ry continued talking. "She's stressed out—what with the wedding, her studies, and trying to get the ranch prepared for guests."

"Well, I'll certainly do my best to help her as much as I can."

"Thanks." He tipped his Stetson to her. "I've gotta go. Cows to herd."

"Nice to see you again, Ry."

"Right back at you." He turned and walked out, the clink of spurs hitting the wooden floor as he finally left.

Avery sat down with a rush, and pressed a hand to her heated cheek. Darn it. He was supposed to have left for good! What was he doing herding cows and helping women with their bags?

January came in, her face lighting up when she spotted Avery. She wore her usual uniform of jeans and a cute T-shirt, her fair hair caught up in a ponytail on the top of her head. There were dark circles under her eyes and her smile looked a little strained.

"Hey!" She came around the table to give Avery a

hug. "Want some coffee? I'm practically mainlining the stuff at the moment."

"Sure." Avery cleared her throat. "I saw Ry. I thought he'd gone back to Sacramento."

January came back with the coffee, sugar, and creamer and dumped them all on the table. Avery helped herself and stirred in some sugar. A lot of sugar. It always made her feel better.

"He did, but he came back. He's living here now."

"Living here, as in *permanently*?"

"Yes, he's done with the rodeo. He's going to work with Roy. Chase is superpleased because he was worried about Roy coping with all the changes. Ry coming back right now was perfect timing."

"Perfect," Avery echoed, her fingers gripping the spoon so hard they hurt. "What about HW?"

January sighed. "He's still caught up with the rodeo. Ry says he has a chance to go to the finals in Vegas this year, so he can't get away."

"Wow, he's doing really well if that's in the cards."

"So I gathered, although you'd know all about that, wouldn't you, being a barrel riding champion?"

"I never got to the national finals," Avery admitted. "But I've been there as a spectator. It's amazing. I wonder if HW will settle down here eventually?"

"It's possible. Look at the rest of them. Blue's busy building a house for himself, Maria, and Jenna, and Ry's come home." January hesitated. "You knew both of them, didn't you?"

"Ry and HW? We went to the same school and competed in the same rodeos, so yes, I know them."

"Are they really identical?"

"To look at? Pretty much. It's hard to tell them apart. They used to drive the teachers crazy. But Ry was always . . . sweeter, friendlier, you know? HW was always too busy being charming and getting noticed."

"You didn't like him?"

Avery sipped her coffee. "Sometimes he made it hard to like him, but he's grown up now. I bet he's changed."

She damn well hoped so, or she might have a few words to say to him on a few sore subjects. Not that he would remember her or what he'd done.

The kitchen door opened and Yvonne appeared, dressed in her working clothes—a black dress with a white collar, like some sexy parlor maid from a different era. She was tall, elegant, and made cakes and pastries that flew off the shelves of her local coffee shop and bakery. She also had a faint French accent and an air of mystery that Avery totally envied.

"Sorry I'm late. I had to go over everything with Elizabeth again before I could leave the shop." She groaned as she sat down and pushed a pink box over to January. "Éclairs. Put them in the refrigerator for later."

January peered inside the box. "Or we could just eat them now?"

Yvonne waved her hand in an airy gesture. "Up to you. You're the bride who's got to fit into that fancy wedding dress you just bought, in eight weeks' time."

January pouted as she closed the lid. "I hate it when you bring facts into an argument about chocolate. I'll put them away—for now."

Yvonne winked at Avery. "Like she won't fit in her dress. Every bride I've ever known loses weight before the big day."

"Not all of them." Avery sipped her coffee. "I've

seen a couple who indulged in a lot of comfort eating and had to be shoehorned into their dresses."

"You've probably dealt with a lot more brides than I have," Yvonne conceded. "I'm really glad you're helping us out here. It's nice to have someone who knows what they are doing."

"I know what I'm doing." January sat back down and refilled their coffees. "I'm getting married to the most wonderful man in the world."

"While trying to finish your thesis and transform this ranch into a dude ranch." Yvonne shook her head. "That's why I'm glad we've got Avery on board."

"I'm enjoying it," Avery said and realized how much she meant it. "I can practically organize an event at the hotel in my sleep now, so this was a great opportunity to branch out."

"You could always take your skill set and move to a bigger place," Yvonne suggested. "I know a lot of hotels and restaurants in the Bay Area that would snap you up."

"I'm not sure I'm quite ready for that yet." Avery smiled at her friends. "But you never know. One day, if my parents decide to ditch the hotel, I might have no choice but to move on."

"They're thinking about leaving?"

"I think my dad would like to retire somewhere, but my mom? She's such a dynamo, I don't think she'll ever slow down."

Yvonne started sorting through her huge bag, laying piles of makeup and perfume and even a spare pair of flip-flops on the table. "I suppose Tucker could take over if he wanted to."

"He'd definitely do a great job."

Avery stared at Yvonne's fancy makeup brands.

She barely managed mascara and sunblock every morning, while Yvonne always looked glamorous. Maybe if you lived in France for a while, like Yvonne had, you picked up that effortlessly chic vibe without realizing it.

Yvonne located her notebook and shoveled everything else back into her bag.

"So you wanted to discuss where to set everything up, right?" She flipped open her pad. "We have several different things going on at different times of the day, so we need to make sure that the waitstaff and the caterers can get everywhere without the food getting cold, or spoiling, or any other of the ten million things that can go wrong."

Avery nodded. "I was thinking about that last night, and I drew up a brief plan of how I thought it might work. Do you want to see it?"

January and Yvonne came to stand behind her chair as she located her sketch. "Here you go. What do you think?"

Ry saddled Dolittle and made his way down to Roy's place. He took his time checking where the cattle were, and automatically inspected the fence line as he rode. The air had a nice sharp bite to it, and the sky was clear. This far out of town there was almost no noise apart from the natural wildlife and the occasional tractor or four-wheel-drive vehicle.

Roy, the ranch foreman who'd lived on the Morgan ranch since dinosaurs roamed, didn't like the all-terrain vehicles, but even he admitted that sometimes they were vital to get to an inaccessible section of the ranch fast. Secretly, Ry agreed with him. He'd much rather ride horses. It was much better for the environment and his peace of mind.

It had been cool to see Avery again—although she hadn't seemed that excited to see him—which was a shame because he'd always liked her at school. She'd been different from the rest of the Hayes siblings, more outgoing, more fiery, something he'd secretly admired as he desperately tried to differentiate himself from his twin.

As he approached the small square house nestled against the hill, he spotted Roy in his usual position, leaning over the wall of the sty talking to his pigs. Man, he loved those suckers. No one quite knew why, but as Ry loved bacon more than life, he was quite willing to put up with Roy's current obsession.

He slowed his horse and dismounted, tying Dolittle up in the shade, where he promptly went to sleep.

"Morning, Roy. Reporting for duty."

Roy turned toward him, squinting into the sun. His face was tanned the same color as saddle leather and he seemed to shrink further into his boots every year. "Ry. Didn't you just get back? I wasn't expecting you down here for another couple of days."

"I've got nothing else to do, so I might as well get started." Ry took a quick look at the pigs and stepped back from the god-awful stench. "What's the plan?"

"Come into the house, and I'll check the schedule."

Ry picked up the empty bowl Roy used for his food scraps and brought it along with him. "You have a schedule now? You used to have it all in your head or written on a chalkboard in the barn."

"TC, I mean Chase, has been getting at me." Roy sighed. "He says I've got to set goals, and be accountable, whatever the hell that means."

"That sounds like my big brother." Ry paused as he noted the brand-new laptop on Roy's countertop. "Wow, he's really serious about this, isn't he? Are you using that thing?"

"Yup, some spreadsheet or *something*." Roy gestured at the laptop. "Take a look. Chase set it up so even an idiot like me could understand it."

"Then I should be fine." Ry clicked the space bar and a calendar opened up. "Cool."

He read through the list of tasks while Roy pottered around the kitchen making a fresh pot of coffee.

"What needs doing the most?" Ry asked.

"Fences."

Ry groaned. "Figures. I'll get on that if you like."

Roy handed him a cup of coffee. "You sure?"

"That's what I'm here for." He paused. "Anything else?"

"Talk to January about the wedding."

"Which particular part of it?"

"Where she's going to hold the ceremony, and all that kind of thing. I guess she won't want to share a field with a herd of cows and cowpats on her big day."

"Okay." Ry sipped at the scalding coffee.

"HW wouldn't come, then?"

"He's angling to get to the finals in Vegas."

"Do you think he'll make it?"

Ry shrugged. "He's got the talent."

"But—"

"He's a bit full of himself at the moment."

"Fame gone to his head?" Roy nodded wisely. "See it all the time on the TV. One little bitty part in a reality show, and some folks think they're God Almighty."

Ry deliberately changed tack. He was sick and tired of talking about his brother. "I saw Avery Hayes up at the ranch."

"Yeah? Good to see her getting out and about. Her mom says she works too hard."

Ry considered his next question. It wasn't like him to pry, but he felt a certain kind of responsibility for Avery from way back when, and didn't want to mess things up with her again.

"Did she get hurt?"

"Didn't you know?" Roy sat down at the table and decanted the rest of the coffee into a metal flask. "I suppose it was just after you boys left home. Barrel racing."

"Damn." Ry had seen way too many riders come to grief barrel racing to be surprised that she'd been injured. "I remember she was really good at it as well."

"Yeah. She was all set to go pro." Roy shook his head. "Her mom says she's still in pain, but she gets by."

Ry pictured the giggling teenager he'd once known and contrasted it with the woman he'd watched struggling to climb three steps up to the porch. It was like something had leeched all the light out of her.

"She works at the hotel, right?"

"Works there twenty-four seven. Never does anything else." Roy sighed. "Poor girl. You should take her out sometime."

Ry raised an eyebrow. "I just got back, and I doubt she'd want to hang out with me."

"Why not?"

"Because HW's the one with the good looks and the charm."

"And he's not here." Roy drained his cup. "So maybe it's time for you to step out of his shadow." He nodded at Ry. "You coming? I've got all the supplies you need in the barn."

Avery leaned more of her weight on her cane as January considered the square Yvonne had helpfully spray-painted on the grass.

"If you put the caterers' tent here in the center of everything, right beside the welcome center, which has power and water, then I think we'll be okay." Yvonne walked back toward January and Avery. "What do you think?"

"Looks good to me." Avery shifted her right hip and angled her body toward the ranch. She was already worried about making it back up the slope. If she stood still any longer she might not make it at all. She was normally a lot more capable than this, but the bang on her hip the day before had shaken her up, and she needed her cane for the first time in a long while.

Yvonne checked her cell. "I'm going to have to go soon, January. I've got baking to do."

"I think we've got it all sorted." January nodded decisively. "Time to eat those éclairs."

She started back up the slope toward the house with Yvonne beside her. Avery slowly turned as well and took a couple of faltering steps.

Yeah. This wasn't going to be fun. She set her jaw
and kept going, her attention focused downward on
the rugged terrain.

"You okay, Avery?" January called back.

"I'm good. I just need to take my time. Don't eat
all the chocolate."

January's laugh floated back down to her. She'd
trained her friends not to hover over her and make
her feel worse. For once she wished she hadn't.

A pair of scuffed brown cowboy boots came into
view and she looked up into Ry Morgan's unsmiling face. He was standing on the slope above her,
slightly to her right.

"Need a hand?"

She wanted so badly to say no—to say she was
fine—especially to this man, who more than anyone
made her remember the silly girl with silly dreams
she'd once been. She didn't want him to see her like
this. She wanted . . . But she wasn't quite that dumb.

"Sure."

He came around to her left side and she grabbed
his forearm, his hard muscles flexing under the
sleeve of his shirt. Although he was considerably
taller than she was, he matched her halting gait as
if he had all the time in the world. Neither of them
spoke; him because he could never be described as
chatty, and her because she didn't have the breath
for it.

When they reached level ground, she carefully
released his arm and tried to sound casual.

"Thanks."

"You're welcome." He stayed where he was, as if
assessing her ability to keep going without him.

Avery raised her chin. "Are you coming in the house?"

"Yeah. I need to talk to January."

Damn.

She nodded and started walking again, putting all her energy into making it look as easy as possible. The three steps up to the veranda looked like Mount Everest. She slowed as she approached them, and then his hand cupped her elbow again, and he silently and effortlessly added his support to getting her where she needed to be.

"You look a bit stiff."

He had to spoil it by saying something now? She refused to turn around, and focused on hobbling toward the door. "I'm fine. I fell down the stairs yesterday."

"Ouch." He winced. "You've got to stop drinking so much."

Wait up . . . Had Ry Morgan just made a joke?

She looked over her shoulder to find him watching her. "Ha. I fell over the cat."

"Yeah, right."

Incredibly, he smiled at her, and her stomach did a complete flip.

"I've got some emu or ostrich cream that one of HW's sponsors claims is the best thing for sore muscles and stiffness. I'll bring it over."

"Eew. You're not smearing anything on me."

His smile deepened, showing the dimple low on his left cheek. "Could be fun."

Dude, he so wasn't eighteen anymore. This level of flirting was totally beyond her. Sure, she'd had a couple of boyfriends over the years, but none of them held a candle to Ry Morgan. Without attempting an answer, she kept moving.

Before she even got to the door, his hand appeared over her head and held back the screen while she wrestled with the inner latch.

"Thanks."

"You're welcome."

She didn't take off her boots, which weren't muddy, but headed straight for the kitchen, where January and Yvonne were already chatting with Ruth. Ry turned left toward the mudroom, giving her a moment to compose herself.

He was just being kind. He always had been.

So why did it bother her so much?

She hesitated at the kitchen door, but Ruth saw her, and that was that. She was made to sit at the table, and eat and drink while Ruth plied her with questions about her parents and her siblings. It almost kept her from noticing when Ry came in and started talking quietly to January.

Yvonne was the first to leave, blowing kisses at everyone as she promised to introduce Avery to the chef who was coming to help her out with the actual cooking. As the chef would be using the Hayes kitchen as well as Yvonne's, Avery was looking forward to meeting him and laying down a few ground rules. The last thing they needed was to upset the slightly temperamental, but very talented hotel chef by misusing his space.

Although Avery wished she could leave with Yvonne, she needed more downtime before she could get out of her chair, squeeze herself into her car, and drive home. Not that anyone seemed to mind her sitting there. That was one of the things she'd always loved about the Morgans. Ruth had always welcomed her grandkids' friends, and nothing had changed.

Eventually, though, she had to move or she'd stiffen up completely. She checked her cell, saw a text from Nancy about meeting her at the hotel, and stood up to make her excuses.

January came around to hug her. "Thanks so much. You were so helpful!" She grinned at Ry. "If you have any more questions about the wedding, talk to Avery. She's got a map of where everything needs to be set up."

"Will do." Ry rose as well. "I have to get back to my favorite job in the world—mending fences. Let me walk you to your car."

She made it down the three steps unaided and over to her car, Ry strolling at her heels.

"*Is* it okay if I talk to you about wedding plans?" Ry asked.

"Sure. Especially if it saves January some time." She hesitated, one hand on her car door. "She does seem a little . . . stressed."

He opened the door, took her bag out of her unresisting fingers, and placed it on the passenger seat within easy reach.

"Cane in the back?"

"Yes." He held out his hand and she relinquished the cane. "Thanks."

She slipped her sunglasses down on her nose and got in, waiting for him to slam the door. Instead he leaned down so he could see her face.

"Speaking of mending fences. You busy tomorrow night?"

"Why?"

He raised his eyebrows. "I'll be in town. I was hoping to see you while I'm there. I can meet you at the hotel."

"What for?"

He smiled. "Clearing the air?" He took a step back and closed the car door. "See you tomorrow, Avery."

She immediately wound down the window. "I don't think there's anything left to say, is there?"

"Maybe not from your point of view, but I'd like to give it a try." His hazel gaze was fixed on her. "Will you be there?"

Avery nodded. She was always there. The hotel was her life.

He touched the brim of his Stetson. "Good. I'll look forward to it."

Chapter Four

"Ry Morgan wants to talk to you?" Nancy put down her mug. "So what?"

"You *know* what."

"That all happened years ago."

"I *know*. That's exactly what I've been trying to tell you. Why on earth would he want to talk about it now?"

"Maybe it's something else entirely."

"Like what?" Avery asked.

"I dunno." Nancy waved a vague hand in the air. "Maybe he wants to book a function at the hotel."

"Yeah, right. Thanks, friend."

They were sitting on her bed, curled up in their usual spots at either end, a cat settled in between them. Nancy was due at her second job at the Red Dragon bar, and often popped in to see Avery before her shift. Nancy had persuaded Manolo, the hotel chef, to make them burritos for dinner, which were so awesome Avery was thinking of asking him to put them on the buffet menu.

Nancy was good with people. She said it was due

to a lifetime of dealing with tourists in the main—
and for a long time, only—Morgantown store, but it
was more than that. She genuinely liked her cus-
tomers, and had an amazing ability to draw out their
life stories within seconds of meeting them. Also
working in the bar meant she had the best and most
scandalous gossip in town.

"Manolo said this is his mother's recipe." Nancy
wiped her mouth with her napkin. "He has written
down a whole lot of her recipes that he'd love to try
out in the restaurant."

"Then why didn't he say something to me? He's
been here for two years."

"He's shy." Nancy belched discreetly.

"Yeah, I can tell that by the way he bellows at all
the other guys in the kitchen when they're not
moving fast enough." Avery took another bite, and
almost sighed with bliss. "This is *really* good."

"Being a chef is like performance art these days.
They all think they have to behave like Gordon
Ramsey. Manolo really is the sweetest guy."

Avery stared hard at her friend. "You like him?"

"I like his food."

"And the rest of him?"

Nancy licked her lips. "He's . . . okay."

"Does he like you?"

"He made us burritos, didn't he?" Nancy uncurled her long legs and stood up. Her blond hair
was in a high ponytail and she wore her usual jeans
and Red Dragon bar T-shirt. She didn't really believe
in long-term boyfriends and had half the local population just waiting for her to change her mind and
pick them for more than one night of fun.

"I've got to go. How about you worry about your love life instead of mine?"

"I have no love life."

"Exactly." Nancy pointed at her. "Come to the bar with me. I'll fix you up."

"That's very sweet of you." Avery fake-smiled. "But I have to meet Ry Morgan downstairs in twenty minutes."

Nancy grabbed her backpack, and then spun around to look at Avery. "I just remembered. You had a crush on him at school."

"*All* the girls had a crush on him."

"Nope, most of us preferred HW. He was more fun." Nancy studied Avery's face. "Is that what's worrying you? That you might still like him?"

"Of course not. He's *way* out of my league."

"He is not."

Avery fixed her friend with her best stare. "You're going to be late."

"And you're avoiding the subject." Nancy came over to kiss the top of Avery's head. "Have fun with Ry, and say hi to him from me, won't you?"

"Sure."

Nancy held her gaze. "Just let yourself enjoy his company, okay? He's a nice guy."

She waved as she went out, leaving Avery with the task of collecting the plates and silverware and sticking them outside the door. Yet another advantage of living in a hotel. She never had to wash a dish in her life.

Checking the time, she brushed her straight brown hair, braided it, and made a face in the mirror. If Ry was expecting her to make an effort, he was going to be disappointed. She wore her Hayes

Historic Hotel T-shirt, name badge, black pants, and her most comfortable boots. She looked competent, professional, and way too tense. He'd pick up on that in a second. He always had.

Time to go.

She hesitated. Maybe she should take the name badge off?

If they were both going to live in this small town, getting everything settled between them was probably a good idea. He'd feel more comfortable and she . . . Avery paused at the door. What would she gain? Her hard-won serenity back? She liked her life just how it was, and just wished everyone else would understand that. Seeing Ry again had brought back too many memories of the fun they'd shared growing up together. She firmly closed her bedroom door. It was time to stop looking backward and move on.

"Nice to see you, sir." Ry grinned at Mr. Hayes, who was serving behind the bar in the old-fashioned saloon in the hotel. He hadn't changed much in the years since Ry had left, and bore a strong resemblance to his oldest daughter.

"No need for the sir, Ry, you can call me Tom." Avery's father extended his hand and shook Ry's. "Now what can I get you to drink?"

"A beer would be good."

Ry went to hand over some money, but it was waved away.

"This one's on the house. Welcome home, son."

"Thanks . . . um, Tom." Ry took the beer. "Is Avery around?"

"*Avery?*"

"Yeah, your daughter, Avery. She said she'd meet me here at six." Tom was staring at him as if he'd never seen him before, and Ry hastened to add, "I wanted to ask her something about the upcoming wedding."

"Oh, a *business* meeting." Tom occupied himself wiping down the old mahogany bar. "Do you want me to see if I can find her?"

Ry was just about to reply in the negative when he spotted Avery coming through the double doors from the lobby. She smiled at one of the guests as she passed by and he was struck by how it changed her face, letting him see that vibrant girl again— the one who had apparently disappeared since her accident.

She was listening attentively as the woman gesticulated and pointed upward. Ry took his beer and walked toward her, catching the end of the conversation.

"Of course, I'll send someone up to check on that for you right now, Mrs. Bryson. What room number are you in again?"

She saw Ry, and briefly acknowledged him before walking back to the front desk with the still babbling guest.

"Tucker, can you help Mrs. Bryson? Her grandson's gotten his toe stuck in the faucet. Apparently he's never been in a bath before, only a shower."

Ry fought a grin as Tucker expressed just the right amount of sympathy and concern, and followed the guest over to the elevators. Avery swung back toward Ry and rolled her eyes.

"Dear God, why do boys do stupid stuff like that?"

"Sexist much?"

"Come on, Ry, nine times out of ten, it's the boys who do the most ridiculous things."

"True," he acknowledged. "Not that me and HW ever did anything wrong. We were little angels."

"Yeah, right. I went to school with you both, re-member?" She turned back toward the bar and he followed her. "I knew I should've taken off my name badge, but according to my dad, if you're a Hayes you're always on duty."

"No cane today."

She looked over her shoulder at him. "Nope."

Dude, she talked less than I do.

"Not so stiff?"

She didn't even bother to answer that and settled into one of the booths. He took the seat opposite, as her father slid a glass of Coke in front of her.

"Here you go, love."

Avery made a face. "I hope there's alcohol in there."

"Not on my watch." Tom handed her a napkin. "Ry said you're having a business meeting, and you know my motto—never mix business with pleasure."

Avery sighed as he walked away. "No chance of me ever getting drunk in this bar. I *suppose* that's a good thing."

Ry held up his beer and clinked it against her glass. "There's always the Red Dragon."

"Nancy works there in the evenings. She's just as overprotective as my dad."

"It's a small town. By the time I used to get home after a night out, Ruth always knew exactly what I'd done, and how I was going to pay for it." He rubbed his ear. "For a small woman she certainly knew how to put the fear of God in all of us."

"Just like my mom." She sipped her drink. "So, what did you want to talk to me about, Ry?"

She was direct. He liked that about her.

"Do you remember the senior prom?"

"Mine or yours?"

"Mine. You were there."

She grimaced. "Do we really have to go through all this again?"

"We didn't go through it the first time. I was an eighteen-year-old idiot."

"You weren't the idiot."

Ry took a slug of beer. "Okay, HW was, but—"

She held up a finger, interrupting him. "So why are you doing the apologizing?"

He stared at her for a long moment. "Because I always—"

"Apologize for your twin. Why *is* that?" She sat back. "You might look like him, but you're not responsible for his mistakes."

"He hurt you."

She shrugged. "Yeah, he did."

"And, at the time, I didn't call him out for it."

This time her smile was brief. "As you said, you were eighteen."

"And you were even younger." He pressed on. "He shouldn't have kissed you."

"No, he shouldn't have pretended to be *you* when he kissed me."

Ry winced. "He just got caught up in the moment, and—"

"Don't make excuses for him. He knew what he was doing. He was peeved because I'd always liked you better than him."

The age-old instinct to defend his brother rose again. For the first time Ry held it back. "You're right. I'm still sorry I didn't stand up for you."

"I didn't stick around to see *what* you did, to be honest. I ran out of there like the place was on fire, and went home." She sipped her soda. "So are we done, now? You've apologized, and I've moved on, okay?"

"You sure about that?"

She shrugged. "Heck, he wasn't that great a kisser, and it's not as if there was anything between us, was there?"

"No?" He looked down at his menu. "Actually, I *was* the first Morgan to kiss you."

She frowned. "When?"

"At recess when you were in first grade."

"Oh . . . yeah, I'd forgotten about that." She shifted uncomfortably in her seat.

"Really?" He fought a smile. "You kicked me so hard in the shins I thought I was going to cry, which would have destroyed my street cred with my seven-year-old crowd. I suppose I should be glad you didn't aim anywhere higher."

"You deserved it."

"I know, but I remember thinking you were something special from that day forward." He hesitated. "I was going to ask you out after the prom. Hell— I was going to *take* you to it except you'd already decided to go with Tucker."

"You were?"

He raised his head to meet her startled gaze as heat washed through her cheeks.

"I thought this meeting was about starting fresh."

"Yeah."

She pushed her drink away. "So we're done, then."

Reaching out, he gently closed his fingers around her wrist. "I'd like to take you out for dinner one night. Will you come with me?"

She went absolutely still. "I don't think that's a good idea."

"Why not?"

She eased her hand away and awkwardly stood up. "Because we're not the same people anymore."

He leaned back in his seat to study her. "You look pretty much the same to me."

She briefly closed her eyes. "But I'm not that girl who had a stupid crush on you."

"And hopefully I'm not that insensitive eighteen-year-old idiot who blew the chance to ask you out."

She looked away. "Don't make me have to say it."

He eased out of the seat to stand beside her. "Say what?"

She stuck out her hand and then patted his sleeve when he didn't reciprocate. "Take care, Ry, and thanks for coming by."

"Wait a minute."

She walked away, her gait slightly uneven as she favored her right leg. He thought about following her, and then imagined Tom's face if he started arguing with his daughter right in the middle of the lobby.

Did she really think he *cared* how she looked? Part of him was slightly insulted that she should think so little of him. He tracked her out of the bar, through the lobby, and watched her go into the elevator before resuming his seat.

She'd looked less offended, and more . . . scared. Maybe it wasn't about him at all. One thing he'd learned from watching HW mess up was to bide his time and not rush into things. The impulse to ask Avery out on a date had come out of nowhere. But once he'd said it, it made perfect sense to him. He'd always liked her and now with school far behind them they were definitely equals.

He finished his beer and put his hat back on. It was a small town. He knew where she lived, and she'd be up at the ranch helping with the wedding of the century for the next couple of months. He nodded to Tom, and stepped out onto the raised wooden sidewalk. Down at the corner of the street was the Red Dragon—the only bar in town. He contemplated dropping in for another beer, and a meet-up with Nancy, who probably knew Avery better than anyone else in the world.

But that was for another day.

He could wait.

The next morning Ry came down the stairs yawning so hard his jaw almost cracked. He hesitated at the kitchen door, aware of raised voices, which took him right back to being a kid and seeing his parents fighting. The memory still made him feel kind of sick.

He loudly cleared his throat and went in.

"Morning, Chase, January."

They were seated at the table, nose-to-nose, glaring

at each other. For a second, neither of them looked away, and then Chase sat back.

"Hell. Morning, Ry."

January shot to her feet, brushed past Ry, and stormed out the back door, slamming it behind her.

Chase winced. "Ouch."

"Problems in paradise, bro?" Ry asked as he helped himself to coffee.

"She's doing too much. I just tried to tactfully point it out to her."

Ry looked at the sheets of paper scattered around the kitchen. "And how exactly did you do that?"

"I've been tracking her time over the last few days, and—"

"Hold up." Ry picked up the nearest piece of paper and scanned it. "What the *hell*?"

"It's just a schematic of her time management skills, and how she's overscheduling herself, and not getting enough sleep. I took the information from the smart watch I bought her."

"You *gave* her that report?"

"I wanted to back up my concerns with facts."

"You gave a stressed-out, sleep-deprived woman a minute-by-minute guide to her whole *life*?"

Chase straightened out one of the crumpled sheets. "From your tone I guess you think that was a mistake?"

"Dude." Ry shoved a hand through his fair hair. "Don't you? Didn't she just storm off muttering something about castrating you?"

"It didn't go well." Chase frowned. "But I am worried about her. I know she's got to finish her thesis herself, and she's determined to continue on with the guest-ranch project, but surely someone can help her with the wedding?"

"She's got Yvonne and Avery helping her."

"I know, but aren't there professional wedding planners around or something? I'm happy to pay for one if it makes January's life less complicated."

"I hear you, but she's got to agree. You can't just make the decision for her."

"You're right." Chase stood up and took a deep breath. "I'd better go and apologize. When she's calmed down I'll suggest the idea of a wedding planner, and we can take it from there."

"Great idea, bro."

Chase paused at the kitchen door. "Sorry about the shouting."

"It's all good."

"No, it's not. Hearing myself getting loud in this particular space?" Chase shook his head. "Brought back too many memories."

"Yeah." Ry kept his attention on his coffee. He really didn't want to go there with his brother. They'd spent twenty years *not* talking about the last fight his parents had in this very kitchen, when his dad had been stabbed and his mom and baby sister disappeared into the night. Why was everyone suddenly willing to talk about it *now*?

"At least you and HW didn't have to see any of that." Chase spoke almost to himself as he went after January, leaving Ry at the table.

Ry took a deep breath. The trouble was, he and HW had never been any good at doing what they were told. And when Blue had snuck out onto the landing to see what was going on, they'd followed him, and seen their father in his bloodstained shirt stagger out of the kitchen and into the yard, shouting for his wife.

At five, Ry had only the haziest memories of the rest of that terrible night, but the image of his wild-eyed father desperately screaming for Annie was seared into his brain.

"What's all this mess?"

He looked up as Ruth came into the kitchen.

"One of Chase's less brilliant ideas in action." He got up and started picking up random pages along-side Ruth. "January's not real happy with him."

Ruth snorted. "She seems fine with him now. I had to drive around them in the yard, they were kiss-ing so hard."

"Wow, he's a quick worker."

"Or January's a saint." Ruth washed her hands and put on her apron. "My vote's on her. Now, what can I get you to eat?"

After a stack of pancakes and bacon, Ry was more than ready to ride off on the range and finish up the repairs to the pasture that ran alongside the Lymond spread. Chase and January hadn't returned to the house, which wasn't a surprise. On a ranch as big as theirs there were plenty of places to go if you didn't want to be found for a while. Or to murder someone if January were so inclined. The aban-doned silver mine was a death trap all by itself.

"Where's BB?" Ry asked.

"Down at Maria's school helping out at the li-brary." Ruth pointed her spatula at him. "Now, don't you laugh. He's being a good parent."

"I know, but BB in a *library*?"

"He's not stupid."

"I never said he was. He's just not exactly the quiet type. He can barely sit still for five seconds."

"Jenna's going with him, so I expect he'll be fine."

"True love."

"She certainly calms him down." Ruth topped up his mug. "Roy said to tell you that when you've finished the repairs to come and find him and Billy at the eastern end of the pasture."

"Will do." Ry considered his grandma as he finished his coffee. "Is January stressed?"

"Well, she's certainly trying to cram thirty hours of work into a twenty-four-hour day, but we've all done that."

"Do you think she'll let Chase persuade her to hire a professional wedding planner?"

Ruth snorted. "Not in a million years."

"Me neither." He contemplated her for a long moment. "What about hiring someone she knows?"

Ruth smiled at him. "Smart boy. Want me to run the idea past her when she comes back?"

"Sure. Now just to prove that Chase isn't the only cowboy in this family, I'm off to mend fences of my own. Real ones." He kissed Ruth, rinsed his mug out in the sink, stowed the packed lunch in his backpack, and got moving.

He liked the slower pace, the chance to get on his horse and spend the day working hard in the open spaces of the ranch. He didn't miss the city at all, or the endless traveling to the various rodeos. In their first couple of years, he and HW had turned up at about a hundred different rodeo events a year, criss-crossing the country in an ancient pickup truck, maybe making a thousand bucks for a thousand miles if they were lucky. Sometimes they made nothing at all.

He hadn't heard from HW. Not that he expected to. Like all the Morgans, HW was as stubborn as a mule, and took his time to work up to an apology. Ry saddled Dolittle and headed out into the crisp morning. HW would be in Poway now, hustling to get those points and prizes to get him to the finals in late October. It was weird not knowing exactly what was going on in his twin's life, but it was also doing great things for Ry's stress levels.

He dismounted to unlock the last gate and closed it behind him and his horse. Chase had some wild plan to operate the ranch gates from some central GPS phone app or something. Ry was skeptical, but knowing his brilliant older brother he wasn't going to bet against him. Farmers and ranchers everywhere would bow down and worship any guy who came up with a cheap system for automatic gate access.

Ry remounted and checked his cell before he moved off. There was nothing from HW, and nothing from Avery. He frowned at the screen. Had he even given her his number? He scrolled through his contacts, looking for hers, and found nothing. Wow, he was smooth. No wonder she wanted nothing to do with him.

Dolittle stamped his feet as if wondering at the delay, and Ry slipped his phone back into his pocket. The last thing he wanted was to lose it. Chase was also on about an alternative method of emergency contacts within the ranch. Blue had pretended to fall asleep when Chase was explaining it, and Ry had ended up laughing.

He smiled now as he contemplated a morning of

twisting uncooperative coils of wire into the right alignment without cutting himself in the process. A man had to concentrate. He might complain, but for the first time in a long while, he felt . . . useful. That, and the thought of solving January's dilemma made him determined to work hard all morning.

Chapter Five

Avery opened the screen door and went toward the kitchen, where she could hear Ruth and January talking. She called out a cheery greeting, and January came to hug her hard. Her friend looked tired, and way too stressed for Avery's liking.

She took a seat at the table and accepted some iced tea before January sat opposite her, her hands clasped together on the table, her enormous engagement ring catching the light coming through the kitchen windows.

"So, what's up?" Avery asked. "Something bugging you about the catering arrangements?"

"It's more than that." January sighed. "I can't do this anymore. I'm spreading myself too thin. Chase suggested we hire a professional wedding planner."

Having dealt with many such people of varying abilities, from the excellent to the insane, at the hotel, Avery gave January a tentative smile. "That's an awesome idea. Who are you going to hire?"

"Well, I was kind of hoping it could be you."

"*Me?*" Avery blinked at her. "Why?"

"Because I trust you." January held her gaze. "I don't want some stranger coming in and telling us we've got it all wrong. I want to stick to the plans we made and carry them through to completion."

"I'm not sure—"

January grabbed her hand. "Please, Avery. I really need you."

"I'll have to talk to my parents about this. Working for you will take time away from my commitments at the hotel."

"I get that. We do want to pay you properly for your time." January fluttered her eyelashes at Avery. "*Please?* I'll love you forever, and so will Chase if it stops me being so grumpy all the time."

"Can I think about it?" Avery glanced from January to Ruth, who had been listening quietly in the corner.

"Sure." January squeezed her fingers and let go. "I understand."

Avery checked her cell and stood up. "Sorry I have to rush off, but I've got to sort out some details for an event at the hotel this evening."

"It was good of you to come out here at such short notice. I wanted to do this face-to-face." January rose, too, and walked with her out of the house. "Let me know when you've made your decision, okay?"

"Will do." Avery paused to get down the steps. "What did Yvonne think?"

"She thought it was a great idea, and the start of a potential new career for you."

"She would," Avery grumbled. "I'm surprised she didn't want to do it herself."

"She hasn't got time, and she also doesn't have your exceptional organizational abilities and eye for detail."

"Flatterer." Avery winked at January.

January kissed her cheek. "Hope to hear from you soon, okay?"

Avery was about to get in her car when she heard hoofbeats and turned to watch Ry loping his horse down the steep slope from the high pasture behind the barn. He was perfectly balanced even on the uneven ground, and so relaxed he made it look like a walk in the park, which she knew from past experience it certainly wasn't.

"Gotta love a cowboy," January breathed. "Those Morgan boys all look so *good* on a horse. It's just not fair."

Avery nodded as he came closer, slowed to a trot and then a walk as he approached the barn. He leaned in to pat the horse and then looked up directly at her. She went still as he kept on moving forward, her gaze fastened on the horse. Her back hit the side of her car, the hot metal shocking her, leaving her nowhere else to go.

She eased a hand behind her, fumbling for the door handle, but it was too late, Ry was practically alongside her now. She inhaled the sweaty, peppery musk of the horse and felt hot equine breath waft over her face.

"Avery?"

She started and forced herself to look up.

"You okay?" Ry's golden gaze narrowed under the brim of his Stetson.

"Yeah, it's just a bit hot out here."

He considered her for a long moment. "I'm just going to take Dolittle back to the barn. Can you hang around?"

She licked her lips, her gaze still on the horse, which was blocking her escape. "Um, no. I have to get going pretty soon."

"Then walk down to the barn with me, and we can talk as I work."

She shook her head. "I . . . don't have time. Sorry."

She finally found the blasted door handle and managed to get herself in the car. Her hand was shaking so badly she could barely start the engine. To her relief he reined his horse back, allowing her the space to reverse her car and leave. She was breathing like she'd run a mile and black spots danced in front of her eyes. She pulled over to the side of the road before she exited the ranch, and sat there shaking quietly until she felt better.

How stupid to react like that after all this time. It wasn't as though Ry had meant to scare her or anything.

"Get a grip, Hayes," she muttered to herself. "Time to move on."

Ry let Dolittle out in the field, and made his way back to the house to shower and change. When he came downstairs Ruth was sitting in the kitchen reading the local newspaper. He got a cold drink and sat opposite her, listening to the clock ticking on the wall and the thunderous hum of the ancient refrigerator.

"What's wrong?" Ruth spoke from behind the paper.

Ry considered what to say. "Does Avery ride anymore?"

"I'm not sure. I don't think I've even seen her helping out anywhere. Why?"

"Just wondering." He sipped his lemonade. "What did she say to January?"

Ruth lowered the paper. "About being the wedding planner? That she'd have to talk to her parents."

"Damn."

"What did you think she was going to do?"

"I was hoping she would just go for it."

Ruth studied him over the top of her glasses. "Why does it matter to you?"

"Because she needs a break."

"And working up here would give her that? Maybe she's happier where she is."

"Where she's comfortable?" Ry sighed. "Yeah, but she's *hiding* from everything."

"Maybe that's all she can manage right now."

"The accident was almost seven years ago."

"And she spent four years having surgery after surgery, and then physical therapy to learn how to walk again."

"We were friends. I just want the best for her."

Ruth patted his hand. "You're a good boy, Ry."

He grimaced at his grandma. "Yeah, right."

Chase came in with Blue and they both sat down at the table. Blue had a pencil stuck behind his ear and the back of his hand was covered in faded pink and blue flowery stamps, probably from his time at the school library.

What the heck was up with Avery? Ry went to get up just as Chase started speaking.

"You got a minute?"

"Sure." He reluctantly sat down again. "Where do you want me to put the cows now, planet Mars?"

"It's not about the cows." Chase opened his laptop. "We just wanted to bring you up-to-date on the search for Mom and Rachel."

Ry glanced from Chase to Blue. "I'm sure you've got it in hand."

BB locked gazes with him. "Is there a problem?"

"About what?"

"You wanting to be involved in this."

Ry held up his hands. "Fine, okay, tell me."

"It's okay to be worried about all this, bro. We're all still in shock that she might still be alive and living in California."

"Seventy miles up the road," Chase added. "I've set our firm of private investigators on finding Mom's last known address. As soon as they have a lead they'll call me, and we can decide how we want to proceed from there." He cleared his throat. "I want us all to be together in this. I know how important it is."

Ry forced himself to contribute to the conversation. "When do you think you'll hear something?"

"Hopefully, soon." Chase shook his head. "I can't believe we might actually get to see her again."

"Me neither," BB agreed. "Rachel will be an adult."

"Do we know if she's still with Annie?" Ry interrupted them.

"As far as we know, yes. Why?"

Ry stood up. "No reason. I've got to go into town and meet the bank manager. Anyone need anything?"

Chase was staring up at him way too intently.

Ry manufactured a smile and tapped his wrist. "Gotta go. I have an appointment."

"Ry, are you okay?"

"I'm good." Grabbing his hat, he made it out of the kitchen, put on his boots, and was on his way before anyone else could ask him about his *feelings*. He really did have a meeting at the bank, but talking about Annie? He could do without that. He had no idea how he'd actually feel if they did find her. His memories were fragmented, and too sharp to uncover. He remembered her long hair and the scrape of her nails against his skin . . .

"Yeah—not going there." He spoke into the air, put his foot on the gas, and set off for town.

Avery looked up as there was a knock on her office door and called, "Come in."

She straightened up as Ry came in dressed for town in jeans and a blue checked shirt slightly unbuttoned to reveal a yellow T-shirt that made his eyes look pure gold.

"Ry, I wasn't expecting you."

He gestured at his shirt. "I was at the bank, trying to look respectable enough to be allowed access to my own money."

"Considering that bank once belonged to your family, you'd think they'd be pleased to see you."

"Not anymore." He took the seat she pointed at and sat down, long legs stretched out in front of him, boots crossed at the ankle. "I practically had to give a blood sample, DNA, and swear some kind of oath to leave my body to science or something."

"Why do you need a bank account?"

He raised an eyebrow. "Because I work for my living. Did you think I'd be happy living off handouts from my millionaire brother?"

"That's not what I meant." She frowned at him. "I *meant*, don't you already have a bank account?"

"Different bank. Chase wanted me to get one here to 'support the local economy' and make it easier for him to pay the wages from one central place. Half the hands still prefer a check, to deposit in person at the bank. So does Roy. He doesn't trust robot internet banking."

"I can just see him saying that." Avery waited a beat and then asked, "So what can I do for you?"

"Take that job January offered you."

She folded her arms across her chest. "That's got nothing to do with you."

"Hell, it was my idea."

"Yours?"

"I thought you'd enjoy it."

"I would, but—"

"You have your work here. Work you told January you could do with your eyes closed."

"That's not exactly true. I'm just very efficient."

"I bet you are—which is why you could easily do the wedding for January and Chase."

She eyed him suspiciously. "Have you been talking to Yvonne?"

"From the coffee shop? No, why?"

"Because she keeps pushing me to expand my business as well."

"Smart woman." Ry paused. "Is it because you don't want to work up at the ranch?"

Inwardly Avery cringed. She should've known he would pick up on her sudden desire to flee earlier.

She tried to sound nonchalant. "I wouldn't be working up there much, anyway. Most of the wedding planning can be done right here."

He regarded her steadily for a long moment. "Did you talk to your parents?"

"Not yet. As I said, I'm still thinking things through."

He sat back, his head angled to one side. "Is it me?"

"Is it you, what?"

"That you're trying to avoid?"

She raised her eyebrows. "Conceited much?"

His mouth quirked up at one corner. "I didn't think it was."

"Which still confirms that you *are* a conceited ass, right? Just for asking the question."

"Defensive much?"

"I'm just saying that I have no problem with seeing you anywhere, okay?"

"So if it isn't me, and the job wouldn't be difficult for you, what is it?"

She didn't bother to answer, and just glared back at him. Why didn't he take the hint and let it go?

"When did you last ride a horse?"

Her breath stuttered in her throat. "What's that got to do with anything?"

"That's it, isn't it? You don't want to come up to the ranch because of the horses."

Silence filled her office, broken only by the cheery sound of Tucker whistling as he went past her door. Avery focused her gaze on her laptop keyboard.

"I am totally capable of being the wedding planner for January and Chase's wedding."

Ry slowly stood up, sauntered over, and leaned his hands down on the edge of her desk. "Then do it."

When she looked up, his eyes were level with hers, and there was suddenly no place to hide.

"It's not your job to tell me what to do."

"True, but I hate to see you hiding your abilities."

"You have no idea what I am capable of these days."

"You've always been smart." He flicked her forehead with the tip of his finger. "Breaking some bones doesn't change that."

She smacked his finger away. "Don't do that."

"This better?" He swooped in, kissed her gently on the mouth, and stepped away. "You can do this job with one hand tied behind your back, Avery."

"You'll have to tie me up if you try to kiss me again."

"Really?" He winked and then turned toward the door. "That could be fun."

"You—"

He paused at the door. "What time do you get off on Friday?"

"Seven, but why—?"

"I'll pick you up at seven thirty. We can go to the Red Dragon. I'll even buy you a drink with real alcohol in it."

The door closed behind him, and Avery sat down, her mouth open.

"What just happened here?" She said the words out loud even though she was alone. "How the heck did Ry Morgan get to be so . . . so . . ." She couldn't even think of a word to describe him.

She called Nancy, who answered immediately.

"What's up?"

"You'll never guess what Ry Morgan just did to me!"

"I can't tell you right now, because my mom is staring at me and she wouldn't appreciate my language. Hold on." There was a rustling sound and then a door shutting. "Okay, what?"

"He . . ." Avery realized she was flapping her hand around. "He . . ." She stopped to take a much-needed breath. "He told me to take that job with January."

"Is that all?" Nancy sounded way too disappointed.

"No, he asked me out on Friday." She snorted. "Like I'd go after what he said."

"Hold up—he asked you out?"

"Only to the Red Dragon."

"But he *asked* you?"

"No! He *told* me he's picking me up at seven thirty, and then he just walked out without waiting for my answer!"

Nancy chuckled. "Boy, he knows you well, doesn't he?"

"What's that supposed to mean?"

"The only way I ever get you to do anything is by telling you it's going to happen whether you like it or not."

"This isn't the same."

"Sure it is, although you'll probably have much more fun doing it with Ry Morgan."

Avery sank back into her chair. "You make it sound like I'm going."

"Doesn't seem as if you have much choice, does it?" Nancy sounded way too cheerful. "I've got to go, Ave. Mom's waiting for me."

"But—"

Avery stared at her cell. What was wrong with everyone? She felt like she was living in some alternate universe where everyone was trying to push her out of her comfort zone.

There was one quick and easy solution to that.

Getting up, she went next door to her parents' office, where they were going over the bookings for the upcoming week.

"Everything all right, Avery?" her dad asked as he looked up.

She gave them her best concerned, professional, I'm-doing-this-for-the-family smile. "I just wanted to run something by you both. I know this isn't a good time for any of us to not be putting one hundred percent of our efforts into the hotel, but I had an offer from January to take over as her wedding planner. Paid and everything." She managed to take a breath. "I know it's not going to work for you, but I just wanted to put it out there."

Her dad looked at her mom, who smiled.

"Actually I think it's a great idea."

"Wh-what?" Avery stuttered. Okay, she was officially still asleep and dreaming.

"You can widen your skill set, and we can start Marley off learning your job."

"My sister Marley?"

Mom blinked at her. "Who else? She's just finished her catering and management degree, so this will be perfect training for her."

"So you wouldn't mind?"

"No, not at all, you go ahead." Dad nodded. "This works out really well for all of us. We were wondering how we were going to broach the subject of Marley's return with you. She's going to have some *great* new ideas for the hotel."

"So why doesn't Marley do the wedding instead?" Avery suspected she was pouting, and was that just the hint of a whine in her voice?

"Because January wants and trusts you, love." Her parents exchanged a glance. "She called this morning, and had such great things to say about you, we couldn't possibly stand in your way."

"Okay, then." Avery nodded. "I'll tell her I can do it. Thanks for being so understanding."

She managed to get back to her own office, where she locked the door and put her head down on her desk. Maybe if she banged it hard enough she'd wake up.

Chapter Six

Ry frowned down at his phone and checked his messages. There were six silent messages, all from HW's number, and a seventh with just a muttered curse word. Either HW was butt dialing him, or butt drunk. It was Friday morning. Two weeks since he'd left Sacramento, and two weeks since he'd heard a thing from his twin. He'd checked the rodeo standings the previous night. HW was almost certain to qualify for nationals if he could just keep it together.

That wasn't a given with his brother, and it wasn't the kind of sport where you could ever count on your luck. You might draw a series of lousy horses, or get injured, or a million other things that stopped you in your tracks. He'd seen it all before. Just thinking about what had happened to a talented barrel racer like Avery made him shudder. He'd searched online, but there was no record of her accident. He felt like a heel for even looking.

She was still spooked around horses, which was a real shame. He remembered her riding the herd with him and his brothers. She'd been an excellent rider, as were most of her family. Living out in the sticks meant all the ranching families and towns-people helped each other out with spring branding, cattle drives, and all the other backbreaking tasks a rancher had to accomplish every year. The Hayes family had always pitched in.

Ry put his cell away and urged Dolittle into a lope. The sooner he reported to Roy, the quicker he could get back to the house and clean up for his ap-proaching date with Avery. *If* she was at the hotel waiting for him, which wasn't a sure thing.

As he approached Roy's place, he noticed the truck was gone, but someone was out there feeding the pigs.

"Hey." His dad, Billy, waved at him as he dis-mounted. "Roy had to go and check in with one of the ranch hands, who got in the way of an uncoop-erative yearling."

"Is he all right?"

"I think so. Just bruised ribs from what Roy could tell, but he's taking him down to Dr. Mendez at the clinic for a proper checkup."

Billy finished with the pigs, his silver gray hair and beard catching sparks from the sun. The harsh lines bracketing his mouth hinted at his troubled past, and didn't reflect the man he'd somehow managed to become.

"You okay, son?"

"I finished repairing the fencing on the Lymond side of the property."

"That wasn't what I meant." Billy turned toward him. His bright blue gaze, so much like Chase's, was careful. "You doing okay out here without your brother?"

Ry rested his forearms against the high back wall of the sty and looked out toward the mountains. Chase and BB had difficulty dealing with Billy, who had walked out just after Annie's disappearance, but Ry had always found him easy company. They were the quieter members of the family. Neither of them ever had a lot to say for themselves.

"It's still . . . weird. Not having him around, you know?" He risked a quick glance at his dad, who was leaning on the wall beside him. "In some ways I feel like I'm free, and in others . . ."

"He's your twin. You two were literally inseparable. Sometimes Annie and I had to wash and feed you as a unit because you had your arms wrapped around each other so tight." Billy paused. "Was he drinking?"

"And the rest."

"Damn." Billy sighed.

Ry refocused on the horizon, where the sun was deciding whether to go down or not. "Should I have stayed?"

"No," Billy said simply. "I had to conquer my demons myself, and no amount of anyone telling me to stop drinking and face my responsibilities made me want to change a damn thing."

"But you had reasons for drinking."

"I had an *excuse*, sure, but millions of people deal with tragedy in their lives and they don't all find solace in the bottom of a bottle. I took the easy way out, and I almost lost it all."

Ry took off his hat and dragged a hand through his flattened hair. "I don't know *why* he drinks and does all the other stuff. We're identical, and booze does nothing for me. Hell, I tried to keep up with him for a while, but I didn't like myself, you know?"

Billy patted his shoulder. "He'll work it out."

"You think so?"

"Sure. Let him get the rodeo finals out of the way first."

"If he gets there."

"You don't think he'll make it?" Billy straightened and turned toward the barn.

"HW said I was jealous of his success and was walking out just when he needed me most."

Billy looked over his shoulder. "I hope you didn't believe that pile of horseshit."

"He said I'd promised Mom never to leave him."

"Did you?"

"I don't remember doing so, but it sounds about right. She was always on at me to keep him safe."

"You remember much about her?"

Ry caught up with his father and they ambled toward the barn. "Not really."

"You looking forward to seeing her?"

"I'm not sure. How about you?"

Billy half smiled. "No one's asking me what I think."

"They should've. Do you want to see her again?" Ry asked as they entered the barn. "I can't imagine this is easy for you, either."

"I'd like to apologize. I know that."

"But Chase says *she* attacked *you* with the knife."

Billy met his gaze. "She did, but she had her reasons. I'm partly to blame for not seeing how depressed she was, and getting her some help."

Something stirred deep in Ry's gut. "Yeah." He

fumbled with the latch of the door to the tack room. "I'm going to put my saddlebag in here, okay? There's no point carrying it up to the main barn."

"Sure, I'll tell Roy tomorrow. You want a ride back to the house?"

"Nah, I'll take Dolittle. He needs the exercise."

Billy laughed. "True. I'll see you back there then—and Ry?"

Ry looked up. "What?"

"HW will work it out and come home one day. You did."

Ry nodded, and replaced the wire cutters on the shelf, making sure he retained his thick leather working gloves. Billy went to check Roy's house was secure, leaving him alone. The thing was, he was far more anxious about the potential return of his mother than the welfare of his brother, and yet he didn't have the faintest idea why. The more everyone talked about Annie, the less he liked it. What if Chase *did* find her? What would that feel like?

Ry stuffed his gloves in his back pocket and went to where Dolittle was happily dozing in the shade. When the dude ranch started taking in guests, he'd volunteer his horse to anyone with a nervous disposition. Nothing bothered the gelding, who took every opportunity to chill out. If a horse could ever be described as bombproof, then Dolittle should be on the poster.

He mounted up, gathered the reins in one hand, and clicked to the horse, who eventually woke up and started moving. A wave to Billy, who was now getting into his truck, and Ry was off, cutting through the pastureland, riding way too fast, but he needed to push back against whatever was bugging him. And he needed to get ready to face Avery.

He rammed his Stetson down on his head and with a whoop, settled low in the saddle, concentrating on the power of the horse beneath him and the suddenly downhill terrain, which made everything pass in a blur. He knew this land with his soul, knew every clod of soil and pothole, and yet he still concentrated hard because you never knew what might come back to bite you in the ass—especially on the back of a horse.

The anticipation of seeing Avery pushed the rest of his troubling thoughts back into his head. As he slowed down to approach the barn, he tried to remember the last time he'd been so excited to see a woman.

The answer hit him as he dismounted and started taking off the heavy saddle.

"My senior prom."

Dolittle didn't look very impressed with the revelation, and nudged Ry with his nose to get a move on.

"Looking for Avery to ask her to dance."

Dolittle sneezed, covering Ry in snot, but he almost didn't notice. Wiping absently at his face, he finished with the horse and put him in his stall. It would all clean off in the shower . . .

She wasn't actually contemplating going out with Ry, was she? Avery stared at the growing pile of clothes she'd already tried on and discarded. Somehow she was getting ready even while she battled with herself about how dictatorial he'd been, and how much she wanted to tell him where to stuff his date.

And she had nothing to wear. The last time she'd been out was two years ago with Nate Turner, who had decided she wasn't The One five minutes after their appetizers arrived, and never asked her out again. Not that she minded. They were still friends. She envied Nate's ability to know exactly what he wanted and when it wasn't working.

"I don't know what I want," she wailed, and picked up her cell.

She didn't even have Ry's number to call and tell him not to come. Sure, she could call the ranch and let his grandma know what he was up to, but that seemed rather unfair. She went for her backup instead.

"Nancy?"

"What's up?"

"I'm conflicted."

"You're going on this date."

"But—"

"You're going. I expect to see you in the bar within the next hour. If I don't, I will have to piss off my boss, leave my shift, and come and get you. Do you want to see me coming through your door?"

Avery imagined it. "No."

"Then I'll see you soon. Suck it up, girlfriend."

"Easy for you to say." Avery realized she was talking to herself as her screen went black. She surveyed the clothes on her bed. "So what does a girl wear for a night out in the only bar in Morgantown?"

Her cell buzzed, showing she had voice mail. It was Nancy.

"Wear the black T-shirt with the silver sparkly

heart on it, and your best bra. And when I say best, I mean sexiest rather than sturdiest, got it? You're welcome."

Avery found the T-shirt, which did nice things for her boobs *and* her brown eyes, and put it on over her fanciest bra. She brushed her long straight hair, leaving it loose for a change, and put on mascara and lipstick.

God, she was actually going to do it.

Checking the time, she eased into her jeans and short boots, found her one and only girly purse and filled it with essentials. She'd pay her own way and make sure she had her phone with her in case of emergency.

She snorted as she left her room. Like Ry Morgan was going to turn into some kind of psycho serial killer. Ignoring the elevators, which were busy with guests, she chose to walk along to the main staircase to stretch out her leg. She paused on the landing and saw Ry down in the lobby, chatting to her youngest brother, Mark. Ry was leaning against the concierge's desk, his wheat-colored hair shining in the light, all his attention on whatever Mark was telling him.

She grasped the banister and started down the stairs and he looked up, holding her gaze as she carefully descended. After a final word with Mark, he walked toward her, his expression serious.

"Hey."

She stayed two steps up so she could see into his face. "Good evening, Ry."

His slow smile almost stopped her breath. "I wasn't sure you would be coming."

"I wasn't sure myself."

He nodded slowly. "You look beautiful."

"I do not."

"You're not the one doing the looking." He offered her his arm. "Are you ready to go?"

She placed her fingers on the sleeve of his freshly ironed going-to-town shirt, and came down the last two steps. Instead of letting go, he tucked her hand into the crook of his elbow. Tucker held the door open for them and winked at Avery as she passed him.

"Have a good evening, sis. Don't rush back."

She stuck her tongue out at him and he laughed. Outside, it was just starting to get dark. The long lines of tourists had disappeared, allowing the town to settle back into comparative silence. Avery let out a slow breath as they strolled down the wooden walkway toward the red and pink lights of the local bar.

"If we go in there, everyone will be gossiping about us." Avery eased down the steps and prepared to cross the street.

"Not a problem for me."

"Someone will tell Ruth."

He shrugged. "It's a small town."

"And we're only having one drink."

He glanced down at her as they neared the bar. "You can have as many as you like. You're not the one driving."

"That wasn't what I meant." She paused as he opened the door into the bar for her, and a blast of air smelling of stale fried chicken and booze streamed past.

She spotted Nancy expertly pouring about fifteen drinks at once and simultaneously chatting with two locals and a bunch of tourists who were sitting at the bar. On one side were the pool tables and a couple of dartboards, on the other were tables and cozy nooks where you could get food to go with your alcohol.

Ry placed a hand low on her spine and eased her forward toward the bar.

"Hey, Nancy, Jay. I'll have a beer when you're ready." He glanced down at Avery. "What can I get you?"

"Beer's fine."

Nancy was already on it, handing over two frosted bottles, glasses, and two menus. "Here you go. Nice shirt, Ave."

"Thanks." Avery let Ry take the beers, she grabbed the glasses and menus, and they wove their way through the tables to one of the booths at the back.

They settled into the comfy seats that gave them a bit of privacy. It wasn't that busy yet. The locals would still be working on the outlying ranches or finishing up jobs that catered to the tourist trade. By ten the place would be heaving and *loud*.

Ry handed her a menu. "Are you hungry?"

"I haven't eaten yet, but I can wait until I get home, if you're on a schedule."

He looked at her over the top of the menu. "I'm done for the week. I've got all night."

"Oh." Avery hastily looked down.

"You trying to get rid of me or something?"

"I'm just trying to make sure I'm not monopolizing your time." Wow, now she sounded like an old prude.

"I wanted to take you out."

She snorted. "You *told* me you were taking me out."

"It worked though, didn't it?" His grin was as

charming as it was unexpected. "Here you are, out with me in the Red Dragon."

"For one drink."

"Sure, as I said, I'm driving." He turned his attention back to the menu. "Is the burger still good? Ruth told me we're supplying the organic beef."

"She's right, and it is very good if you like that kind of thing."

His head came up. "You've haven't gone vegetarian like BB's fiancée, have you?"

"No."

"Thank God."

"It's much healthier for you."

"Not according to Ruth and Chase. They have all kinds of statistics about how home-reared organic produce is the best thing ever. And now that I'm a rancher rather than a cowboy, I suppose I should get with the program."

Avery rested one elbow on the table. "Are you really done with the rodeo?"

"Yeah. I was never that good at it."

She frowned. "I saw you and HW ride when we were competing at the same events. You were just as good as him—maybe even better—because you were way more consistent."

"Things change."

She studied him for a long moment. "In what way?"

"He wanted it more."

"And what HW wants, HW gets, right?"

Just when the conversation was getting interesting, one of the servers came up and took their food orders.

Ry took a sip of beer. "So what did you decide about the job?"

Avery let him change the subject. Talking about HW never ended well, and she hated seeing Ry's face close down like that.

"I'm going to take it."

"Really?" His grin made her want to smile right back at him. "That's *awesome*. They're both going to be so pleased."

"I hope they haven't made a huge mistake. I was going to call January tomorrow, but you can tell her when you get back if you like."

"I think she'd prefer to hear it from you. So your parents were okay with it?"

"Yes. Everyone seems really keen on getting rid of me." He went to speak, but Avery kept talking. "Marley's coming back from college, and my parents want to squeeze her into the Hayes empire, so she's going to take over some of my work."

"That's good, isn't it?"

"I suppose so, but what about when I'm done with the wedding?"

He sat back, his beer in his hand. "What about it?"

"Marley might be better than me." She bit her lip. "She's getting a proper degree in hotel administration and all that useful stuff. Maybe my parents won't need me anymore."

He shrugged. "Then you do something else. Set up your own business."

"Like it's that easy."

"I'm just trying to help here, and anyway, Marley might suck at your job, or hate this town, and she'll be the one leaving."

"Unlikely. She's way smarter than me."

He slowly shook his head, and Avery looked him right in the eye.

"What?"

"Why do you always assume the worst?"

"I do *not*. I was just saying . . ."

"That Marley's going to steal your job, and leave you penniless."

"I didn't say that."

"That's what it sounded like from here. You used to be one of the most positive people I knew."

She grabbed her purse. "And this is why I told you it was pointless, us going out for a drink together. What I used to be is not who I am anymore." She found ten bucks and slid it under her bottle of beer. "Thanks for a great evening. I can walk myself home."

She managed to get out of the seat and marched toward the exit, aware that Ry had also stood but hadn't yet moved. She felt Nancy's inquiring gaze on her as she left without acknowledging her friend. If she stopped there was no telling what might happen, and she still liked Ry enough not to offer him up to Nancy's wrath,

Snaps of cold in the night air made her catch her breath. There was still almost no one around, so she was fairly certain she could navigate the five-minute walk in perfect safety.

"Avery, wait up."

She didn't look around and just kept on going.

"*Avery*. This is stupid."

She finally stopped on the corner of the intersection where she intended to cross, and scanned the street for traffic. He was right behind her now.

"Go away, Ry."

He caught her elbow, gently drawing her round to face him.

"So you're going to run away every time I say something you don't like?"

"Works for me."

His gaze searched her face. "The thing is, I'm not exactly sure what I said to make you duck out on me in the first place."

"You *insinuated* that I was negative about everything."

"You damn well *are.*"

She gaped at him. "How dare you?"

He shrugged. "Tell me one positive thing you said tonight. I said you looked beautiful, you said you didn't. I said January and Chase were going to be thrilled you'd taken the job, you weren't sure, and *then* you suggested your sister was going to come in and steal your job."

She slowly closed her mouth. Was that really how she sounded these days?

"I have positive things to say."

He raised an eyebrow. "Well, I'm not hearing them."

"So what? Maybe you caught me on a bad night."

He sighed. "I don't want to fight with you, Avery."

"Then I'll just go right on home and spare you the possibility, okay?" She smiled brightly. "Is that a *positive* enough attitude for you?"

He let go of her arm. "Sure. Go back home. Hide out in your room." He tipped his Stetson to her. "I'm going back to the bar."

He turned his back on her and started walking. Avery swallowed hard.

"Ry?"

He stopped and looked over his shoulder.

"I don't know how to be positive, and attractive, and all those things that used to come so easily to me. I feel like I'm stuck, and I don't know how to change anything anymore."

He came back and stood looking down at her, his expression unreadable. Just to add to her total humiliation, she wanted to burst into tears and throw herself at his chest. Where the heck had all that come from, and why had she just dumped it on Ry Morgan of all people?

"Avery . . ." He slid one warm hand behind her neck, bringing her close so she had to look up at him. "I want to help, so stop snapping at me, and *let* me, okay?"

"You can't—"

He put his finger over her lips. "I *want* to. You're my friend, you've always been my friend. I don't like the thought of you staying in that room night after night with nothing but work the next morning to look forward to."

"I'm not that pathetic. Nancy would never let that happen. She'd drag me out by the hair."

"Good for Nancy." He brushed a kiss over her forehead. "So will you come back to the bar, eat your burger, and just *talk* to me?"

She stared at the buttons of his shirt. "I bet you think I'm an idiot."

"No, I think you've been given a raw deal, and that you need to get back on your horse."

She shuddered. "That's one thing that's definitely not happening."

"Yeah?"

She scowled at him. "You were speaking metaphorically, weren't you?"

His smile wasn't reassuring. "Nope. I'm going to literally get you back on a horse." He took her hand and started walking toward the bar.

"That's supposed to make me feel positive?"

"I think you miss it more than you realize."

She snorted. "Then you're completely wrong. I hardly even think about it anymore."

Liar, liar, pants on fire. She dreamed about galloping away from all her worries every single night.

For the second time that evening, he held open the door to the bar. "Yeah, I could see that at the ranch, by the way you tried to climb inside your car without resorting to using a door."

"You surprised me."

"Bullshit. You watched me ride down the hill. I saw you looking."

Their booth was exactly as they'd left it, beer bottles, silverware, and all. As soon as they sat down, Nancy appeared with their food order, her gaze on Avery as she placed the food on the table.

"You okay, hon?"

"I'm good."

Nancy gave Ry the best-friend scowl, but he winked at her.

"Nice to see you again, Nancy. How's life?"

"Great, if you don't upset my bestie."

Avery patted her arm. "He didn't upset me, Nance, I upset myself."

"Then that's okay then." She picked up the tray. "As long as he's making you feel better."

"I'm trying," Ry said. "Can we have two more beers, make mine nonalcoholic, and whatever you're drinking yourself?"

"Sure. I'll bring them right over, and thank you."

Ry watched Avery's best friend walk back to the bar. He'd forgotten how pretty Nancy was, and she was no pushover. At school she'd been one of the few brave souls willing to take on his fiercely competitive brother Blue at any sport. She'd beaten him a few times as well . . .

"Nancy hasn't changed a bit."

"Yeah. Still stubborn as a mule."

Ry grinned. "Just like a Morgan."

Avery considered him. "You're not as bullheaded as the rest of them."

"I have my moments."

"You're more like Billy." She dipped a fry in her ketchup and slowly sucked it clean. "Was your mom stubborn?"

"I don't really remember much about her."

"That's right, you were only five when she disappeared." Avery shook her head and licked more ketchup off another fry. It was quite hypnotic. Ry couldn't decide if he wanted to lean over and suck her fingers, or kiss her lips.

"What?"

He jumped. "You're getting ketchup on your shirt."

"Darn it." She rubbed at the spot, pulling her

T-shirt away from her skin, giving him an eye-popping view of her excellent cleavage. "I think some of it went down my cleavage."

"I could help you with that."

She slapped a hand over her bosom. "Ry Morgan, behave yourself."

"Why? You're not seventeen anymore."

"I know."

The amusement faded from her face and he kicked himself for being so insensitive.

"How's the burger?"

"It's good." Avery licked her lips. "I'll have to talk to Ruth about supplying the hotel. I've always wanted to do a locally sourced type of menu, and Manolo would probably go for it."

"Who's Manolo?"

"Our chef. He's really talented. I'm going to get him involved in January's wedding buffet if Yvonne agrees."

Ry finished his own burger in three more bites. Working outside gave a man an appetite, and the beef was good. He must remember to tell Ruth.

"Is HW coming to the wedding?" Avery asked.

He avoided her gaze and sorted through his fries with one long finger. "He said he would."

"But . . . ?"

"He's pretty mad at me right now."

"Because you came home without him?"

"Trust me, he didn't want to leave."

"And, I bet, knowing HW, he had a tantrum when you wouldn't stay."

The nice thing about Avery knowing both of

them was that he didn't have to explain everything. She totally got it.

"He said I was doing it to spite him—that if he didn't qualify for the finals it would be my fault."

She was silent for so long that he wanted to look up, but instead dipped a fry in his ketchup. She probably thought he was such a wuss.

"What a *jackass*."

His gaze locked on hers and he blinked.

"He didn't—"

She reached across and grabbed his wrist. Now he was the one getting covered in sauce. "Don't you *dare* defend him. What a selfish, inconsiderate *jerk* to lay that on you."

He contemplated the unexpected strength of her grip and the pink polish on her well-trimmed nails.

"Thanks for the support." He took her hand and kissed her knuckles before returning it to her. "It means a lot."

"Ry—I know he's your twin, but sometimes even you must want to strangle him, right?"

"I left, didn't I?"

"And you shouldn't feel bad about that at all," she said fiercely. "I bet he was treating you like dirt."

He wanted to tell her the whole of it—to lay it out there in all its messy glory, but he *never* did that with anyone. His loyalty had always been to HW. The idea that he even wanted to share was startling in itself.

"Dad says HW has to work it out for himself."

"And he's right." There was a strength and conviction in Avery's words that she totally lacked when talking about herself. "You're not your brother's keeper."

Yeah, I am. . . .

His mother's voice as she cracked him round the ear resonated through his head. *You look after your brother, do you hear me? You take care of him.*

"Ry? Are you okay?"

He shook off the strange memory and refocused his attention on Avery. Ever since he'd found out that his mom might still be alive, he'd been having these flashbacks, or whatever the hell you'd call them. He sure as heck wished they'd go away.

"I'm good." He offered Avery a smile. "Do you want dessert?"

She made a humming sound that went straight to his groin. "Only if you'll share something with me?"

"Sure."

"Banana split?"

He pictured her eating that and wondered how much extra room there was in his jeans.

"That would be awesome."

Chapter Seven

"HW, it's four thirty in the morning. What the hell do you want?"

Ry blinked hard and settled back on his pillow, his cell now clamped to his ear. He'd forgotten to turn the ringer off, and was now regretting it.

"Just checking in with you, bro."

There was the sound of loud music, voices, and lots of whooping, which made Ry think his twin *wasn't* settled in for the night.

"Call me in the morning."

"Come on, Ry, give me a break. Just . . . talk to me."

"About what? I can barely hear you." HW's sigh was loud enough to get through, making Ry open his eyes. "What's up?"

"Nothing."

"You hurt?"

"You'd know if I'd broken anything. You always do."

"So what's wrong?"

There was a long pause. "Why do you always assume something's wrong, bro? Maybe I just called to tell you I'm almost certain to qualify for the finals."

"That's awesome." Ry hesitated. "I'm really proud of you."

"Yeah, which is why you assumed I only called because I screwed up."

Ry thought about his lecture to Avery. Was he just as bad? Only seeing the negatives?

"I'm really pleased for you. I mean it."

"Right."

"You out celebrating with Lally?"

"Yeah."

There was another silence and Ry wondered how it had come to this—that they couldn't even string a few words together. HW was supposed to be the outgoing, chatty one.

"When will it all be made official?"

"In the next week or so. Don't you remember?"

"I haven't had much time to keep up with the rodeo schedule since I've been home."

"Home? Is that what you're calling it now?"

"Yeah. The ranch is doing really well, and I'm working with Roy." Not that HW had asked a thing about how he was doing.

"You don't sound like you miss the rodeo."

"I don't." Ry let out his breath. "I miss you, though."

"So come back."

"I don't think Lally would like that."

"It's nothing to do with her. Come back for me. I—need the support."

"Yeah?"

HW's laugh sounded forced. "Hell, no. I don't *need* anyone. You're like my lucky charm, you know?"

"Like something you dangle from your key chain or rub for luck? I'm worth way more than that, bro, and you seem to be having plenty of luck without me being around. Didn't you just say you'd qualified for the finals?"

"Ry, what the hell's wrong with you? I said I'll forgive you, and I want you back—what more can I say?"

"Number one, I haven't done anything that requires forgiveness, and number two, *please* don't say any more or I'm going to end this call. I'm happy here, HW. *Happy.* Do you get that? I'm doing good work and good people surround me. I wish you all the best, and if you want me to come and watch you compete in Vegas? Let me know and I'll be there in the stands, cheering you on."

The silence this time went on so long Ry would've ended the call if he hadn't still heard HW breathing.

"I just wanted to tell you I finaled. It seemed important to do that."

His twin's voice was flat.

"HW . . ."

"Thanks for the lecture. Later."

"Typical." Ry snorted and resisted the impulse to throw his cell across the room. "He calls *me* in the middle of the night, makes the whole conversation about him, and I end up feeling guilty."

He lay back on the bed and stared up at the ceiling. There was no chance of getting back to sleep now. What the hell had just happened? HW had been way out of line, as usual, but there had been something beneath what he'd been saying. Some sense of him reaching out that was still eluding Ry. Was it as simple as HW wanting to hear a familiar voice? Ry rolled onto his front and stuck his pillow over his head.

He'd stood up for himself, and refused to rush back into his brother's orbit. That was good. But he still felt damn guilty.

Of course HW hadn't liked it. That was why they were in this hole in the first place. But if their positions were reversed, and he needed someone to talk to, who was the first person he would call?

His twin.

Hell.

Should he call back? Ry considered it for a second. He didn't regret what he'd said. HW was just pissed that Ry wasn't prepared to drop everything and come running.

Even though it was still dark, one of the roosters started crowing and Ry decided he might as well get up and get an early start. He might not have hundreds of adoring fans like his brother did, but at least the chickens would be pleased to see him.

"So Mom's not in Eureka anymore?"

Ry forced himself to ask the question as he forked up another piece of bacon and tried to sip coffee at the same time. It was now eight in the morning and he was ravenous. Billy had an appointment in town and had taken Maria to school, so it was just Chase, BB, and Ruth who sat with Ry at the table.

"Apparently not." Chase grimaced. "But they do have another lead to chase down, so all is not lost."

"Good." Blue nodded. "I really want this sorted out soon."

"You think I don't?" Chase asked. "It's costing me a fortune, and more importantly my wedding day's creeping up, and I'd much rather be focused on that."

"Then why don't we drop it?" Ry heard himself speak before he'd even thought it through. "Start looking again after the wedding."

He raised his gaze from his plate to find both his brothers staring at him.

"What's up?" BB eventually asked.

"Nothing. It's just that Chase's wedding should be more important."

"It's more than you worrying about the wedding," BB persisted. "We all want this, don't we?"

"What about Ruth and Dad?"

BB frowned. "What about them?"

"Have you ever considered asking *them* how they feel about all this?"

Chase and BB exchanged a puzzled look. "Ruth wants to find Annie and Rachel as much as we do."

"True," Ruth said.

"And what about Dad?" Ry demanded. "Have you even asked him what he thinks?"

Chase sat back, his gaze focused on his laptop. "I can't say I have."

"He lives here, too, you know."

"I'm well aware of that, Ry."

"Then maybe you should consider *his* feelings. Mom tried to stab him, and walked out, making him think he'd killed her!" Ry looked at his brothers and stood. "You don't consult him about ranch affairs, even though technically he owns this place, so why the hell should you care what he thinks about locating his wife?"

Ry pushed away from the table. "I'm going down

to see Roy. If anyone wants me, we'll be working out near the ghost town today."

He was halfway to the barn before he calmed down and Chase caught up with him. Ignoring his brother, Ry went into the tack room, grabbed his saddle, carried it out to the yard, and heaved it onto the top rail of the fence.

Chase hooked the heel of his boot on the bottom rail and looked out at the mountains. "Dad asked me to run the place and make the decisions for him. I have the official paperwork if you want to see it."

Ry didn't bother to answer and got his bridle ready, hanging it on the post beside the saddle.

"But you're right about one thing. I didn't ask him how he felt about us finding Mom."

Ry finally glanced at him. "Maybe you should."

"Yeah. I get that." Chase scrubbed his hand over his jaw. "I'm sorry."

"For what?"

"Assuming shit." His smile was crooked. "Or worse—not even *noticing* I should be assuming shit. Has Dad said anything to you?"

"Not really." Ry waited, the halter swinging in his hand.

"Then I'll talk to him."

Ry was about to go and fetch Dolittle when a familiar car pulled up in front of the barn.

"Is January here today?" Ry asked.

"Nope, she's in town at the historical society meeting." Chase noticed the vehicle as well. "Is that Avery?"

"It's her car. I'll go see what she wants."

"She'll come down here, won't she?"

"I doubt it." Ry started walking up the slope. "She keeps well away from the barn."

She turned as if she'd heard his voice, shielding her eyes against the sun. She wore her usual jeans and Hayes Hotel T-shirt, and her brown hair was tied back in a severe ponytail. She came toward him, the slight hitch in her gait barely noticeable on the flat surface.

"Hey!" It took him a moment to realize her gaze wasn't on his face but on the halter swinging from his hand. He held it up. "I was just about to get Dolittle. Why don't you keep me company?"

She took a step back. "I just came to check out the kitchen facilities."

"You can do that after you've seen me ride off into the sunset."

"It's morning."

He shrugged. "You know what I mean." He held out his hand. "Just walk down with me? I won't make you touch anything you don't want to."

Her eyebrows rose, and he was pleased to see some color returning to her cheeks.

"Okay, now you sound like a perv."

"You wish."

"No tricks?"

He solemnly crossed his heart. "I wouldn't do that to you."

"Okay." She nodded at him to move on. "I'll follow you."

For once he was glad that Dolittle's stall was at the far side of the barn. It meant he could walk Avery around the outside, past the chickens, and the feral cats sunning themselves on the retaining wall and in the other entrance.

When he reached the stall he took a tentative look inside and grinned. Perfect. Without turning around, he said. "Do you know why we named him Dolittle?"

"After the talking-to-the-animals-guy movie?"

"Nope." He made no effort to open the door but leaned against it, inviting Avery with a jerk of his head to join him. She took two tentative steps, her breathing already uneven.

He pointed at the horse. "Because look at him."

"He's asleep."

"I could get his food bucket and bang on it for half an hour, and he probably wouldn't even blink. If you want to know anything about conserving energy? Talk to Dolittle."

She studied the horse, her expression wary as if expecting an explosion. It made Ry's chest hurt. "So why do you ride him?"

He shrugged. "Because it makes a nice change from a saddle bronc or a bull." He tried not to react as she joined him, leaning over the gate, her shoulder wedged against his. "I don't like surprises anymore."

Dolittle smacked his lips and one eyelid flicked open in their direction and then closed again. Even in that second Avery tensed.

Ry transferred the halter into his left hand and carefully put his right arm around her shoulders. "The other reason I'm riding him is because we're trying out all the new horses for the guest ranch and writing profiles on them."

"Profiles?"

"Yeah, you know, about their good and bad points. What kind of rider would suit them best, that kind of thing."

"That's a great idea."

"Chase came up with it. He even created some

kind of shared document where we can all upload our opinions about each horse, and then add to it when we get feedback from the guests."

"He's a smart guy."

"Chase? Supersmart and super rich."

She looked up at him, the horse forgotten. "Do you wish you'd gone to college like he did?"

"Nope. Not my thing." He smiled down at her. "How about you?"

"I had a rodeo scholarship to a place in Texas, but obviously I couldn't go."

"That sucks." He kissed her nose and then, more gently, her mouth.

She gave a quivery sigh and he kissed her again, licking the seam of her lips until she opened her mouth to him. He dove in, seeking her warmth, pressing her closer to him as he explored and luxuriated in her unique taste.

His hat fell off as she shoved a hand into his hair, scraping her nails against his scalp, making him arch his back and purr . . .

A long, wet lick to his ear made him jerk away to find Dolittle right in his face. He shoved the horse's head away.

"You have terrible timing, dude."

Avery's laugh was shaky. "But a much longer tongue." She attempted to pull out of his embrace, and he immediately let her go. "I'll stand over there."

"How about you go grab my saddle blanket and meet me by the mounting block?"

"Sure. Where is it?"

"In the tack room, hanging on the appropriately named pegs since Chase got in there and put everything in order."

Her laugh this time was more genuine, but then she was walking away from him and the horse, right down the center of the barn, which meant she was going by eleven occupied stalls. He held his breath as she slowed and a few inquisitive heads popped out to watch her progress. But she kept going and he got down to the business of coaxing Dolittle out of his stall and into the sunlight.

She met him outside and placed the blanket beside his saddle, keeping well clear of Dolittle, who had immediately gone back to sleep the moment Ry tied him up.

"Thanks."

"You weren't kidding about the tack being organized, were you? I've never seen anything like it."

Ry threw the blanket on Dolittle's back. "We used to keep all the blankets in one big pile and hang the saddles and bridles wherever we found a space. Chase said we needed a more organized system, especially when the guests arrive, and made us redo the whole thing."

"It's kind of neat."

"I know, but don't tell him I said that." He checked the blanket was level and then hefted the saddle on top of it before automatically checking the cinch and the length of the stirrups. "Want to hand me the bridle?"

He reached out his hand, keeping his back to her,

and smiled as it landed in his palm the right way up, the reins trailing neatly on the ground. "Thanks."

Dolittle yawned, and Ry slipped the bit between his teeth, fastening the leather straps in place.

"Damn." He held on to the reins. "I left my saddlebags on the kitchen table."

"I suppose you want me to hold the horse while you go and get them."

He stiffened at her sharp reply and turned to study her. All Avery's ease had disappeared. Her arms were crossed over her chest and her tone was downright dripping with sarcasm underpinned with a whole lot of fear.

He blinked at her. "I was going to ask you to go fetch them, actually."

She let out a breath. "Sorry, I've had too many well-meaning people play stupid tricks on me with horses."

"I said I wouldn't do that."

She stomped off toward the house, leaving him looking at Dolittle. "She's a tough crowd." The horse chewed on his bit as if he was contemplating his answer. "We're going to have to take this slow, okay? Which should be a piece of cake for you, seeing as *slow* is your middle name."

Ry checked the cinch and all the buckles again, untied Dolittle, and walked him up and down beside the barn.

"I've got your saddlebags."

He turned slowly, keeping his body in between Avery and the horse. He hoped they hadn't been too heavy for her to carry. Keeping his promise not to leave her alone with the horse had seemed the most important thing to honor. "You're a sweetheart. Ruth really doesn't like it when we bring the horses into the house; otherwise I would've gone myself."

"So she said." Avery slung the saddlebags over the fence. "She also said to tell you your memory is terrible, and that she made you beef sandwiches."

"What a woman." Dropping the reins to the ground, which was Dolittle's signal to stand, Ry picked up the saddlebags and attached them to the back of his saddle. With one last covert look at Avery, who seemed to be doing okay, he mounted up and tipped his Stetson low over his eyes against the glare.

"Where are you working today?"

Good, she was still talking to him. "Up by Morgansville."

"You're running cattle there?"

"No, we, along with the 'save the ghost town' historical society, are working on ways to keep them out. We're mapping out fences and boundary lines for what land is going to be left untouched, and what land we can use for grazing." He hesitated. "Want to come along?"

"I'm not riding up there with you, Ry."

"I meant in your car."

"Not on that road." She paused. "You really mean it about not scaring me, don't you?"

"Yeah."

"It's very kind of you, but I'm not going to change my mind."

"We'll see." He blew her a kiss and reined Dolittle back just to remind him who was boss. "Have a nice day."

With a click and a nudge with his heels, Ry moved

Dolittle off in the right direction, leaving Avery standing there in front of the barn. Ry could've sworn her mouth was hanging open. He patted the horse.

"Good job, buddy. Just keep on being your dozy, nonthreatening self, and we'll have her eating out of your hand within a week."

Chapter Eight

Avery hugged Marley hard. After her tumultuous day at the ranch she'd woken to find her sister had returned to her family home. "It's so good to have you back."

Her baby sister, who was at least five inches taller than her, kissed the top of her head. "It's nice to be home."

Marley dumped her backpack on the bed and surveyed the small attic bedroom. "I don't suppose Dad's had an epiphany and put air-con in up here?"

"Nope. Not for family." Avery moved over to open one of the sash windows. "But you do have cross ventilation."

She sat on the bed as Marley unpacked the basics from her backpack with her usual calm efficiency. Her brown hair had been layered and lightened to a soft gold that Avery wondered if she could carry off herself. But would she be willing to keep it looking as good as Marley did? She had a feeling it involved more than just shampoo, conditioner, and a comb.

The rest of Marley's stuff was en route from her college digs and would arrive the next day. She'd persuaded some poor guy to drive it down for her.

"How are you doing?" Marley flopped down on the bed beside Avery.

"I'm good."

"Mom said you were working up at Morgan Ranch?"

"I'm coordinating Chase Morgan's wedding."

"Chase is getting married?" Marley pouted. "Damn, I was hoping I was the only one who'd seen his potential, and that he was up there waiting for me."

"You're too late. He's not only superhot now, but super rich."

"So I heard. Is his fiancée nice?"

"January's lovely. You'll like her a lot."

Marley avoided Avery's gaze and smoothed a hand over the pillow. "So you're okay about me muscling in on the family business?"

"The hotel stuff? Sure. I've been doing it for quite a while. I can help you get up to speed pretty fast."

"You're really okay about it? I could probably find a job somewhere else if it bothers you. You've done a great job getting the Hayes family into the twenty-first century as it is."

"I'm good." Avery hoped she sounded as certain as she felt. "I want you to be successful as well."

"Then I'll do my best to follow in your footsteps." Marley grinned. "Dad won't know what's hit him."

"Good." Avery smiled back. "You show him."

Marley started talking about all the things she intended to change, and Avery sat back and listened. She had no doubt her sister would shake things up.

Marley was something of a perfectionist. Her drive would free Avery up to work on the Morgan wedding, which was becoming more complicated every day. With Marley on board at the hotel, Avery would be able to spend two or three full days up at the ranch on double pay.

Chase had given her office privileges in the newly constructed welcome center, which had high-speed internet and excellent cell reception. How he'd managed that on a ranch in the middle of nowhere she had no idea, but she wasn't about to complain. It was much easier to coordinate her efforts from the ranch than she'd anticipated. And then there was the added attraction of a certain soft-spoken cowboy.

In her head, she couldn't stop replaying his kisses—the way he'd focused entirely on her, the lush taste of him . . .

Marley stood up. "I'm ready to start right now, sis."

Avery groaned and hauled herself off the bed. "I'd forgotten what you're like. Let's start with a tour of the place to meet the new staff, and then you can take it from there."

Later that day as she drove up to the ranch, Avery smiled as she remembered how quickly her sister had fitted in. Marley was not only smart, but very likeable, and had made a great first impression on everyone. Avery didn't mind one bit, which was something of a surprise. It made her feel less guilty about wanting to be up at the ranch.

She parked in front of the house next to Ry's old truck and went down toward the barn. The new welcome center was right behind it, and wide paths connected the house, the barn, and the as-yet-to-be-constructed guest cabins. The center had been designed to fit in with the original clapboard house and barn and, to Avery's amusement, looked as if it had always been there.

It was quiet, and Avery decided to take the short-cut through the middle of the barn between the stalls. She'd started doing it as a kind of test for herself, and now didn't even notice the number of horses she had to pass. It wasn't as if she was going to jump on one and start riding again, but at least she wasn't frightened every time one of them moved.

Progress was progress. She'd learned that the hard way.

The last stall was empty, and, hearing voices, Avery carried on walking until she came out into the paved yard between the barn and the fenced pasture. The area had been extended to meet up with the welcome center and now held new hitching posts and mounting blocks for the anticipated dude-ranch guests.

Both Ry and his horse had their backs to her and she paused to admire the sight of her favorite cowboy talking away to Dolittle as he brushed him down. The saddle and bridle were sitting on the fence, and from the muddied state of the horse, it looked as if they'd already been out.

"I think you need a bath, old fella." Ry smoothed a hand down the horse's neck. "Let me get the hose."

Avery stayed where she was as he turned toward the corner of the barn where the hose was connected to a standing pipe, and turned the water on. It was no hardship watching him work with the big animal. He talked more to the horse than he did to most people, and his voice was so soothing she was more than willing to fall under his spell.

She still wasn't sure how her friendly feelings for him had evolved into something quite different. She felt . . . safe. But a few kisses—outstanding as they had been—didn't make a relationship.

"Grab me a bucket and some soap, would you, Avery?"

She jumped as he addressed her directly, and checked the time. She should've known he would spot her. She was early, and there was no reason why she couldn't help out—except it meant getting closer to the horse. Without answering him, she backtracked to the tack room and found what he needed, along with a couple of sponges and cloths. When she got back he was gently playing the water around Dolittle's hocks and feet, getting rid of the worst of the muck.

"Thanks. He's scared of the bucket, so when you bring it round here could you put it on a cloth?"

Avery tightened her grip on the handle. "Where exactly do you want it?"

He looked up and her throat tightened as she realized his shirt was unbuttoned, displaying his chest and tight abs. It was a riveting sight. For a second she imagined grabbing the hose and directing the water at his chest, and lower, until he had no choice but to strip naked and let her towel him dry . . .

"Avery?"

She averted her gaze from his chest to the hose. "Yeah?"

"You okay? Dolittle's not going anywhere, I promise."

He thought she was scared of the horse. For the

first time in years he was wrong. She was more scared
by the throb of excitement running through her.

"I'm fine. Where do you want me to put the
bucket?"

"Over here beside the fence."

"Sure."

She walked in a wide circle around the horse, and
carefully placed the bucket on top of one of the
cloths she'd brought out with her.

"Thanks." He turned toward her and used the
hose to fill up the bucket, adding some soap as
the level rose. "It's all good. Dolittle's tied up. He's
not getting loose at any time."

"Okay." Avery took two careful steps back, her
gaze drifting to Ry's chest where a happy trail of
golden hair disappeared down into his jeans. He was
a good man in so many ways. He'd kept his promise
and never once tried to force her to come anywhere
near his horse.

He dunked one of the sponges in the bucket and
straightened, rubbing his palm over his collarbone,
which almost pushed his shirt off his muscled shoulder. She knew cowboys were fit—especially the ones
who competed—but she hadn't seen one up close
and personal for quite a while, and the sight was
mouthwateringly good.

Or maybe it was because it was Ry . . .

He came toward her, his gaze steady, and started
stripping off his shirt. His jeans were held up with a
leather belt with a modest silver buckle on it pro-
claiming him runner-up in some long-forgotten
rodeo. And why was she staring at his belt buckle?

"Better take my shirt off before I ruin it and Ruth

kills me." He hung it on the gatepost beside her. "You sure you're okay? You're making me look like the chatty one, here."

Reaching out one trembling hand, she touched the curve of his bicep with her fingertip, and he went still.

"Avery . . ."

With a soft groan he leaned into the press of her fingers, his muscles bunching under his sun-warmed skin. She got a firm grip of his upper arm and reeled him in. The sudden heat and press of his naked chest against her was a delicious shock, as were his lips as they met hers in a deep and thorough kiss.

She slid her hand up his arm to his shoulder and just held on as the kiss turned molten, pressing her body against his, all too aware of the rigid length trapped within his jeans between them. His hands moved over her back, molding her against him, soft to hard, demanding heat to her yielding welcome.

"God . . ." she whimpered against his mouth as he hitched her higher against him, her back to the fence post, her right thigh falling to the side so that he could rub himself harder against her denim-covered core.

He was like a drug—so important to her right now that breathing, standing, and maybe even wearing clothes seemed like stupid ideas. Oh God, if he kept that up she was going to . . .

"Don't stop." She moaned as his hips rocked into hers. Her fingers tangled with the back of his belt,

locking him against her, keeping him exactly where she needed him.

"*Yeah*," he breathed, and rolled his hips. "Not stopping sounds good right now."

She barely heard him, her focus all on the incredible, unbelievable evidence that she was about to come right here, right now. She flattened her palm against his ass and climaxed, gasping her pleasure into his mouth as she shuddered and rocked against him.

Oh dear God . . .

It took her a long time to peel her eyes open, and even longer to extract her nails from his skin and lower her right leg to the ground. Around them the birds still sang, the chickens pecked away around her feet, and . . . someone was walking down from the house.

Avery shoved hard at Ry's chest and he stumbled backward, his golden eyes dazed, his mouth reddened from her kisses.

"What's wrong?"

"Someone's coming!" she hissed.

He blinked and looked down at himself, one hand cupping the hard evidence of his arousal.

"Crap," he muttered and picked up the bucket of cold water. She winced as he doused himself with it, shivering with the shock.

"You okay there, son?" Billy called out as he came out of the barn with Roy. Both of them stopped to look at Ry.

"I picked up the wrong bucket of water," Ry said. "Didn't mean to freeze my assets off."

Roy cackled. "That'll teach you." He tipped his hat to Avery. "Morning, my dear. Don't leave that

horse standing around too long, will you, Ry? There's
a cold wind blowing through."

Billy winked at her as they both went into the
welcome center, leaving her alone with Ry and the
horse.

"I'm sorry," Avery blurted out.

"For what?" Ry gave a convulsive shiver.

She gestured at his now soaked jeans. "I didn't
mean—"

"To turn me on?" He grabbed one of the cloths
and mopped his face before looking at her. "You
do that without even trying. Turning *you* on—now
that's way more exciting."

Heat gathered on her cheeks. "I didn't mean that
to happen either." Some of the amused warmth
faded from his eyes, and she hastened to continue.
"Not that it wasn't . . . *lovely*, but my timing sucks."

"Yeah." He shivered again as a sharp breeze cut
between the barn and the welcome center.

She found his shirt and tossed it to him. "Go and
take a warm shower before you catch something."

He considered her for a long moment. "You going
to be here when I get back?"

"Yes, I'll be in the welcome center all day."

He nodded. "Then I'll catch up with you later."

He jogged away toward the house. It wasn't until
he was out of sight that Avery remembered the
horse—a horse that needed to be rubbed down and
let out to graze. Had Ry done that deliberately? She
didn't think so. His mind had definitely been on
other things. There was no one else around. She supposed she could fetch Roy or Billy from the center if
she had to.

She eyed Dolittle, who was taking a nap, and

circled around checking him out. Most of the mud had been washed off. All he really needed was to be rubbed down and let out into the field—a field that was about ten feet from where the horse was tied up.

Swallowing hard, she grabbed one of the cloths and advanced toward Dolittle. Her hand was shaking so much it looked like she was waving a flag.

"Okay, then. You can do this, Avery. You can . . ." She reached out and dabbed the cloth against Dolittle's long neck. "That's it. Nice horsey. Stay asleep." Was that her pathetic, breathy voice? She studied Dolittle's long eyelashes and thought he snored. Did horses snore?

One step closer, and she swiped the cloth down over the horse's back and withers. His muscles rippled as she worked and the chestnut shine of his coat caught the sun. She was breathing too fast and inhaling way too much horse, but she was getting it done.

Ry was halfway to the house before he remembered Dolittle, and doubled back. The last thing he wanted was for Avery to think he'd left her to deal with the horse. Sure, he was freezing his nuts off and soaked to the skin, but Avery was way more important than that. He paused in the shadow thrown by the barn and halted, his attention riveted by the unexpected sight of Avery drying Dolittle off.

She was talking as she worked, her voice way too high-pitched with an edge of panic that if Dolittle were any other horse would've set his ears twitching and tail swishing. Ry took another step forward, and then stopped. Should he let her continue? See how far she could go before she lost it? Was that being cruel or kind?

Even as he considered, she went to Dolittle's head to untie the halter rope securing him to the hitching post. It seemed to take her a long time. Part of Ry wanted to get out there and do it for her, to tell her it was okay and that she could let it go, could let him do it. She was still talking to herself—or maybe to the horse as she led Dolittle toward the gate into the pasture.

Ry readied himself as Dolittle finally woke up, blew on Avery's hair, and allowed her to lead him on. She took another long minute to open the gate. Ry let out his breath as she and the horse went through, and she unclipped the rope from Dolittle's halter. Most horses moved off immediately, but Dolittle settled in for another nap right there.

Avery gave the horse a tentative pat, and turned back to the gate. Her face was white, her brown eyes huge, and her mouth tight. Ry took one last look at her and quietly retraced his steps toward the house. God, he was so damn *proud* of her. He wanted to hold her in his arms and tell her how brave she was, but had a feeling she'd be better off not knowing he'd been watching her.

He was grinning like a loon. Some things had to be done alone, and this was probably one of them. He'd take a quick shower, get dressed, and find her at the welcome center. Then he'd make damn sure she knew just how much he appreciated her.

She was definitely going to throw up.
Avery had locked herself in the restroom and

stared at her pale, sweating reflection as she leaned over the sink. She'd gotten Dolittle into the field.

By herself.

It was the first time she'd voluntarily touched a horse in years. She blinked back tears as she started to shake, gripping the edge of the sink until her fingers hurt. She took several deep, gulping breaths, but couldn't seem to stop crying.

A knock at the door made her jump like a wild deer.

"Avery? You okay in there?"

It was Ry's voice. She debated what to do. It was obvious that she'd been crying, and she didn't want to face an inquiry about why.

"Avery?"

She washed her face and hands, unlocked the door, and walked straight into Ry's arms. He held her close without saying a thing, his thumb rubbing small, comforting circles on the back of her neck as she simply breathed him in.

"What's up?" he murmured into her hair.

She spoke into his shirt. "I put Dolittle in the field."

"You did?"

She slowly looked up at him. "Is that all you've got to say?"

"Nope."

Taking her hand, he drew her back into her office, closed the door and locked it. He walked her backward, sat her on the edge of her desk, and framed her face with his hands.

"You are awesome." He kissed her forehead, then her nose, then each cheek, and finally her mouth. He smelled like pine and sea salt from his shower. "You *rock*."

She smiled even though she was still close to tears. "Yeah?"

He kissed her again, this time less gently, until she opened to him and kissed him back. With a soft groan, his hands slid to her shoulders.

"I didn't mean to leave you alone with Dolittle."

"I know."

"I came back as fast as I could, but I guess you'd already taken care of everything."

She shrugged. "I couldn't leave him standing there all day."

"You could've." He searched her face, his hazel eyes intent. "Or you could've called Roy or Dad."

"I thought about it," she confessed. "But I wanted to see if I *could* do it."

He kissed her again. "My hero."

She pushed on his chest. "Don't. There's nothing heroic about me. I almost threw up. Can we stop talking about it now?"

His smile was slow in coming and made her all too aware that she was female—something that hadn't happened to her since her accident.

"Sure. How about we clarify something else?"

"Like what?"

"You touched me first, didn't you?"

She blinked at him. "What?"

"When I took my shirt off, you touched my arm, right?"

"I suppose I did. So what?"

He grinned. "You want me, don't you?"

"I wanted to touch you at that moment, sure."

"Just like I want to touch you, hands, tongues, and other body parts."

"It was just an impulse."

"So you don't want anything else?"

Her heart rate sped up. "I didn't quite say that, but—"

He placed a finger over her lips. "No buts. I want to make you come again. Will you let me?"

She held his heated stare as her body swayed toward him, offering itself before she could even attempt to frame the necessary words.

"I would've thought it was your turn."

"I can wait." He kissed her slowly and thoroughly until she could barely remember her name, as he eased her knees apart, his hand cupping her mound.

She was lost in his taste and his texture again, moving against his hand as he kissed and fondled her, raising her hips in an urgent plea for him to take more, *do* more.

"Damn, Avery, you're so beautiful." He kept on kissing her as he worked the button and zipper of her jeans free, and fitted his palm against her already damp panties. "So brave, so pretty, and so wet and ready for me."

He eased a finger beneath the elastic of her terribly sensible panties, homing in on her already needy center and stroking her there until she almost lost her mind. When he finally slid a finger deep inside she came almost immediately. He didn't stop, just murmured his appreciation and brought her to a second more intense peak, which left her gasping his name.

She wanted more, she wanted *everything* . . . She rocked against the heel of his hand, lifting into each stroke and grinding herself against him until a small persistent ache from her hip impinged on her sensual haze. She tried to shift her weight and her breath hissed out. Ry immediately went still, easing her back onto the desktop and slowing his fingers.

"Time to stop, I think."

She managed to open her eyes. "I'm fine. I really am."

His smile was crooked as he pulled his hand free. "You might be, but I'm about to come in my jeans. I haven't done that since I was a teenager."

She sat up straight and the pain on her side eased. He was right in front of her so it was easy to run one finger over the hardness behind his fly and feel his helpless response.

"My turn, I think," Avery whispered

"You sure about that? Because I'm not asking . . ." He stopped talking as she attacked his zipper to rcvcal whitc boxcrs clinging to the thick shape of his arousal. Avery sighed and rubbed her thumb over the crown, which was already attempting to push its way out of the confining cotton.

"Nice."

"Yeah?"

He sounded almost as breathy as she did, which was kind of endearing. She dipped inside the boxers and stroked the length of him, making him buck against her hand.

"Jeez, I think I'm gonna . . ."

With a hoarse cry he came into her hand and she held him close as he rocked and pulsed against her. His forehead came to rest on her shoulder as the last few shudders racked through him.

She was smiling when she removed her hand, and he hastily set himself to rights. She slid off the desk to do the same, and her left knee buckled. He immediately caught her elbow, holding her steady until the cramp eased.

"I'm sorry, Avery. I wasn't thinking straight."

"I'm fine." She shook off his hand, turned her back, and zipped up her jeans.

"But—"

She could hear it in his voice, the fear, the worry, the same tone she endured day in and day out from everyone around her.

"I'm *fine*, okay?"

And now she didn't want to turn around because she knew what she'd see—the honest concern for her, the *sympathy*.

But he didn't say a word, so eventually she sat down at her desk, hands clasped together in front of her, and raised her chin.

He retrieved his hat from the floor and took a while putting it back on. God, he was beautiful, so golden, and languorous, and easy on the eye . . .

"Was there anything else you needed, Ry?"

He angled his head and studied her for a long while. "Why won't you let me apologize?"

"Because I don't like being reminded that I'm a stupid invalid?"

His mouth quirked up at the corner. "Ah."

"What's so funny?"

"You are."

She sat up straight and glared at him. "Because I want to be treated like a normal woman?"

He rubbed a hand over his jaw. "I thought I *was* treating you like one."

"You *were*, and then you had to spoil it all by apologizing."

This time she got the whole smile and wanted to

growl at him—might actually have done it, considering his startled expression.

"I was apologizing for *my* lack of control." He shrugged. "A guy likes to last more than two minutes, you know? It was embarrassing."

She gaped at him. "You . . . were?"

"Sure."

She eyed him suspiciously. "Really?"

He winked at her. "Just promise me you won't tell your friends, and I promise I'll do better next time, okay?"

"You think there'll be a next time?"

He hesitated, his gaze meeting hers. "I'd sure like to get a second chance."

"You would?" Wow, he sounded as if he really meant it. "This isn't the best place to be doing any of this."

He looked around her office. "Agreed, but I doubt your parents are going to let me stay the night with you at the hotel."

"You'd be surprised what they miss. I have a key to my room and instructions about how to get there without anyone ever knowing." She hesitated. "If you want to try, that is."

"Didn't I just say that I did?" He sauntered closer and perched on the corner of her desk. "I want you naked and screaming my name."

"Okay." She refused to meet his gaze and rearranged the pens on her desk. "Then I'll call you."

"That's not going to work."

Startled, she looked up right into his amused golden eyes. "Why not?"

"Because you don't have my new number."

Now she was blushing. She handed him her cell. "Put it in for me."

He complied and she called him, making his jeans pocket buzz against his thigh. He took out his cell and checked the number. "Got it."

"Then we're good." She risked a smile. "I'm sure you have work to do, so I'll see you soon, Ry."

He stood and looked down at her before touching the brim of his Stetson and turning to the door. "Bye, Avery."

She pretended to be busy as he unlocked the door and walked down the hallway, his spurs clinking on the new tile. When the sound faded, she sat back and let out a long breath. Her morning so far had been rather unexpected. She'd touched a horse and had her first climax in years. Actually, several climaxes. Both of these things were closely related to her interactions with Ry Morgan.

Were they a couple now? She imagined him naked, and licked her lips. Maybe they were—or maybe he was just scratching an old itch, replaying the lost years of their past before moving on again.

Her smile died. Maybe he was just feeling sorry for her.

But if that was true—and despite what he said, she still couldn't discount the possibility—what the hell was she doing encouraging him?

Chapter Nine

"Hey, wait up, bro!"

Ry paused in the hallway and then poked his head around the door to the kitchen, where BB was sitting at the table drinking coffee and texting on his phone. He'd spent a restless night thinking about Avery instead of sleeping and was not in the best of moods.

"What's up?"

"I've got new data about Mom."

"Yeah?" Ry didn't go any farther into the kitchen, but he didn't retreat either. He leaned against the doorjamb. "What's happened?"

"Chase's guy reported back. They think they've traced her to Humboldt."

"The university town up north?"

"Yeah, that's the one. I've no idea what she might be doing there, but I wanted to warn you that Chase is probably planning a trip."

"Before the wedding?"

"I should imagine so." BB sighed. "He's so damn focused on finding her."

Ry grimaced. "I got that." He hesitated. "The thing is, BB, if she was so close, why didn't she come back? Even if it was just to visit? It wasn't as if we were a thousand miles away or anything."

"I asked Chase the same question. He didn't have an answer either . . ." BB finished his coffee in one gulp. "I guess she had her reasons. Dad said she was depressed after Rachel was born, and that maybe she wasn't responsible for her actions."

Ry let that sink in. It didn't help.

BB put down his mug and stood, stretching his arms over his head. He was shorter than Ry and had blue eyes like Chase and Billy, whereas the twins favored their fair-haired mother. After his years in the Marines he was also superfit and not the kind of guy to mess with. He was a straight shooter and easier to understand than Chase, who could overcomplicate things sometimes.

"Look, if you don't want to come with us to Humboldt, I'll tell Chase and make it okay."

"I haven't decided yet. I don't expect you to make excuses for me," Ry replied as evenly as he could.

"But you're not keen on seeing her, are you?" BB held his gaze. "I didn't think you remembered her that well."

"I don't. Maybe that's why I'm not as interested in pursuing this as you two are."

"Makes sense." BB nodded. "But I know Chase would appreciate your support. He talked to Dad and made things right with him after what you said."

"Yeah?" Ry didn't want to get into that. "Cool. I gotta go, okay? Let me know what Chase decides."

He put on his boots and went out to his truck. Today, he and Roy were building fences out by the old abandoned silver mine and ghost town. Apparently both places had to be protected from the cattle and the expected influx of guests to the dude ranch. Morgansville was gradually dissolving into the dust, so a task force, headed by January and the local historical society, were working with the ranch to preserve what was there. It would make the ghost town safe and secure forever, which meant a lot to Ry.

The old mine was something of a death trap, and there were very few maps of the underground workings. The consensus had been to fence the place off completely, and just hope no one had the bright idea of getting up close and accidentally falling down an unknown shaft. Roy said anyone who did that deserved what they got, but current California health and safety laws meant the ranch would be facing a lawsuit, and Chase wasn't going to let that happen.

One of Ruth's dogs followed Ry out of the house and barked at him encouragingly. It was some kind of hound crossed with spaniel and possibly Chihuahua, which meant its ears were all over the place.

"You coming, Dog?" Ry held the back door of his king cab truck open, and the dog jumped in. He'd missed having a dog. Traveling between rodeos meant it hadn't been a good idea. But now he was home and this dog seemed to have adopted him, so all was good. Before he set off, he checked his cell. There was nothing from Avery.

After watching her deal with Dolittle and then get down and dirty with him in her office, Ry had decided to give her some space. The last thing he wanted was to push her into *anything*, although being with her and not touching her was harder than he'd anticipated. Did she even want to be in a relationship? She certainly hadn't asked for clarification, but neither had he. They'd always been friends, and somewhere in his heart he'd always hoped for more. But HW had spoiled those early adolescent dreams, and then they'd left town.

He'd been too shy at school, assuming that anyone with any sense would prefer his twin to him, while taking every opportunity to hang out with Avery at school and at any event that involved horses. He was pretty sure she'd seen him as a friend and never thought of him as anything special. But he'd always admired her outgoing personality and her determination to not be just "one of the Hayes kids," but her own person.

He fired up the engine of his truck and the dog barked and jumped into the front passenger seat. In his more reflective moments, he was glad he hadn't started something with Avery back then, because he was pretty sure the relationship wouldn't have lasted, what with his crazy rodeo schedule, and her accident . . .

The thing was, he still liked her, and maybe if he took things slow and steady she'd work out that she liked him, too. If he could just keep his hands off her. He hadn't bargained for the heat between them.

Succumbing to temptation, he sent her a text.

You okay?
Yup, you?

He grinned at his cell like an idiot. All good here. Just heading out.

More fences?

How did you guess? You free for dinner tonight?

The pause this time was longer, and the dog nudged his shoulder as if telling him to get a move on.

Could be. What time?

7? I'll call you when I get to town.

OK C U later x

He eased off the brake, and drove off. His canine buddy put his head out of the window, his tongue hanging out, huge ears flapping in the breeze. Ruth said the dog hadn't told her his name yet, and that Ry was welcome to listen in and take the critter on if he wanted. Looking at the dog's goofy grin, Ry decided to take Ruth up on her offer. But if the dog didn't come up with something soon for his name, Ry had a few ideas of his own . . .

Life was good. It really was.

"What in thunderation is that?" Roy shaded his eyes as the roar of a helicopter drowned out everything around them in the dusty, sunbaked pasture. "The landing strip's on the other side of the darned ranch."

Ry spat out a mouthful of dirt the chopper had stirred up. "Maybe they aren't landing."

"They'd better not be. Scaring my cattle like that." Roy scowled at the large silver helicopter that made another pass, and then flew to the east.

"Probably some of Chase's buddies from Silicon Valley."

"Fools," Roy muttered as he put down his hammer. "I'll give them a piece of my mind."

"Looks as if your wish will be granted." Ry shaded his eyes. "Yeah—they're landing down by your house. You sure you aren't expecting anyone?"

"We'll find out. You coming?" Roy stomped over to the truck and got in.

As Ry was driving, he guessed he was.

He didn't know much about helicopters. This one was new and had lettering on the side that looked like a TV station or something similar. By the time they arrived, several people were emerging from the helicopter, some of them in cowboy hats.

He glanced at Roy, who shrugged.

"I have no clue who these folks are, but that's a California TV channel that features local sporting events."

Ry didn't doubt his boss's knowledge. Ruth and Roy were TV addicts and watched every reality show, soap opera, game show, and sport known to mankind.

"Better see what they want, then."

Ry parked, left the window open for the dog, and got out. The hot, dry wind swirled around him like a desert storm, coating him in fine white dust. He put his Stetson on and strolled behind Roy to the group gathered just beyond the helicopter.

One of the women was pinching her nose. "Oh my God, the *smell*! How can anyone live in a place like this?"

Seeing as she was standing directly downwind of Roy's pigs, Ry wanted to smile.

"Can I help you folks?" Roy raised his voice to be heard above the winding-down whine of the helicopter.

"Roy! *Dude!*"

Ry's gut tightened as the tallest of the guys turned and came toward them, hand outstretched.

"That you, HW?" Roy didn't sound any more welcoming than Ry was feeling. "Don't you know better than to scare every living creature on a ranch?"

HW's grin widened. "Nice to see you haven't changed, Roy. How are you doing?"

He clapped an unresponsive Roy on the shoulder and turned to Ry.

"Hey. What's up, bro?"

"Nothing much."

HW turned back to Roy. "I'm sorry about the landing. The team just wanted to get a sense of the ranch from the air, so I was giving them the tour. I had no idea where the cattle were running."

"Team?" Roy asked.

HW made a sweeping gesture with his hand. "Yeah, these guys are from the Cally4Nya network. They wanted to do a piece about me before the rodeo finals." He glanced between Roy and Ry. "When they found out I grew up here? They really wanted to see the place."

"Your cell not working, HW?" Ry contemplated his brother for a long moment.

"You mean why didn't I call?" HW grinned. "It was a last-minute decision. I really didn't think anyone would mind. Ruth is here, isn't she?"

"At the main house." Ry stuck a hand in his pocket. "How are you expecting to get up there?"

"Ry . . ." HW lowered his voice. "Could you just get

over yourself for a few minutes? This is important to me. I want to make a good impression so I can attract more local sponsors. How hard is it to give us all a ride up to the ranch?"

Ry glanced at Roy, who shrugged. "We can take them. You okay with that?"

"Sure." Ry was already walking back to his truck. "I can take three in the back. The front passenger seat is already taken."

Two of the people were carrying big items that looked like cameras and lights. He helped them load their gear in the bed of his and Roy's trucks. They were nice and polite and thanked him for his help. Meanwhile HW continued to hold court with the other three, two females and one guy, who all seemed to think the sun shone out of his ass. Roy could take those guys. He'd settle for the real workers.

Before he left he called Ruth. She didn't hold with texting or with the internet in general.

"Hey, HW's turned up with a TV crew. You okay about him coming up to see you?"

"A TV crew?"

Ruth sounded way too thrilled for Ry's liking. "Yeah. Cally4Nya. Roy says he knows them."

"So do I! How exciting. I'll set the table."

Ry ended the call as the two techies got in the truck and immediately petted his big slobbery dog. Roy was still talking to HW, who was smiling his sweet golden grin. His twin was looking leaner than usual, his blond hair cut short and tight. Ry ran a hand over his unshaven jaw and grimaced. He wasn't going to compete with his brother. It never ended well.

It didn't take long to reach the ranch house. The two guys in the back spent every moment exclaiming over the views and the emptiness and the silence. Ry couldn't decide whether they were horrified or intrigued. A lot of people couldn't deal with the isolation. His mom had hated it.

A memory crept over him: He was standing at the foot of the bed watching his mom dump clothes in a suitcase while the baby was crying. They hadn't had anything to eat for a long while, and he was hungry and had come looking for her. Whatever he'd said had made her angry. Her face had contorted with rage and she'd grabbed hold of him by his T-shirt . . .

"Wow! You grew up here? It's *awesome*!"

Ry turned off the engine, got out of the truck with Dog, and helped the guys unload.

"Leave your stuff on the porch and come in and meet my grandma."

He led the crew into the house, where Ruth was waiting in the kitchen. She immediately sat them down and started simultaneously feeding them and asking questions. Ry left her to it and headed back out, bumping into Roy and HW as they came in.

HW's fingers closed around his upper arm. "Where're you going, Ry?"

"Back to work."

"But I need you here. Francesca wants to interview you."

"So?"

"*Please*, Ry. Help me out? I need the exposure before the finals. You know how it goes."

Ry met his brother's gaze properly for the first

time, noticing the shadows under his eyes and the worry lines bracketing his mouth.

He sighed. "Sure. I'll hang around if it's okay with Roy."

"Thanks, bro." HW grinned. "Roy's down with it. He's dying to be on TV."

"Figures." Ry made for the stairs. "I'll just go and clean up."

Avery checked her cell and found a message from Ry.

Sorry, change of plans. Can't get into town tonight.

"What's up?" Marley came into their shared office, a pile of folders in one hand.

"Ry said he'd be coming into town this evening and now he can't make it."

"Ry Morgan?"

"Yeah." Avery contemplated her phone with a sense of real disappointment.

"Brother to multimillionaire Chase, superhot Marine Blue, and twin to HW?"

"That's the one."

Marley sank into the chair with a sigh. "You lucky thing. Are you going out with him now? Why didn't you *tell* me? Why didn't anyone tell me?"

"Because there's nothing to tell."

"Just a business thing, then?"

"Yes." Avery hoped she wasn't blushing at that downright lie. "But he's had a change of plans, and he's not coming."

Which meant she wouldn't be coming either . . .

Oh God, he was corrupting her without even trying. They weren't even officially dating, and yet they'd both had their hands down each other's pants. Were they just hooking up now? Was it totally about sex for him?

Not that they'd had sex . . . but oh God, she wanted to . . .

"Avery?"

She hastily collected herself. "It's a shame he won't be here. I have some financial information for January and Chase I was hoping he could pass along."

"Then why don't you meet at the ranch instead?"

"I could do that." Avery's thumb hovered over the keyboard of her cell.

"Then go and see him. I'll manage here."

"I know you will." She checked the time. One hour before she was due to meet Ry. "I suppose I *could* go up there."

"I would." Marley winked at her. "You never know when business might turn to *lurve*."

"You read too many romance novels."

"So do you. In fact, you were the person who got me hooked on them."

"That was Mom's fault. She started it."

She texted Ry back. Have paperwork to deliver so might come up there, okay?

The door burst open to reveal her brother Mark. "Tucker's out, and there's a snake on the back porch. Can one of you catch it?"

Marley shuddered and Avery stood up. "Sure. Can't have the guests getting all scared like your big sister, Marley. But you're going to have to help me, okay? Get the net and the bag."

* * *

Ry shielded his eyes from the glare of the lights the TV crew had put up facing the pile of straw bales where he was supposed to sit to be interviewed by the very beautiful Francesca. The sun was going down and the sky was tinged with purple, a spectacular backdrop to the set. Ruth and Roy had already done their pieces and were now busy making up beds for the guests and planning a sumptuous dinner.

Now it was Ry's turn.

He'd always hated being hauled up in front of the lights to speak after a rodeo win. Sometimes he'd sent HW along to pretend to be him.

Francesca sat beside him and patted his arm. "You look *so* like your brother!"

"We're identical twins, ma'am."

Her smile thinned. "You don't have to call me ma'am. I'm probably the same age as you are."

Ry doubted that, but he'd been brought up to be polite.

"It's a shame your oldest brother isn't here right now. I would've loved to have interviewed the great Chase Morgan of Give Me A Leg Up."

Blue had conveniently disappeared with Jenna, and Maria and Billy had muttered something about going to check on the new house site, leaving Ry to stand in for the rest of the family. He wished the others were around. They'd be far better at getting publicity for the new and improved Morgan Ranch. He felt inadequate just sitting there, his tongue stuck to the roof of his mouth and his throat dry. HW had always done the talking.

He made an effort. "You can probably catch up with Chase in San Francisco. He's there once a month."

"So I heard." Francesca looked over at Tom, who was in charge of the shoot. "Ready to go? I'd like to get this done before the light goes. It's so pretty out here."

"Ready when you are," Tom called.

She smiled at Ry again. "Okay, just be yourself, and don't worry about getting everything right. We can always edit stuff out. We'll start with you, and then bring HW in so our viewers can take in the sight of the two of you."

"Great," Ry murmured.

If it was up to him it was going to be a damn short interview, and a very long night.

Avery approached the unnatural circle of lights down by the barn with all the trepidation of a girl in an alien movie. What the heck was going on? Ry had said he was busy. He might have explained that something extraordinary was happening at the ranch. But maybe he hadn't wanted her to come up. She checked her cell. He hadn't replied to her last text, so she'd assumed everything was fine. She slowed down. Maybe this was a mistake.

"That you, Miss Avery?"

She jumped and slapped a hand over her heart as Roy's voice came from behind her. He was standing on the porch of the house, looking down at her.

"Hi! I was looking for Ry. Is he busy?"

Roy nodded at the barn. "He's being interviewed.

Go on down, and when they wrap up remind everyone to come on in for dinner. Ruth's expecting them."

"Will do."

Avery carried on down the slope, aware of a group of people behind the lights, all staring inward. She edged closer until she was right alongside them, but no one noticed her. Ry was sitting on a bale beside a beautiful blond woman who looked vaguely familiar. It was so quiet out on the ranch that she could hear what was going on quite clearly.

"I think it's time to introduce your brother—the saddle bronc rider bound for the national rodeo finals, HW Morgan."

Avery moved a step nearer as HW sauntered onto the set, tipping his hat to the interviewer and taking a seat beside his brother, who hardly acknowledged him.

Seeing them together only emphasized the differences between them that most people would never see. HW looked relaxed, confident, and golden . . . as if nothing could ever go wrong in his life. Ry smiled less and held himself more tightly, his hand clenched on his thigh as HW chatted to the woman.

She'd seen Ry being interviewed over the years, and he'd never looked comfortable. Now—with HW beside him—he looked downright miserable. The woman took the twins through a brief review of their childhood and early careers before turning to Ry.

"So, Ry, how does it feel having a superstar for a brother?"

Avery winced at the question, but Ry shrugged.

"He's done amazingly well."

"But how does it *feel* to have your identical twin succeed where you have failed?"

"I guess I just didn't want it as much as he did."

The woman leaned in. "And you're okay with that? Rumor has it that you walked out when you heard your twin had qualified for the finals and you hadn't."

HW opened his mouth, but Ry got in first.

"Yeah? I don't remember it that way myself. I'd already decided to come home to help restore the family ranch before I knew HW had qualified. I don't like to break my promises."

The woman turned to HW. "And what did you do when your brother deserted you at this crucial moment in your career?"

HW's smile was a study in patience and humility. "I just wanted my brother to be happy, Francesca. I knew *I'd* be okay. I'd done most of the hard part."

"Do you plan on going to watch your brother compete in Vegas, Ry?"

"If he wants me, I'll be there cheering him on. It's a great achievement."

"I'm hoping my whole family can come out," HW added.

"That includes your oldest brother, Chase Morgan, who runs a tech company in San Francisco, correct?"

"Yup. He's already told me he'll be coming." HW grinned. "He's been awesome."

Ry said nothing, easing back so that all the light fell on his twin like the sun reflecting back the moon. Avery came from a big family. She knew how easy it was to get lost among a crowd of siblings, but Ry seemed to be intent on disappearing altogether. He was worth twenty of HW. Why couldn't he see that?

Francesca turned to the camera. "Let's wish HW Morgan all the best at the national finals, and many thanks to the Morgan family for hosting us today. We've had such fun!"

"Cut!"

One of the men beside Avery shouted, and she jumped. Attempting to avoid being seen, she circled around the cameras deeper into the shadows, and came out close to where the brothers were standing by the bales.

"Why did you tell her that bullshit, HW?" Ry was speaking.

"I didn't. I swear it."

"Then somebody did. I don't care if you want your face on TV, but I don't want mine on there or anyone judging me, get it?"

"Calm down, Ry. I'll talk to Francesca and Tom. I'm sure they'll edit out anything you don't like."

"Tell them to edit me out completely. What the *hell* were you thinking, HW?"

Avery stumbled over the pebbled drain gully and Ry's head whipped around.

"Avery?"

"Hey." She tried to smile at him. "Ruth says dinner's ready, and don't be late."

HW was staring at her, his brow furrowed. "Avery *Hayes*?"

Ry moved over and took her hand. "Yeah. Shall we go up to the house? We can talk on the way."

His grasp was little short of brutal and his stride way too long. After a couple of steps, Avery dug in her heels and attempted to slow him down.

"You're going too fast."

"Sorry." He immediately eased up and muttered a curse under his breath. "I just needed to get away from my brother."

She pushed gently on his chest until he took two reluctant steps backward and hit the outside wall of the barn, deep in the shadows.

"What's wrong?"

"HW's here."

"So I saw. Is he doing some kind of documentary or something?"

"He says it's for a local news channel that wants to follow a hometown hero through to the national finals in Vegas."

"And he decided to turn up here and get some family time in."

"Exactly."

"Typical HW."

He let out a breath and leaned back against the wall, looking up at the sky. "How much did you hear?"

"Just the interviewer suggesting you were consumed with sour grapes and green with envy over your brother's success."

He groaned.

She cupped his cheek. "You handled it really well."

"Didn't feel like it. It felt like a sucker punch."

"I wonder who told *that* story out of class."

"HW has plenty of people around him who want him to look like the golden boy. The more fans are invested in him as a personality, the more sponsors he'll attract and the better his chances of success at the finals."

She went up on tiptoe and kissed his mouth. "It still sucks."

"Only for me."

She kissed him again, and this time he rested his hands on her hips and held her close.

"You're worth a dozen of him, Ry. Why do you let him get away with crap like this?"

"Because I'm stupid? And he's not all bad." He sighed. "I was born first. I'm supposed to look out for him."

"Says who?"

"My mom, my dad, everyone. That's all I heard when I was a kid."

"I know what that's like, but these days my siblings are all adults. So is HW. You can't save him from the consequences of his own choices."

"You sound like Blue's Jenna. She's always trying to psychoanalyze me." He dropped a quick kiss on her nose. "Come on, let's go eat."

"Are you sure you don't mind that I just turned up?"

He smiled for the first time and took her hand. "You're kidding, right? You're the best thing that's happened to me all day."

Avery was still grinning as he drew her into the kitchen, which was already filled with people. There was no sign of Blue and his family, but Ruth, Roy, and HW were present as well as all the film crew.

HW pulled out the chair next to him. "Room for two more up this end."

"Figures," Ry murmured as they moved down the room.

Avery took the seat right next to HW and Ry slipped in beside her. On the table already was a huge pan of lasagna, a dish of gnocchi, and one of garlic bread. Avery's mouth watered as the scent of melted butter and roasted garlic reached her.

"Make some space, Ry. There's green salad." Ruth leaned between them and Avery took the bowl from her and placed it on the table. "Anyone want more iced tea or a beer?"

There was a chorus of no's and everyone settled in to eat, sharing the dishes between them. The TV crew were soon exclaiming over Ruth's cooking—all except Francesca, who looked like she wanted to cry.

"Are you okay?" HW called out to her.

"I'm not supposed to eat carbs." Francesca sighed.

Ruth looked up. "This is pasta and potatoes. No carbs in there."

Francesca tasted the lasagna and moaned. "You're right, Mrs. Morgan. I don't see a single carb among all that protein and fat."

"Good organic Morgan beef, as well."

"Really?" Francesca took another bite. "Well, I can't be rude and not eat that. I *love* organic produce."

Avery nudged Ry, who had filled his plate and was now adding a second layer to the arrangement.

"You must be starving."

"I was out all day. Roy packed us some lunch, but it was hours ago."

"You look good, bro." HW broke into their conversation.

"You look worn out," Ry replied.

"I've been busy getting those qualifying points. No time to sleep."

Avery caught his gaze. "It's awesome that you qualified. Congratulations."

"Thanks." HW's vivid golden gaze swept over her. "You live at the hotel, right?"

"Live there, work there." Avery spread her napkin over her knees. "It's the family business."

"So we must've gone to school together."

"I was in the class below yours. We mostly saw each other on the rodeo circuit on the weekends."

Ry leaned forward, one hand on her shoulder. "Avery used to be a barrel racer."

"That's a crazy occupation for any female." HW shook his head. "I wouldn't do it if you paid me." He paused to drink some beer. "Do you still compete?"

"I don't."

"Wise woman." His gaze flicked toward Ry. "Are you two dating?"

Ry's hand slid down her arm, and he drew her close against his side.

"Yeah."

"Quick work, bro. Although I seem to remember you had the hots for one of the Hayes girls back in school."

"Yeah. This one." Ry's tone was flat and edged with something that almost sounded like a challenge.

HW held up his hands. "Back off, Ry. I've no intention of stealing your woman."

"Again?" Avery gave him her sweetest smile. "I don't suppose you remember pretending to be your brother at the school prom, and spoiling my first kiss?"

"Did I?"

Avery nodded, and HW burst out laughing.

"Dude, I'm sorry. I don't even remember that."

"Remember what?" Francesca asked from the other end of the table.

"That I pretended to be Ry at our school prom, and got his girl to kiss me."

"Oh my God, that's hilarious!" Francesca said. "Did you call him out on it, Ry?"

"Nope, but maybe I should've."

"Lighten up, dude. It was a joke. You got the girl in the end, didn't you?" HW winked at Avery. "My brother has a really long memory, so don't go doing anything wrong, because he'll never let you forget it."

Avery refused to smile back, but she did lower her voice. "Glad to see that one of you has a conscience."

"Wow, you're as touchy as he is. I can see why you two get along."

Beside her Ry tensed. She reached under the table and grabbed his denim-clad knee before turning as far away from HW as she could.

"Just ignore him," she whispered in Ry's ear. "He's been drinking a lot more than beer this evening. I can smell it on his breath, and his pupils are seriously dilated."

"I noticed that," Ry murmured back. "Do you want to switch seats? I can shut him up if you like."

"No, I'm good. He's got a far bigger audience to worry about winning over than me. He's going to have to be on his best behavior."

"You really get him, don't you?"

"Doesn't everyone?" Confused, Avery looked right into Ry's face.

"Sometimes I think I'm the one with the problem."

"That's because he's so charming that most people don't notice what's going on underneath. Why is he like that, when you aren't?"

"That's a really good question."

Ry's gaze went to his twin, who was laughing and talking to Tom, the director. Even Avery had to acknowledge that his smile was dazzling, and he was funny as hell. He had everyone in stitches, apart from her and Ry, who sat there like some isolated island in the middle of a sea of hilarity.

Ruth produced three different kinds of pie for dessert, and ice cream. Despite a lot of groaning, the pies were all eaten up. Eventually, the TV crew went to bed, leaving HW, Ry, Avery, and Ruth in the kitchen. Roy had gone home earlier to tend to his pigs.

Ry still couldn't get over the fact that HW was sitting in Ruth's kitchen acting like nothing was wrong and they were all one big happy family. But that was HW all over. He'd never liked to talk about the past, and would rather run than have an honest conversation.

HW patted his flat stomach. "No wonder Ry looks so good, if you feed him like this every day."

Ruth took her seat at the table and offered them all more coffee. "He works hard every day. He needs to eat." She gave HW a speculative look. "You look like you could do with a decent meal or two inside you. Doesn't Lally cook?"

"Lally?" HW snorted. "She burns water. Neither of us have time to cook, Ruth, and we're never home."

"You still need to eat." She turned to Ry. "Blue called. They'll be back in an hour or so. You can catch up with him in the morning, HW." Ruth yawned behind her hand. "I think I'll take myself off to bed."

Ry stood up when she did, and kissed her. "Thanks for that amazing food, Ruth."

"Yes, thanks so much, Ruth," Avery said.

"It was my pleasure. I've never fed a TV crew before. Francesca was saying I should have my own cooking show."

"She's right." Ry hugged her hard. "You rock." He looked over at HW, who was engrossed in his phone. "HW, Ruth's going to bed."

He briefly looked up and said, "Yeah? Thanks for everything. It was awesome," before returning to his texting.

Ruth sighed and gave Ry a telling look before going out the door. She hadn't given HW much of her time, and he certainly hadn't made much of an effort to speak to the woman who had basically brought him up.

Ry sat back beside Avery, who smiled at him.

"I should be getting along as well. I have to come back up here tomorrow to see January."

Ry lowered his voice. "Why don't you stay over? Ruth won't mind."

She looked up at him, her brown eyes wide. "You sure about that? You have quite a houseful already."

"Please?"

She squeezed his hand. "Sure. I just need to call Mom and let her know what I'm doing. I'll get the paperwork I have for January out of my truck. I'll be back in a minute, okay?"

"Cool."

She maneuvered her way around the table and chairs, leaving Ry alone with his brother. The screen door shut behind her, and HW looked up.

"She's limping."

"Yeah."

"Why's that?"

"Not my story to tell."

"Is it permanent?"

"Ask Avery."

HW abruptly stood. "Maybe I will. I need some fresh air."

Ry looked up at him. "What's up?"

"Nothing you can fix." HW's smile was strained. "By the way, I kicked Lally out last week, and I'm not going to renew the lease on the apartment."

"Seems a bit extreme."

"The two events were unrelated. She was screwing around with someone and I haven't decided where I'll be based after the finals. If I do well I might have to move anyway."

"True." Ry couldn't help but notice the way HW constantly fidgeted with everything. "Maybe it's for the best."

"It's not the same without you there." Ry didn't say anything and HW sighed. "I miss you. It's hard not having anyone I can trust around—especially now." His smile was rueful. "Don't they always say that you don't appreciate what you have until it's gone? Bit like our mom, right?"

Ry pulled out the chair next to him. "As to that. Maybe you should sit down. There's something you need to know . . ."

Chapter Ten

"Why the hell didn't you tell me about this before?"

Avery hesitated outside the kitchen door, her file clutched to her chest as she heard raised voices.

"Because I only just found out myself. I wanted to tell you in person."

That was definitely Ry. HW was the angry one.

"So you're all going up to Humboldt to see if this rumor is true? And what are you expecting to find? Mom and Rachel? That's *bullshit*, Ry, and you know it!"

Avery froze and slowly closed her mouth.

"I'm not expecting anything. I'm as doubtful as you are that this is true, but Chase is determined to follow the trail to the end. You know what he's like."

"But if Mom's alive, then—" HW left the end of the sentence incomplete.

"Then what?"

"Nothing."

A chair scraped against the floor. Avery looked around desperately for an escape, and ran back to the mudroom, where she'd just taken off her boots. HW stomped up the stairs, his smile gone, his expression bleached of color in the moonlight streaming through the landing window.

Avery let out a slow breath, and tiptoed into the kitchen. Ry sat at the table, his head in his hands and his back to her.

"Ry? she whispered. "You okay?"

"Just peachy."

She came up behind him and rested her hands on his bowed shoulders. She didn't ask the questions she was dying to, and concentrated instead on the other important thing—the feel of him beneath her hands, the tightness of his muscles. It might even distract him from whatever had just gone down with HW.

"Are you going to take me to bed? I don't even know where your room is."

He twisted around, picked her up, and dumped her in his lap, burying his face in the curve of her neck. She stroked his hair as he gave a long, shuddering sigh.

"What a day."

"Yeah." His voice was muffled against her skin.

"I can go home if you'd like."

His arms tightened around her. "Nope. Stay."

She kissed the top of his head. "Okay."

Closing her eyes, she just relaxed against him, listening as his breathing evened out and the kitchen clock ticked on. After a long while he stirred.

"We'd better move. Blue's going to be back soon."

"Fine by me."

He stood and brought her carefully down to the floor, holding her steady until she took her own weight. She reached up to kiss his unsmiling mouth. He looked older and more like HW than usual.

"Come on, cowboy. I'm really looking forward to seeing you naked."

"You are?" He took her hand and they went up the stairs together, the oak steps creaking and sighing as they passed. The moon was full and bright, and Avery had no problem seeing where she was going.

Ry stopped at the end of the hallway. "I'm in here."

"Sweet. It's even got your name on the door. I could've found it by myself after all."

"Ruth left everything pretty much as it was when we left." He closed the door behind her and locked it. "She had more faith in us all coming back than we did."

"Of course she did." She walked farther into the room, noting the cowboy posters on the wall, and one of Sigourney Weaver half out of her spacesuit. The bed wasn't that large, and was covered with a homemade quilt in shades of blue and brown. "Did she keep all your schoolwork as well?"

"Yeah. It's all wrapped up in plastic in the closet."

"Just like my parents. I told them they should just scan everything in and save it that way, but they looked at me as if I was crazy."

"I can just see Ruth's face if I suggested that. She doesn't have time for technology."

Avery went over to him and started on the buttons of his shirt. He dealt with the cuffs, and then his hands fell to his sides, letting her do as she wanted. He shivered when she unbuckled his belt, the leather whispering through the loops as she took it off and dropped it to the floor. She eased one finger beneath the waistband of his jeans, and carefully undid the button and zipper.

"Hey," he said softly.

Startled, she looked up, and he kissed her, her fingers stilling over the hot, hard bulge in his boxers.

"You still okay about this, Avery?"

She nipped his lip. "No, I'm totally against it. That's why I'm taking your clothes off."

"Just making sure."

The smile was back in his voice, and for a moment she was so damn amazed that she had done that to him that she kissed him again. He let her in, and they swayed together, bodies locked as tight as their mouths in an endless kiss that only made her want him even more.

His callused fingers moved to the small of her back, and the next minute her T-shirt came over her head and he was working on her bra. She didn't stop kissing him. She couldn't. With a soft sound he cupped her breast and then bent his head to take it in his mouth. Her knees almost buckled as he drew on her, sending needle-sharp sensations straight to her girl parts.

"Ry . . ."

"Hmm?"

"Can we lie down?"

In answer he backed her up against his bed and laid her on the quilt, straddling her hips. Before she got much of a chance to appreciate the skin she'd uncovered, he leaned in and licked between her breasts, making her breath catch. Even as he used his mouth his hands were busy stripping her out of her jeans and panties, leaving her naked to his gaze.

He knelt, his gaze devouring her. She resisted the urge to cover the scars from her many surgeries, and dug her fingers into the fabric of the quilt. If he didn't like what he saw, he wasn't who she thought he was. And if he said a single thing she didn't like, she was in the perfect position to kick him somewhere it would really hurt.

"Avery, honey." He kissed her left hip and ran a line of kisses along the worst of her scars—the one that went all the way down to her knee. She jumped when his mouth dipped into her belly button and then lower, the tip of his tongue teasing and exploring her most sensitive places, bringing everything back to sudden, shocking life.

"Nice." He dipped his head lower, easing her thighs wider as he took her with his tongue and his fingers and . . . oh God. She grabbed a handful of his hair as she climaxed, turning her head to stifle the sound against his pillow.

He rose over her and stripped off his jeans and boxers, letting her see just how hard and ready he was for her. Leaning across the bed, he found protection and covered himself before coming down back over her.

"You want me?"

"Yes please."

His smile was beautiful as he eased inside, making her moan, while he stretched and learned her, rocking back and forth, taking it so slowly that she almost wanted to scream at him. But oh God, the pleasure of that leisurely, so-like-Ry penetration made everything feel even better.

She climaxed immediately and he went still, holding himself deep until she gasped for breath and managed to open her eyes. He was watching her, his gaze molten in the silver moonlight, his mouth a sensual treasure she wanted to plunder forever.

"Selfish," she gasped.

"What, you?" His smile was so hot she was surprised she didn't come again. "Nope, I can take it."

"Really?"

He rolled his hips, and she clutched his biceps. "As many as you want, princess."

She mock-frowned at him. "Don't call me that. Marley's the princess in my family."

"She's not as pretty as you."

"You're obviously delusional, but that's okay." She smoothed her hand over his muscled chest. "I am pretty spectacular."

"That's my girl."

He started moving again, and she rapidly forgot her name, and everything except the grinding rhythm of his body over hers, and the need to take him, and keep him, and bring him with her into a climax that would rock his world.

"Avery . . ."

He bucked against her one last time, driving so deep she instinctively curled her legs higher around his hips and just held on, her third climax catching her unawares, drawing a strangled groan from Ry as she clenched around him.

After one last, lingering kiss, he moved away and set himself to rights. She lay still, experimentally moving her limbs, checking that beneath her sexual high her bones were all present and in working order.

"You okay?" He drew the covers back and got into bed, pulling her in with him.

"Yes, I'm good."

He spooned her from behind; his hand curved over her belly, her rounded butt against his flat stomach. She breathed in the smell of sex, and sweat, and them, and let out a big contented sigh.

"Thank you."

He kissed the top of her head. "No, thank *you*. I was having a hell of a day until you came and saved me."

"HW didn't mention he planned to bring a film crew with him?"

"He didn't tell us anything at all. He just arrived."

"When's he leaving?"

"Tomorrow."

"Good." She turned her head to kiss his shoulder.

"Yeah." He kissed her again, his hand sliding lower until he cupped her mound. "Why are we talking about him right now?"

"Because he has the amazing ability to make himself the subject of every conversation when he's around?"

"I don't want to think about him." He paused. "You okay about us being a couple?"

She rolled onto her back to stare up at him. "You're asking me that *now*?"

He shrugged. "You know how it is, Avery. A lot of people prefer to hook up or—"

"Stop right there." She slapped her hand over his mouth. "I don't."

His golden eyes crinkled at the corners and he bit her fingers. "Neither do I."

"Then we're going out together, okay?"

"Officially. If you like, I'll get Dad to take out an ad in the local paper."

She grinned at him. "Local rancher snares hot hotelier in his lasso of love."

"Sounds good—although my roping could do with some work."

"Maybe you can practice on me."

"Yeah?" He raised his eyebrows. "Sounds like fun."

"But maybe not right now."

She yawned and covered her mouth, and he immediately cuddled down behind her. How come she felt so comfortable when they'd only slept together once? But she *knew* him, knew the serious boy inside the strong man, at some bone-deep level that made being with him feel so right.

Her eyes were beginning to close. "You've had a busy day, what with the ranch, and HW, and being interviewed, and your mom . . ."

His hand stilled on her shoulder. "What about my mom?"

She winced. "I, um, overheard HW saying something about your mother maybe being alive?"

He was quiet for so long she contemplated either apologizing or leaving.

"Yeah. Chase has been looking into what happened that night my mom and sister disappeared. He thinks they might still be alive and living in Humboldt."

Avery slowly closed her mouth and attempted to match his calm tone. "That's pretty major. How do you feel about that?"

"I'm not sure. I don't remember her very well. HW and I were five when she left. I do remember that it was the day after our birthday party. I think that's what they were arguing about."

"Wasn't your dad suspected of killing them?"

"Yeah, but there was no evidence to tie him to any crime. Eventually when no bodies showed up the police gave up trying to pin it on him. It almost broke him anyway. He was never the same, and he left us as well." He sighed. "Took him twenty years to find his way back here, and Chase and BB still haven't quite forgiven him."

"So, what's the plan now?" Avery asked.

"We're supposed to go up to Humboldt to check this woman out."

"But you don't think it's her, do you?"

"I doubt it, but Chase seems convinced, and he's the one with the money."

He turned onto his back and she came up on one elbow to observe him. He looked his usual calm self, but . . .

"You don't want to go, do you?"

He glanced at her, his golden gaze hooded. "Nope."

"Do you have to?"

"Chase says it's up to me." He smoothed a hand over his unshaven jaw. "There's no reason why I shouldn't go, especially when I don't even know why I'm so reluctant in the first place."

"Ry, she left you when you were *five years old.*"

His smile was sweet. "She left us all, Avery. It hurt Chase and BB the most, and it almost destroyed my dad. They all want to find her."

"What about HW?"

He blinked at her. "What about him?"

"He didn't look very happy."

"I'd only just told him. Once he calms down, he'll

be all for it. He was always Mom's favorite." He stopped talking, his gaze drawing inward. "I'd forgotten that."

"And now I've gotten us back around to talking about your twin again." Avery groaned. "I'm so sorry."

He smiled back and she kissed him. God, she could spend a whole day just kissing him . . .

"I'm sure I can think of plenty of ways to stop you thinking about HW," Ry murmured, as he rolled her beneath him and kicked the covers to the bottom of the bed.

"I'm absolutely sure . . . you can." Avery let him bear her down onto the mattress again and concentrated on far more exciting things than poor Ry's ancient family history. "In fact, that will do very nicely."

Ry woke up early to an armful of lush woman . . . snoring in his ear, and he simply buried his face in her neck and inhaled her sweetness. He'd slept right through the night, which rarely happened, and hadn't been bothered by any of those weird nightmares about his brother or his mom. Maybe he was getting used to the idea that she might not be dead after all . . .

Avery muttered something in her sleep and smacked her lips. Her brown hair was stuck to the side of her face, and she might have been drooling. Ry didn't care. Having her in his bed—*being* with her—felt right.

He kissed her shoulder and went to have a shower. With so many guests in the house, it would have to be quick. Chase was already talking about installing more bathrooms in the main house. Ruth and Billy weren't too keen on the idea, thinking it would destroy the old-world charm of the place.

As far as he was concerned, the lure of endless hot water and a good shower far outweighed Ruth's objections. A two-minute rinse standing inside a slippery enamel bathtub was not his idea of fun. He wrapped a towel around his waist and ran back to his bedroom barefoot and shivering. Avery was still asleep. He sat on the bed beside her and stroked her hair.

"Avery? You ready to get up?"

She muttered something unintelligible, and rolled onto her other side, away from him. Ry tried again.

"Avery?"

She pulled the covers over her head and made a very specific gesture with her finger that encouraged him to leave her alone.

Fighting a grin, Ry went over to his desk, wrote her a note, and stuck it on the pillow beside her. He found his jeans, a clean T-shirt, and some socks, and padded down the stairs into the kitchen.

"Hey."

He pulled up short as HW called out to him from where he was sitting at the table. His twin looked as if he hadn't slept at all. Ry got some coffee and scooped out a bowl of the oatmeal Ruth always left to cook overnight in the slow cooker. He added cream, raisins, and brown sugar and took his loaded bowl to sit next to HW.

"Jeez." HW shuddered. "Don't you care about your arteries?"

"I burn up a lot of calories. A good breakfast keeps me going all day. By the time I've gotten through this, Ruth might be up making pancakes, eggs, and bacon."

HW looked like he was going to heave.

Ry kept on eating, aware for the first time that he wasn't inclined to ask HW what was wrong, let alone fix everything for him. His brother sipped at his black coffee and stared into space.

"You and Avery going to stay together?"

Ry looked up. "Why do you want to know?"

"You look happy."

"And . . . ?"

HW shrugged. "I just don't want you to get hurt."

"How specific are you being here, bro?" Ry slowly put his spoon down. "By any woman, or by Avery specifically?"

"I'm not saying—"

Ry interrupted his brother. "You just can't help yourself, can you? Interfering in my life—trying to tell me who I can date, and whether I'm allowed to be happy."

"Hell, you interfere in my life all the time! You hated Lally!"

"Because she wasn't good for you." He glared at his twin. "Well, I am damn happy with Avery, so don't you come around here trying to screw things up, okay?"

HW was the first to look away. "I thought Mom and Dad were happy, didn't you?"

"What does that have to do with anything?"

"Because I couldn't sleep last night. Being back here brought out all my memories. How can you stay here and not dream?"

Ry almost stopped breathing. "What the heck are you talking about?"

"That last night? When Mom and Dad were fighting?"

Ry held up a hand. "Dude, we were five, neither of us remember it clearly, okay? Why do you suddenly want to talk about it now, twenty years later?"

HW shoved a hand through his hair. "I'm sorry."

"It's okay. Coming back here messed with my head as well, at first."

"That's not what I'm apologizing for."

Ry reluctantly looked into his brother's eyes. "I don't understand."

"Yeah, you do. You know how she was with us. What she did that last night. You *know*, Ry."

Ry stood up. "I have to get to work."

HW kept on talking. "I should've stopped her. I should've . . . I dunno, done *something*."

"How about you shut up?" Ry only realized he was shouting when HW winced. "How about you get out of here, and never come back?"

He pushed past Ruth and Billy, who had both appeared in the doorway, made for the mudroom, and then went out to the barn. Dolittle wasn't pleased to see him at all, but Ry saddled up, and they were away, out into the pasture where no one could find him if he didn't want them to. The only thing was—he couldn't escape the demons that HW had raised in his mind—and now he knew he never would.

Aware that she was in someone else's house, Avery woke up in a fright right after Ry left the room, and rushed to the bathroom to wash and put her clothes back on. She tiptoed down the stairs, wondering if she could get away without being seen. The bottom stair creaked loudly and she winced.

"That you, Avery? Come and get something to eat."

Ruth sounded her usual self, so Avery turned around and went into the kitchen. HW was sitting at the table with Billy.

"Good morning," Avery flashed them all a quick smile. "Ruth, I hope you didn't mind—"

"You staying over? I've gotten used to all these comings and goings, what with Jenna, and BB, and January . . ."

Avery's face heated as she grabbed a mug of coffee and sat down at the table. "Is Ry around?"

HW stirred. "Nope, he left."

There was a flatness to his voice that made Avery instantly worried.

"Is he okay?"

Billy patted her shoulder. "I saw him heading out on Dolittle. He'll come back when he's ready."

She turned toward him. "Did something happen?"

"I dunno. I was just going to ask you the same question," Billy said.

"There was nothing wrong between us."

She didn't want to mention that the thought of Ry fleeing his home after their first time making love was a little depressing.

"It wasn't you." HW looked up. "He was pissed with me. What's new? I can't talk to him these days without him getting angry."

"Ry doesn't get angry here, HW. Why do you think that is?" Ruth put a plate of eggs and bacon in front of Avery.

"I know you think everything's my fault, Ruth, so

why don't you just come out and say it?" HW gripped his mug so hard his knuckles shone white. "I didn't ask him to stay with me all these years. He did it because he wanted to."

"He did it because he loves you, and wanted to keep you safe," Ruth said. "You know that."

HW stood up. "Then maybe he should have developed some balls, and gone after what *he* wanted. I'm not taking all the blame here."

"No one's blaming you for anything, son," Billy pointed out. "We're just trying to work out why Ry headed out without telling anyone where he was going."

"Seems obvious to me." HW shrugged. "He told me about Mom maybe being alive."

Billy shot a quick glance at Ruth. "Yeah? How do you feel about that?"

"It sucks." HW picked up his cell phone and stuck it in his back pocket. "And why didn't anyone mention it sooner?"

"Because we decided it was something that needed to be said face-to-face, and this was the first opportunity Ry had to share the news with you."

"He's not happy about it," HW stated.

"We all gathered that, but why?" Ruth asked. "It's not as if you can remember her that well, is it?"

"We remember her, all right. If Ry's saying something different, he's a big fat liar, but that's his business." HW started toward the door. "I'd better get packed and ready to leave. Tell Ry I said good-bye, and give my best to Chase."

Ruth barred his way, her spatula raised like a weapon. "Are you coming back for the wedding?"

"I hope so. It's right before the finals, but I should be able to make it." He nodded at Billy and Avery. "I'm going to help BB down at the barn. Tell Francesca and the guys that I'm ready to leave whenever they are."

The moment he went out the door, Avery stood up and followed him. To her surprise, he hadn't gone far. He was standing on the porch, staring out at the mountains, his expression grim as he fumbled for a cigarette in his jeans pocket.

"May I ask you something?" Avery approached him carefully, aware that after a night of lovemaking her stiff hip was making her gait extra awkward.

He gave her his famous golden smile, and stuck the unlit cigarette behind his ear. "Sure. What's up?"

"Was Ry really okay?"

He studied her, leaning back against the Victorian railings, his gaze drifting lower to her lagging left foot. "You like him, don't you?"

"Well, duh, I wouldn't be going out with him if I didn't."

"He's not as easygoing as most people think, so maybe you should be careful."

"Are you trying to warn me off?"

"It depends." He eyed her consideringly. "I don't want him to get hurt."

"So who should be worried here? Him or me?"

"Maybe both of you." He sighed. "This thing with our mom?"

"What about it?"

"It's all kinds of messed up."

"In what way?"

"If she's still alive, it . . . changes things. If she

comes back here"—he winced—"I don't know what's going to happen."

"But you won't be here anyway, will you?"

"True. But Ry will." He looked past her at the screen door. "Francesca's up. I can hear her coming down the stairs. Do you want to walk down to the barn with me?"

"I'd rather not." Avery found a smile somewhere. "I have to go to the new welcome center and get to work."

"Then I'll walk with you. It's on my way, and I'm not that keen to get a list of chores from BB, and another lecture."

She took her time descending the steps and he waited for her. "They're all worried about you."

"Because I'm successful?" He snorted. "Strange family, right?"

"I think Ruth just wants you to come home, and Ry misses you a lot."

He glanced down at her. "You're an expert on my brother now, are you?"

"HW, don't be an idiot. I went to school with both of you. You might be bigger these days, but you haven't changed that much."

The welcome center came into view, and she was *so* glad. Talking about Ry when he wasn't present didn't feel right.

"You don't think we've changed?"

"Not really. Ry was always quieter than you." She stopped walking and turned to HW, holding out her hand. "It was great to see you. Safe trip back to wherever you're going, and all the best in the finals."

Staring right at him, she registered both the similarities between him and Ry and the differences, so clearly. When HW was miserable, which he clearly was right now, he looked just like his twin.

On impulse she kept hold of his hand. "Are you okay?"

He started to speak, and then stopped and smiled before kissing her on the cheek. "I'm good. You take care of Ry for me, and I'll see you at the wedding."

With a tip of his hat he was gone, walking away to the barn with long, confident strides.

Avery stared after him for quite a while. Whatever HW was *saying*, he was as unhappy about what was going on as his twin. Whether that was because Ry had left him right before the finals, or because the news about their mother had hit him hard, she wasn't sure. He wasn't as carefree about everything as he pretended to be. He concealed things just like Ry did, albeit behind a different kind of mask.

Maybe he always had.

Chapter Eleven

"Mom, no . . . *don't* . . . don't do that . . . Mom!"

"Ry? What's up? *Ry?*"

He sat up with a jerk and Avery rolled off him and onto her back with a thump. He took several deep breaths as his heart continued to jackhammer in his chest, and slowly unclenched his fists.

He turned to Avery, who was lying where he'd literally thrown her off him, her hair in disarray on the pillow.

"God, I'm sorry. You okay?"

"I'm good. How about you?"

He scrubbed a hand over his eyes. They were in his bed at the ranch for their fourth night together in two weeks. He still hadn't mustered the courage to go up to Avery's room in the hotel. "I must've had a bad dream or something."

"I should say so." She hesitated. "Do you remember what it was about?"

Stretching out beside her, he searched for her hand and found it waiting for him. "Nope."

He'd just had a terrible sense that if he didn't

wake up and force the lid back on all that crap HW had stirred up, he'd go nuts.

"Have you had the dream before?"

"Yeah."

She waited him out, but he wasn't inclined to say another damn thing.

"It's not surprising that all this new information about your mom has unsettled you." She rolled onto her right side and curled against his still tense body. "I think I'd be a basket case."

I am. He shut his mouth. Had he said that out loud?

She stroked her hand over his chest in slow circles, her nails gently scratching his skin in an oddly soothing way. "Even if it isn't your mom up there in Humboldt, this is still stressful for you all. January says Chase is really struggling."

Ry opened his eyes. "Chase is?"

"And Blue."

"I hadn't noticed."

She jabbed him with one fingernail. "They probably think the same about you. Men are so useless at being emotional."

"Maybe we just don't want to be."

"Emotional? Why not?"

"Because it's not manly."

She snorted. "Seriously? You might be a cowboy on a historic ranch, but you don't have to act like one of your ancestors. It's the twenty-first century."

He swallowed hard. "Maybe if I give in to it, I won't be able to stop."

She went still and then came up on one elbow to stare into his face, her soft hair falling over her shoulder and tickling his chest.

"We're friends, right?"

He nodded.

"And you know you can tell me anything?"

He looked deep into her whisky-brown eyes. "I don't know what to say."

"Just try," she said softly.

"It's not that simple. I don't *know* what's wrong. It's like I'm aware something bad happened, but I can't remember it. I get glimpses of *something*, and then it's gone."

He tensed, waiting to see what she'd make of such a lame answer, amazed that he'd even tried to offer her one. He'd always had HW to confide in—not that he'd needed to do it much, because they'd always known how the other was feeling, but this time—he couldn't bear to talk to HW at all.

"I guess it's got something to do with my mom," Ry said reluctantly.

"I got that, seeing as you were screaming her name. Was she hurting you?"

Ry blinked hard as an echo of pain hit him. "I don't know."

"Did she hurt HW?"

"She never hurt him. He was the golden boy." Hell, where had that come from? He tensed again, but Avery didn't say anything.

"January told me your mom might have been suffering from postnatal depression after your sister, Rachel, was born."

"It's possible, I suppose. I was just a kid. I just knew she wasn't happy."

"That must have sucked. How was she with your sister?"

"With Rachel?"

"Yes."

"She . . ." Ry frowned. "She took her with her when she left."

"So Rachel might be out there as well?"

"Yeah, if my mom didn't . . ." Ry stopped speaking.

"Didn't what, Ry?" Avery's question fell into the silence.

"BB said that the last guy who saw Mom didn't mention seeing Rachel. But Mom was at work, so it's possible she was in day care or something, I suppose."

"Very possible. How old would Rachel be now?"

Ry considered. "Around twenty. Wow."

"She might be at college somewhere."

"Yeah. I could've passed her on the street and never known it." Ry raised his hand and cupped Avery's cheek. "I'm sorry to dump all this on you."

She mock frowned at him. "Like I'm not intending to bend your ear about my family in the near future."

"But my family are way more out there than yours."

"We're competing now?" She leaned down and kissed his nose. "I bet I can take your mind off your bad dreams, and make you sleep like a baby."

She kissed his mouth, then his chin, and then his collarbone, her lips soft and her teeth . . . not so gentle, and he shivered as she went lower.

"You're good to me, Avery."

She looked up at him, her eyebrows raised. "I am?"

"Yeah. Probably too good for me."

"Don't start that again. I chose you, Ry." She nipped his hip bone and growled. "You're all mine now, and you're just going to have to lie back and take it."

He pushed the sheet down so that nothing would get in her way and gripped the headboard with both hands as her tongue feathered over his abs and went lower. He rolled his hips, inviting her to take more of him, and she obliged in a long, slow, gliding rush that almost made him swallow his tongue.

"Avery . . ." He breathed out real slow, and looked down at one of the most glorious sights he had ever seen—her mouth on him, her eyes on his face, watching his reaction. "That's . . ."

He tried not to surge forward, but she took more anyway, engulfing him in sweetness and tightness until he forgot about anything except that he wanted to come, wanted everything she was willing to give him.

"You know that lie-back-and-take-it bit?" Ry said hoarsely. "I think I'm done with that."

She made some kind of humming noise in her throat that made the situation even more critical. Reaching down, he threaded one hand through her long hair.

"Avery, honey, you don't have to . . ."

But it was too late. Even as he was begging, he was coming, and she was taking everything he had to give her, leaving him spent and exhausted, and so damn grateful that he wanted to curl up and die happy.

She snuck back up to lie beside him. He held her close, kissing the top of her head as she settled over him like a warm blanket.

"How about your turn?"

She yawned like a delicate kitten. "I'm done. You can owe me, okay?"

He considered that. "Sure, as long as I get to pick the time and the place."

"Agreeing to that sounds like something I might come to regret."

"You'll enjoy every moment. I guarantee it."

"I know I will, but I also know you."

Hell, she really did. She'd worked him out when she was six. He closed his eyes and smiled, and that was the last thing he knew until the alarm went off at five thirty the next morning.

"Avery? Can I talk to you?"

"Sure! What's up?"

Avery looked up as her dad came into her office and shut the door firmly behind him. Was he going to ask her where she kept disappearing to at night? She'd been expecting the question for days, and sneaking down the back stairs was really not her thing.

She frowned. "Did you just lock that door?"

He took the chair in front of the desk she now shared with Marley and looked slyly over his shoulder.

"Yes. I don't want your sister hearing what I have to say."

Avery's spirits sank. "Let me guess. You're firing me."

"I'd never fire a Hayes." He looked furtively back at the door and lowered his voice. "Marley is driving me and your Mom to drink. She's reorganizing everything, changing the way we've done things for years, making us more *efficient*, she says . . ."

Avery sat back in her chair. "So? Wasn't that what you wanted her to do?"

"Not all in two weeks! The staff are complaining and threatening to leave en masse. We can't have that, Avery. You know how busy it gets around the holidays, and with the Morgan wedding we're booked solid."

"Why are you talking to me about it?" Avery asked. "You should talk to Marley."

"We've tried, but she doesn't listen. She just pats my head and tells me that change is a process and that I've got to get used to it."

"She's right."

"Avery . . ."

"Everything up at Morgan Ranch is changing as well. Chase has them all running in circles, updating everything from the way they graze the cattle to the crops they raise, and then there's all the new stuff for the dude ranch . . ."

"Which is going to take our business away, young lady, don't forget that."

Avery ignored the interruption. "But they are all doing their best to change, Dad. They know they have no choice. You wanted Marley to give you the cutting edge of hotel economics, and that's what she's doing. And she's so happy right now."

"I know, but maybe you were better suited for the hotel."

"In what way?"

"You're more conservative, less of a risk taker."

"Those aren't always good things, Dad. As Chase keeps telling us, if we stand still we might lose everything." A shadow crossed her father's face, and for the first time he looked old and worn down. Avery suppressed a sigh. "Do you want me to talk to Marley?"

"Would you? We'd be so grateful. And maybe

today you could just walk around the place and smooth a few ruffled feathers? You're so good at that." He came up to the desk and kissed her forehead. "After all, you'll be back here full-time soon, and Marley will have to make a decision about what she plans to do next."

She raised an eyebrow. "I thought you said you would never fire a Hayes."

"I have no intention of *firing* her. I'm just going to encourage her to look for a different kind of job with better pay and more scope for her talents."

"But she wants to be home with her family."

Her father sighed. "Nice way to make me feel guilty, eldest daughter. But there isn't enough work for both of you. I can't afford to pay two events managers."

"Maybe I'm the one who should leave."

He patted her shoulder. "You're funny. Where are you going to go?" Something must have shown on her face as he immediately started speaking again. "Not that you couldn't do anything you wanted, Avery, just that you've always seemed happier here where we all know you and . . . understand."

"Understand that I'm crippled?"

"That's a bit harsh, love, don't you think? I only meant that we like to keep you safe, and that we'll always give you a home."

And now she'd hurt his feelings . . . Avery managed a smile, but he'd made her feel like a much-loved pet. "It's okay, I get what you mean. I'll talk to Marley."

"Thanks, darling." He kissed the top of her head, and left.

Avery stared into space and tried to unscramble

the jumble of her emotions. Was she more hurt that her dad didn't think she would ever leave the hotel and needed protecting, or that he assumed she had no plans for advancing her career?

Okay, so she hadn't done anything to disabuse him of the notion that she wasn't going anywhere. She'd never applied for another job even for the fun of it, and she'd continued to run the hotel events just as her parents had, rarely offering up new suggestions of her own. The most daring thing she'd done lately was accept the offer to coordinate January's wedding.

And date Ry Morgan, but her parents didn't seem to know about that yet.

She sent Nancy a quick text.

Am I boring?

You can be. Why what's up?

Nothing.

You broke up with Ry?

Avery grinned at the screen. Ry who?

Give it up GF, you're def getting some. Want me to come over before work?

Can you?

Sure. C u later x.

Avery put her cell down and focused on the spreadsheet for the golden wedding anniversary party the hotel was hosting that evening. So far everything looked good. Marley was working her ass off to make sure it all came together. She was *way* better at the job than Avery. Why couldn't her parents see that? She'd wait until after the event to talk to Marley. There was no way she wanted to upset her sister right now.

Her thoughts turned to Ry, and how he looked sleeping naked in his bed, all sprawled out and golden and . . .

Yeah . . .

She shut down her laptop. That was just the kind of image that would help her make it through another day. She still couldn't quite believe how well they were getting along, both in bed and out of it. There was still a strain of tension running through him because of the business about his mom and sister, which she couldn't seem to help him resolve. He had nightmares he refused to talk about, and was ignoring HW, who kept calling him.

That was the part she didn't understand. Ry had always been there for his twin, so why was he so determined to shut him out now? Having seen HW, Avery was fairly convinced he was struggling to deal with their fractured relationship as much as Ry was. And for once, Ry didn't seem inclined to play the peacemaker. Avery paused to close the door behind her. In fact, he seemed determined to keep his twin at arm's length.

She walked down toward the lobby, but heard yelling in Spanish and turned toward the kitchen. It seemed their temperamental chef might need to have his feelings validated . . .

* * *

Ry put away his saddle and bridle, and turned Dolittle out into the field with Nolly, who danced around his barn buddy like a young foal. He moved out of the way so that BB could let Messi through the gate, and grinned when Nolly received a sharp nip on his ear when he barged into the other horse.

BB closed the gate and stood next to Ry, watching the horses fool around.

"Nolly's an idiot. I don't know why Chase is so fond of him."

"Maybe because Chase is an idiot, too?"

"True." BB's smile dimmed. "He just sent me a text, that's why I was delayed. He wants us to meet him at the landing strip in half an hour for a flight to Humboldt."

"Seriously?" Ry said as the bottom dropped out of his stomach.

"Yeah." BB's bright blue gaze searched his. "You okay?"

"I'm good."

"You don't have to come."

Ry turned and started walking back up to the house. BB caught up with him in about five seconds.

"It's okay, Ry. HW said—"

"What the hell does HW have to do with anything?"

His brother held up his hands. "Don't get at me. I'm just the messenger here, but the fact that you get so angry about this speaks for itself. You're the *calm* one in the family. You're the one who keeps everything together."

"Which is why I'm coming with you." Ry set his jaw. "If I don't, what am I? Some coward? I'm not

going to be that guy. I . . . need to deal with this,
okay?"

BB slowly nodded and then slapped him hard on
the back. "Then let's get a move on."

The plane was small, which Ry hated, but it was
certainly luxurious. Chase was working, and BB had
gone to sleep like he didn't have a care in the world.
Ry settled back in his seat and calculated how long
the four-hundred-and-fifty-mile journey would take,
and how much time after that there would be before
he might have to confront his mother.

Nausea stirred low in his gut. He had to remind
himself that he wasn't a little kid anymore, and that
no matter what she tried to do to him, he could
simply turn around and walk away. He had a terrible
sense that she wouldn't be pleased to see him—that
even if she were alive she'd prefer to see HW.

"Not long now." Ry looked up to see Chase shutting down his laptop. Chase scrubbed his hands over
his face and groaned. "I didn't get much sleep last
night. I was too busy trying to work out what the hell
I intend to say if it really is Mom."

"Hi? I'm your long lost son?" Ry cleared his throat.
"If it is her, she'll take one look at you and think
you're Billy."

"And run off screaming? Great." Chase groaned.
"I'm beginning to wish I hadn't started down this
road."

"Yeah? Then let's go home."

"I promised January I'd see it through. She says I

need 'closure' or something—that we all do. She wants it all sorted before the wedding."

Ry didn't bother to argue. He had a sense that he was set on a path and that nothing was going to stop him going forward. It was like that moment when you strapped your hand into your rope on the back of a bucking bull and nodded at the gateman to let it go. You might get the ride of your life or be bucked off in a second.

The pilot's voice came over the intercom.

"Please take your seats. We will be landing in approximately ten minutes."

Humboldt was smaller than Ry had anticipated and dominated by the university. It had a quaint kind of '60s hippie vibe to it, which made sense with all the students around. Chase had hired a limo, and they were currently en route to the offices of their contact downtown, a law firm, or so Chase said. BB looked so relaxed Ry wanted to kill him, but his bro had been in Afghanistan and other hostile places, so a trip to the far north of his home state was hardly going to rattle his nerves.

Chase looked okay, but he was texting furiously on his phone the entire journey. The most amazing sequoia forest Ry had ever seen surrounded the town. They'd flown over miles of it on their way in. When they got out of the car the scent of eucalyptus and pine still lingered.

The offices of the law firm were situated in a modern five-story building. Chase led the way, BB in the rear, his demeanor that of a soldier protecting his ass in inhospitable territory. Ry kept his head down and kept walking.

The receptionist was very pleasant and took them through into Andrew Gage's office. Chase advanced on the man behind the desk.

"Hey, I'm Chase Morgan and these are my brothers, Blue and Ry."

"Good to finally meet you all." Andrew shook hands and waved them into the chairs in front of his desk. "I understand you have an unsolved missing person case on your hands."

"That's right. We're trying to locate our mother."

Andrew glanced at the open file on his desk. "Your team of private investigators has been very thorough. They contacted our firm when they needed information on Anne Morgan, usually known as Annie. They believed she had taken an alias and ended up here in Humboldt."

Ry slumped in his chair, and BB tapped his fingers against his jeans-clad thigh.

"And?" Chase prompted politely.

"We matched the information with that of a client who dealt with our firm about fifteen years ago. She was using the name Anne Langton at that point."

"That's not even her maiden name," Chase murmured. "Why did she need a law firm?"

"She wanted to obtain a divorce."

"Presumably from our father?" Chase frowned. "I don't remember hearing anything about them getting divorced."

"Can you do that without telling the other person?" BB chimed in.

"Yes." Andrew looked apologetic. "There are legal

ways to get around the desertion or disappearance of a spouse, and California is a no-fault divorce state. In his notes, my colleague mentioned your mother claimed your father had disappeared from the marital home, and she had no idea where he had gone."

Chase nodded. "If she went looking for him five years after *she* left she was probably correct. He'd gone walkabout by then. How come all of this has just come to light?"

"We currently have an intern working with us who is scanning all our old records online, which is probably how your investigators found us."

"Did your firm have an address in Humboldt for Annie back then?" Chase asked.

"We did, but I doubt she's still there. That street is now a parking lot."

"Then where do you suggest we start looking for Anne Langton?"

"I'd start at the university. There's a note here in the file, which suggests your mother was planning on attending college. If she did so, the university will have a record of her."

BB turned to Chase. "Are your guys on this already?"

"Yeah, that's what I was texting about on the ride over. We've got an appointment to meet the registrar next." Chase stood up. "Thanks for your time, Andrew. We appreciate it."

"Glad to help." Andrew shook Chase's hand. "Let me know if you find her, okay?"

Chase didn't commit to anything, and they left the office in silence. The limo was waiting for them in the parking lot, and they all got in.

BB asked the obvious question. "I wonder if Billy ever knew she was trying to divorce him?"

"If he did, he never mentioned it." Chase grimaced. "And it would mean he must've known she was alive. I'll ask him when we get back."

"He might have divorced her," Ry said slowly. "He wanted her to be free."

"Yeah, he did, but back then, I'm not sure he knew *what* he was doing. He was pretty much a full-time drunk."

Ry stopped talking and stared out of the window as they turned toward the university. For some reason he felt steadier now—as if having survived the first few steps he could keep on going. He thought about Avery and her struggle to learn how to walk again after all the damage to her hip and thigh. She'd understand, and she'd definitely tell him to keep moving forward. In fact, she'd probably smack him a good one if he didn't.

The limo stopped again and they all got out. It was raining and Ry wished he'd brought his jacket. Some of the students paused to point and giggle at the sight of him and BB in their cowboy gear. Chase had sensibly left his Stetson on the plane.

The administrator offered them coffee and led them through to her office, which was warm from the earlier sun. Chase explained what they were after, and repeated the bare bones of the story.

"Yes, we do have a record of an Anne Langton who studied here for several years." She searched their faces. "I joined the office just about the time she was admitted and I remember her quite well." She nodded at BB. "She had the same color eyes as you, although her little girl was fair haired, like your brother."

"You remember she had a daughter?" Chase asked.

"Yes, Rachel was in the day care program with one of my daughters for several years."

BB let out his breath and glanced at Ry. "Sounds like we hit the jackpot, guys."

Chase ignored them and leaned forward, his attention all on the woman behind the desk. "Do you have any idea what happened to Anne after she completed her degree?"

"She left for a year or so to do her master's somewhere farther downstate and we lost contact, but I believe she came back."

"To teach here?"

"I *think* so. I left this job to take care of my children, so I missed a few years. I remember one of my colleagues saying that after Anne came back she got married."

"*Married*?" BB asked.

"That's right—to one of the professors here."

Ry turned to Chase. "Did you know about this?"

Chase shook his head. "It's all news to me. Do you have a name and address for this guy?"

The administrator sat back in her seat. "I can't give you that information without clearing it with the university first."

Chase stood and held out his hand. "Okay, then I'll be in touch. Thanks for all your help."

As they walked out to the parking lot, BB patted Chase's shoulder. "You're going to find out who this guy is, and get back to us, right?"

"Yeah, we're close now, can't you feel it?"

"We could ask around and find out whether anyone knows them."

"And risk scaring her into running away again? We'll do this properly and contact her through her new husband."

BB snorted. "Yeah, and as to that—did that lawyer say she was actually divorced from Dad? Because otherwise she's in a whole pig's trough of trouble."

Chapter Twelve

"So what did you find out?" Avery asked Ry as she passed him a bucket of water to put in Dolittle's stall. She'd come up to the ranch to see him after her shift ended, but he wasn't in a particularly chatty mood.

"Well, we didn't bump into her on the street or anything."

She hesitated at the door. "You don't have to tell me if you don't want to."

He filled the water trough and gave her back the bucket. "Nothing much to tell. It seems like she applied for a divorce, changed her name, and went back to college."

He sounded relaxed, but she wasn't fooled.

"Do you think it might be her, then?"

"Possibly. She has a daughter named Rachel."

"Wow." Avoiding Dolittle's swishing tail, she squeezed past to Ry from behind. He was as unyielding as a plank of wood. "You're tense."

"Yeah, well."

She rubbed her cheek against his back and

wrapped her arms around his hips. "What's the plan now?"

"She might have married again. Chase's team is looking into that right now. As soon as we get more information we'll be on it."

"Will you go back there?"

He turned around to stare down at her. "I don't think I have much choice, do you?"

"Not if you want to meet her." Avery took a deep breath. "What did she do to you?"

"I've already told you I don't remember."

"Do you know Dr. Mendez? He operates the physical rehab facility alongside his general practice, and he's a great believer in natural remedies and techniques."

"And?"

"Maybe you could go talk to him."

"About what?"

"About whatever's bothering you."

"I'm fine, Avery."

"You are not. You have nightmares."

He shrugged. "Who doesn't?"

"He could hypnotize you and find out what's going on."

"Avery, are you *kidding* me?"

"No. He managed to stop my mom smoking, and he helped me, so why won't you try it?"

"Because I'm *fine*." He slapped Dolittle's flank to move him out of the way, and squeezed past Avery. "You coming?"

Avery followed him out into the yard. "Why do men think getting help for their issues is like admitting some kind of failure?"

"Because it is?"

"It's a sign that you are mature enough to realize that you need *help*!"

His only reply was a snort as he headed for the tack room. She followed right after him.

"Ry Morgan . . ."

She yelped as he turned around and shut them both in the small space, pinning her against the door.

"Let it go, Avery."

"But—"

He bent down and kissed her hard, one hand moving away from the door and curving around her neck.

"How about you think about something more interesting, like having some barn sex with your favorite cowboy?"

Her body thought that was a fine idea, but she pushed hard on his chest. "I'm not going to let you distract me like that."

"Like what?" He nibbled her ear, and her knees almost gave way with lust.

"With sex. You need to deal with this, Ry, and I don't like being used."

He went still and eased away from her. "What exactly are you saying here?"

"That it's easier to escape into something else than face the truth."

"You think I don't want you?"

"That's not what this is about, and you know it."

"It sure as hell sounded like it."

She folded her arms over her chest. "And now you're going to get mad over that, and use it as another excuse not to face up to your problems."

He took three steps back, which was about as far

as he could go in the cramped tack room, and
smiled.

"The only person who's getting mad around here
is you, honey."

"Don't call me that, and don't *smile* like that—you
look like HW."

He came toward her and she eased back against
the wall, but he pushed open the door, obviously
intending to get as far away from her as possible.

She called after him. "You're always telling me I
can't run away from things, so where are you going?"

He stopped and slowly turned. "You run as well."

"Really, Ry? You're going to do the classic man
thing, and make this all about me?"

"You're still shit-scared of horses. What good has
all that therapy and hypnosis done you, Avery?"

She closed her mouth so hard she snapped her
jaw, and just stared at him. "Wow. Well, it worked.
I'm not going to argue with you about another
damned thing."

And she was damned if she was going to run,
either. She held his furious gaze until he was the one
who walked away. Checking her pocket for her keys,
she headed for her car, stumbling on the uneven
ground, fighting the hot tears that crowded the back
of her throat.

Yeah, she really wasn't the person to lecture
anyone about confronting their fears. He was right
about that. She bit down hard on her lip. She hadn't
expected her even-tempered cowboy to throw that
back in her face. She drove off down the main ranch
road, barely seeing the fences and trees that lined
her way. One thing she'd learned during all her
physical and emotional rehab was that anger hid way

more than most people imagined . . . and that
sometimes what you *thought* you were angry about
wasn't the real truth.

Which made sense of Ry's outburst, but didn't
mean she had to like it.

On impulse, she stopped at the general store and
went inside. Maureen, Nancy's mom, was at the
cashier station patiently giving directions to a group
of obviously lost Japanese tourists. She winked at
Avery and pointed to the family quarters.

"Nancy's out back if you want her."

Avery went on through and found her best friend
lying on the couch watching some soap opera that
Roy and Ruth loved.

She plopped herself on the couch and pressed a
pillow to her stomach.

"I think I just screwed up."

"What did you do?"

"Told Ry to get some therapy."

Nancy sat up. "You told a man to pay out good
money and share his intimate thoughts with a
stranger?"

"Yeah, and he told me I was a fine one to talk because I was scared of his stupid dopey horse."

"Ouch."

Avery flopped back against the arm of the couch.
"I was just trying to help."

"Yeah, sounds like it. You never tell a guy he can't
fix everything by himself. You make suggestions and
keep making them until he thinks he came up with
the idea himself, remember?"

"Sometimes I just don't want to deal with the frag-
ile male ego." Avery closed her eyes. "I've blown it."

"With Ry?"

"Who else?"

"Nah, he's totally into you. He'll be hammering on your door by tonight, begging for forgiveness."

"Nancy, have you met the Morgan brothers? Stubborn Ass should be their middle name."

"So you're going to apologize?"

Avery sighed. "I don't know. I'm not ashamed of anything I said to him. I still think I was right to say it."

"Then let him stew for a while. If he really wants to be with you, he'll find a way to make things right."

Ry stormed over to Dolittle's stall and slammed his fist into the woodwork.

What the hell was wrong with him? Avery didn't deserve such crap. He took a deep breath, turned around, and walked back the way he'd come. By the time he reached the yard, Avery's car was turning out of the gate, and she wasn't slowing down.

"Hell . . ." he breathed.

His temper was so uncertain at the moment—a temper he hadn't even known he possessed—and all because he'd come back to the ranch and had to deal with his past.

"You okay, son?"

He looked over his shoulder to find his dad watching him from the porch of the house.

"Nope."

Billy came down the steps toward him. "Was that you and Avery shouting down at the barn?"

Ry took off his hat and smoothed out the brim. "Might have been."

"Is there anything you want to talk about?"

"Jeez, don't you start."

Billy raised his eyebrows. "I can see why Avery left." He made as if to walk past. "If you'll excuse me, there are chores to do."

His father was halfway to the barn before Ry spoke again.

"Do you think Mom was sick?"

Billy stopped moving and slowly turned around. "Before she left?"

Ry nodded.

"I think she was depressed and hadn't recovered from Rachel's birth. These days they call it severe postnatal depression."

"So does that make what she did okay?"

"Walking out on all of us?" Billy asked. "We all tried to help her, we really did, but she was too far gone to even notice. Poor woman."

"How come you don't hate her, then?"

Billy looked down at his boots and then centered his gaze somewhere past Ry's shoulder. "What's the point? I'm sure she didn't mean to do what she did—no more than I meant to end up too drunk to take care of you all. Nobody's perfect, Ry. We all make mistakes. We just have to learn how to live with them."

"What were you two arguing about on that last night?"

Billy went still. "I don't remember. Why?"

"Was it something to do with our birthday party?"

"What makes you think that?" Billy came toward him, his lined face the picture of concern.

"Because I have this strange memory of you

getting mad because Mom only made one cake or something."

"Yeah? I don't think I remember that," Billy said way too carefully for Ry's liking.

"I'm right, aren't I? She made a cake for HW."

"Maybe she only had the ingredients to make one." Billy paused. "Is it important?"

"You tell me. The next thing I knew she was gone, and you were covered in blood."

Billy winced. "I'm sorry, son."

"Why? She was the one trying to gut you with a kitchen knife."

"I'm sorry you saw that. It was late. I thought you younger boys were asleep and Chase was the only one who knew what was going on."

"We weren't asleep. I was—" Ry frowned. "I was cleaning up the bathroom."

"You two were always getting water everywhere."

"Yeah, but—" Ry shook his head as whatever elusive memory he'd just rediscovered disappeared again. "Anyway, it wasn't your fault."

"It was, because I didn't understand how bad she was feeling until it was almost too late."

Ry had nothing to say to that, and wanted to cheer when Chase pulled up in his enormous blue truck and got out.

"Hey, Dad, you got a moment?"

Billy stayed put and so did Ry as Chase came toward them, his laptop under one arm and his Stetson in his hand.

"Did Ry tell you about what happened in Humboldt?"

Billy looked at them both. "Nope."

"Then can I ask if you and Mom ever got officially divorced?"

Billy sighed. "Yeah. I think we did. I got some paperwork after I got out of jail, telling me what she'd done. It was too late to do much about it at that point."

"But you didn't go after her?"

"I wasn't in any state to go after her. I was barely hanging in there myself, clinging to sobriety, and trying to make a living as an ex-con and a dishwasher."

"You knew all along she wasn't dead?"

"I wasn't certain until that point. I hoped she was okay, but that confirmed it. I was . . . relieved that she'd found a new life."

Chase didn't look happy. "You could've told us."

"I wasn't here, son." Billy's gaze was clear. "It wasn't my place to stir everything up again when I had no way of fixing things."

"Did Ruth know?" Ry asked.

"I wrote to her. She's never mentioned it to me, so it's possible the letter went astray." Billy patted Ry's arm. "There's no point getting mad at your grandma about this. She was too busy bringing you all up and running this ranch to have time to worry about much else."

Chase started walking toward the house. "He's right, Ry. Ruth probably didn't want to make things more complicated than they already were."

Billy winced as Chase slammed the screen door behind him. "He's still mad at me."

"He's getting over it." This time it was Ry who slapped his father on the back. "If he wasn't we'd all be homeless right now instead of working on a new improved future for the ranch. I'm kind of glad that you did know about the divorce—otherwise Mom would have added bigamist to her résumé."

"She married again?"

Ry searched his father's lined face. "You okay with that?"

To his amazement Billy smiled. "Yeah. I'd like to think she got her happy ending after putting up with me."

"You were a good husband and father."

"Before I threw everything away." Billy's smile faded. "I'm just glad she found her place."

"And what about you?"

Billy looked him right in the eye. "I'm back here, on the ranch, and all my sons are talking to me again. I reckon I hit the jackpot, don't you?" He touched the brim of his hat and started walking down toward the barn, leaving Ry staring after him.

He wasn't sure if he would be so forgiving in the same situation. At least his dad was honest enough to admit he'd made a shitload of mistakes of his own. Which led Ry back to thinking about Avery, and how she'd tried to persuade him to get hypnotized or something equally stupid.

But she'd done it because she cared about him— at least he thought she did. And she had a point. He was deeply conflicted about his mother, and he wasn't handling it well.

He took out his phone and stared down at the screen. Should he text her an apology? Nah. This was one time when he had to cowboy up and say the words in person. After dinner he would go into town and find out if she was willing to talk to him.

* * *

Avery smiled at the last guest who trooped past her out of the dining room.

"I hope you enjoyed your dinner, sir. The bar's still open. It's across the lobby and down on the right."

She closed the door and surveyed the candlelit space. The tables were almost cleared and one of the cleaning staff was working the vacuum over the carpet. They were an efficient bunch, and she had no concerns that they wouldn't have the place all nice and sparkly in time for the breakfast rush in the morning.

It was technically her night off. She'd planned to spend it with Ry up at the ranch, but an evening alone watching crummy movies and eating ice cream suddenly seemed incredibly appealing. She checked her cell. Nothing from Ry. Not that she was expecting to hear from him. Beneath his sweetness he was as stubborn as all the Morgan brothers. Nancy had told her to stand firm, and not contact Ry. She hadn't, but she wished she knew if he was okay.

She couldn't forget how he looked when he woke up from one of his nightmares. Something had gone terribly wrong between him and his mother. He didn't seem to know exactly what had happened, and she could hardly go around asking other members of his family.

Was it possible to bury something so deep you couldn't remember it at all?

With a last wave at Marta, who was overseeing the

cleaning, Avery left the dining room and walked toward the lobby. Standing right by the registration desk was hot Dr. Mendez and his grandmother, whom he always took out for dinner once a week.

"Hey, Avery," he called out to her. He whispered something in Portuguese to his grandmother, who answered him. "My *avo* says to tell you the fish was excellent."

"Hi Tio, Mrs. Mendez. Good to know." Avery's Spanish wasn't bad, but her Portuguese had been picked up during her days in the rodeo, and was hardly suitable for a respectable lady like Mrs. Mendez. She dredged up something polite. "*Obrigado.*"

The old lady disappeared toward the restrooms and Avery lingered to keep the doctor company.

"How are you doing these days? I never see you anymore," Tio complained.

"As much as I like you, I'm glad I'm nowhere near your surgery." Avery grinned at him. "I'm feeling really well. I've been working up at Morgan Ranch around all those horses."

"Good for you." Tio's answering smile was warm. "The next thing I know you'll be riding again."

"I'm not sure about that."

He touched her arm and they moved slightly away from the front desk. "Now that you're no longer a patient of mine, would you like to go out for a drink sometime?"

Avery blinked. "That's really sweet of you, but I'm kind of seeing someone right now." Which might be a big fat lie, but she could always hope.

"No harm done. Just thought I'd ask. I've always admired your courage."

"Thanks for that." She smiled back at him and caught a sudden movement over his shoulder. Redirecting her gaze, she locked eyes with Ry, who had just come in the front door. He'd stopped walking and everyone had to go around him like he was a rock in the river.

Mrs. Mendez returned and went off with her grandson, her hand tucked into the crook of his elbow, leaving Avery with two choices. Go and see what Ry wanted or run like hell. Despite her bad hip she was favoring the second option when he came over to her.

"Was that Dr. Mendez?"

She nodded.

"Were you talking to him about me?"

"Do you really think I'm that underhanded?" She poked him in the chest with the tip of her finger. "I didn't even mention you."

He took off his hat and scrubbed his fingers through his corn-blond hair. "I'm sorry."

"For which particular part? That you think I'd go around telling other people your business, or that the last time I saw you, you behaved like a complete ass?"

"All of it."

She wasn't ready to concede quite yet. "And for your information, Ry Morgan, the reason Dr. Mendez was talking to me was to ask me out."

She just about stopped herself from adding the "so there," sticking out her tongue, and stamping her foot, but she hoped she conveyed the same feelings with her patent glare.

"I hope you told him you were already taken."

"Like an empty chair?"

"No, like the most important woman in my life, period."

She frowned at him. "Don't say things like that. You make me want to like you again."

The corner of his mouth twitched. "So, there's hope?"

"It depends. Do you want to come up to my room and talk about it?"

"Here?" He glanced back at the desk, where her brother Tucker was chatting away to one of the guests. "Where are your parents?"

"They're out at some local business thing."

"You sure they won't mind me being here?"

"Trust me—they'll never even know. Come on." She waved at Tucker and made her way through the door into the staff area, bypassed the kitchens, and went up the back stairs, Ry following along behind.

She let him into her bedroom and locked the door, watching as he checked out her big bed, her pink flowered chaise longue, and her ancient posters.

She sat on the chaise and gestured for him to sit opposite her on the bed.

"So?"

He placed his hat on the quilt and sat forward, his head down, staring at his boots, his hands loosely linked together between his knees.

"I never used to get mad about anything."

"I know."

He sighed. "But since I found out about Mom? I've been losing it big-time."

Avery couldn't resist pointing out, "You're not telling me anything I haven't already told you."

"I hate it when people lose their tempers." He

risked a quick glance at her. "I guess that's because of what happened between my parents. They fought all the time that last year. HW and I were so scared, sometimes we'd pack up our clothes and make plans to take two of the horses and run away."

"You were *five*."

"We were scared shitless." He hesitated. "After she had Rachel, my mom . . . changed. We tried to keep out of her way as much as possible, but as you said, we were only five, and we *needed* stuff like regular meals, clean clothes. My dad did his best, and Ruth tried to help, but Mom got so offended that they tried not to upset her."

"I'm so sorry, Ry. I never realized things had gotten that bad."

"No one did." He grimaced. "We weren't going to tell anyone, in case things got worse. But the thing is? When she left? I remember feeling relieved. I didn't tell anyone that—not even HW—because you aren't supposed to be happy your mom has disappeared."

Avery held his gaze. "One thing I've learned since my accident, Ry, is that even if you know you're being irrational, you can't help how you feel." She took an unsteady breath. "I hated what had happened to me, and I hated everyone who was trying to help me. I wanted to be left alone to die." She caught the flash of concern in his eyes. "Yes, even that crossed my mind. I was nineteen, and as far as I was concerned, my life was over."

He didn't say anything, but he reached out and took her hand in a hard grasp.

"So I can kind of understand that your mom might have just . . . given up."

"Yeah, as an adult? I get that she was ill, but as a kid . . . it was terrifying." He cleared his throat. "HW remembers more about what happened than I do. I've been avoiding talking to him—using my decision to come back and work on the ranch as a reason for that, rather than the true one, which is I don't want to have that conversation. So I'm going to do it. When he comes back for the wedding, I'll ask him."

Avery grinned at him like an idiot. "That's really brave of you."

"Hell, it's about time, right?" He shrugged. "Can't have my woman thinking I'm a big old coward."

"I'd never think that, Ry. I was just worried about you." She hesitated. "Maybe I pushed too hard."

His smile faded. "I'm glad you did. But I'm the one who came here to apologize. I should never have said that about you."

"About me being scared of horses? I am scared."

"But you're trying to fix that. I know how much courage it takes. I've watched you force yourself to stick around me and Dolittle, seen every twitch and deep, steadying breath, and I'm so damned *proud* of you."

"Really?" She smiled at him for real this time. "So why exactly are we fighting again?"

"I'm not sure."

"Neither am I, seeing as we're both trying so hard to deal with our own crap." She rose from her seat and walked over to the bed. He looped his arm around her waist, drawing her down onto his knee and buried his face in the crook of her neck.

"I'm sorry, Avery."

"I'm sorry, too," she whispered, and hugged him hard. Not holding him—even if it had only been for one day—had been horrible. She never wanted to let him go. He smelled like horse, and leather, and good honest sweat. He smelled like he belonged just to her.

He kissed his way up her throat and she shivered as his mouth met hers.

"You sure your parents are out?" he murmured into her ear.

"Absolutely sure, and I've locked the door."

"Good thinking." He moved so fast she was suddenly on her back with him straddling her hips. "I used to dream about this."

"About having sex?"

His smile was crooked and so hot she wanted to give him everything.

"About you—in this room. I came up here once just before I left town. I was doing some kind of project with Tucker, and we had to finish it after school. While he was rounding up supplies in the kitchen I waited in the hallway and your door was open so I peeked inside."

She kissed his cheek. "I always knew you were a pervert."

"I always knew I liked you way more than you liked me." He grinned. "All you wanted to talk to me about back then was the rodeo, and your horse."

"That was Mellie. She had to be put down after my accident. Another thing I felt guilty about." She swallowed hard. "It was raining and she slipped on one of the turns and fell, taking me with her. I don't remember much about it."

"At that speed I'm not surprised." Ry kissed her shoulder and slid his work-callused fingers under the hem of her T-shirt. "You ready for some make-up sex?"

"We were only apart for one day."

"Still." He kissed her exposed belly. "It feels like forever to me."

She grabbed a handful of his hair. "Ry, do you want me to argue with you about stuff, or would you prefer me to keep my opinions to myself?"

He studied her, his golden eyes sleepy with lust and warm amusement. "Is that really a serious question?"

"I suppose not. If you told me I had to keep my mouth shut, I'd probably kill you."

He knelt up over her and undid the top button of his jeans. "I can think of far better things for you to do with your mouth."

Avery rolled her eyes. "Wow, you are so smooth."

He winked at her. "Am I? Maybe you'd better find out."

Chapter Thirteen

"Come *on*, Ry," Ruth yelled from the front parlor, loud enough to wake the dead. "Chase has set up a big screen, and I've made popcorn and brownies."

He glanced at Avery, who'd come upstairs to keep him company while he got changed.

"I suppose we'd better go and watch HW's movie debut."

"It's exciting!"

She bounced up and down on his bed, which gave him other ideas completely—especially as her bosom was bouncing close to his face. He was trying to be discreet about how many times they got together, but three days apart was about the longest he could manage without breaking down and calling her.

"Unless you want to hang out up here for a while?" he suggested with a wink.

"You are insatiable."

"Only with you." Which was the God's honest truth. She made him horny just sitting next to him. "We could get the reviews from the family first, and then decide if we want to watch it."

"No. Let's go down." She stood and stretched, smiling down at him. "Come on. You're in the damn thing, aren't you?"

"I told HW to cut me out. Did you hear the questions that reporter asked me?" He took her hand as they walked along the hallway to the stairs. "She was trying to make me out to be some kind of bitter loser."

"That's what the media do these days. They love a scandal, and the idea that you and HW are fighting? She must have eaten that up."

"HW shouldn't have said anything."

"I thought he said he didn't?"

"So he claims." Ry followed Avery down. "I suppose it could've been his ex-girlfriend Lally, or one of the other guys he regularly hangs out with. They all knew how things stood between us, and I can't say I tried to hide how much I disliked that whole bunch of losers."

"Then someone probably told on you both." Avery paused at the bottom of the stairs to look up at him. "I don't think HW's dealing very well with the split either."

"On what basis?"

"I talked to him a bit when he was here. He sounded downright miserable."

"Mainly because he wasn't getting everything his own way." Ry forced a smile. "Come on, let's go in before BB eats all the brownies."

"I heard that," his brother called out from the couch, where he was sitting with Jenna and Maria. "Ruth made enough for everyone, even me."

"Where's Billy?"

"He's at AA. He'll be back soon."

"Shush!" Ruth sat beside Roy. January and Chase were at the table. Ry offered Avery the last comfortable chair and perched on the arm beside her. "It's about to start."

Francesca's beautiful face came on the screen and she spoke directly to the camera. "Welcome to the last of our profiles of local heroes: HW Morgan, finalist in the upcoming national rodeo finals in Las Vegas."

"Hero." Ry snorted, and Avery dug her elbow in his ribs.

A photo of HW caught him in motion on the back of a saddle bronc, his hand held high, his body arched like a bow against the pull of the horse, who had all four feet off the ground.

"Nice," Avery murmured.

The picture faded to show the real-life HW waving and grinning up at the stands as he received an outstanding score. Ry had to admit he looked good on camera—like an all-American cowboy from the old movies.

Francesca appeared again, this time her expression concerned—well, Ry supposed she was *meant* to look concerned, but she didn't seem able to frown due to the Botox in her face.

"But behind this triumph lies a story so shocking that it is amazing HW Morgan has succeeded at all."

Ry tensed. "Holy hell, she's going to make this all about what a shit I've been to my identical twin, isn't she?"

Ruth patted his knee. "Calm down, Ry, and stop cursing. Let's listen to what she has to say."

* * *

Chase turned the TV off and silence fell over the room, broken by the cheerful sound of Billy whistling as he came through the door.

"What's wrong? It looks like you're holding a séance in here. How did the TV special go?"

As Ruth brought out a handkerchief from her pocket, her hand was shaking and for once she looked her years.

Chase cleared his throat. "Ah . . . not too good."

Billy frowned. "Did she do a hatchet job on Ry?"

"She did an exposé of our whole family—including dragging up all the crap that happened when Mom and Rachel disappeared. I didn't even know there was TV footage of that around, but dear old Francesca found it." Chase took out his cell. "Don't worry. I'm going to talk to my lawyers and get this piece of bullshit taken off the air."

"But everything she said was true." Ry finally found his voice. "How the hell can you fight *that*?"

"Sure, some of the facts were right, but the slant she put on them? Making us all look like devils while poor old angelic HW struggled to survive his monstrous family and become a rodeo hero? That's not journalism." Chase was so furious he'd gotten all quiet, and his blue eyes were chips of ice. "That's a hatchet job."

"Holy crap." Billy sucked in a breath, his gaze fixed on Ruth. "Did they mention me?"

"Yeah," Ry answered before Ruth could. "They knew all about you, and Francesca made very sure to leave the question of whether you murdered your own wife and child hanging out there for the entire world to speculate on."

Ruth dabbed at her eyes. "We invited them into our *home*. I made lasagna! We were good to them."

"We didn't invite them," Ry said flatly. "HW did."

Chase tapped out a number on his cell phone. After a few seconds he grimaced.

"He's not answering. I'll leave a message." He waited for the beep and then spoke. "HW? It's Chase. You need to come back here right now, no excuses. You've got some explaining to do to your grandmother and father."

Ry sat at the kitchen table with Chase and BB. They'd persuaded everyone else to go to bed or go home, which hadn't been easy. The shock of seeing all her family tragedies spelled out on TV had made Ruth cry. Ry found that unforgiveable. And his poor father, who was trying so hard to be a good man, was now cast as a villain. The fact that HW had also made Ry out to be a jealous, talentless fool hardly mattered.

BB groaned and poured himself more coffee. "What a mess."

"At least they didn't seem to have much dirt on Maria, or know that Mom might be alive," Chase murmured as he tapped away at his laptop. "My only concern is—what if someone picks up this story, and it goes viral? Then nothing will be sacred, and they'll be digging into January's past, Jenna's, Maria's, and even Avery's."

BB scoffed. "It won't go viral. Who's going to care about one local rodeo cowboy?"

Chase looked at him over the lid of his laptop. "Because news these days is twenty-four seven, and the networks are all desperate for new content, and steal from each other all the time. Something like this, topped with HW's pretty face? Total clickbait."

BB set down his mug with a thump. "If anyone gets in my face about Maria . . ."

"What are you going to do, bro?" Chase said. "Break some bones? That will really help."

Ry sipped his coffee. "If this does get bigger, we've got other problems."

"Like what?"

"Mom up in Humboldt. What if she saw this? She's going to freak out."

Chase shrugged. "She hated the rodeo, she hated this place, why the hell would she bother to watch something about an up-and-coming local rodeo star?"

"Because HW was her favorite?" Silence greeted that remark, and Ry carried on. "If someone mentioned his name, or she saw an ad for the show, she'd watch it."

"The odds are still small that she would, Ry, but I take your point." Chase closed his laptop. "I would worry about all the other people we met in Humboldt—the ones who know we're Morgans and we're searching for our mother. They might be quite happy to talk to the media about that."

"Crap." BB dropped his head into his hands. "We're toast."

"So what do we do?" Ry asked.

"Nothing until we hear back from HW."

Ry leaned back in his chair. "Oh, come on, Chase. You won't hear from him. He'll love all the attention, and he won't care how he got it."

"That's harsh," BB said slowly. "HW isn't the devil

any more than we are. What's up with you, Ry? You used to be the one defending him to the last breath."

"He's right." Chase was also staring at him now. "What's wrong?"

"Maybe I'm tired of defending him."

"Sure, but give him the benefit of the doubt. He'll come back, and we can sit down together and work out exactly how we're going to handle this *as a family*, okay?"

"Right." Ry stood up. "And now I'm going to bed."

Chase held up his hand. "There's one more thing. It has nothing to do with the situation with HW. I was going to tell you earlier, and then I got distracted."

"What's up?"

"Ruth and I have decided we need a full-time events coordinator on board before we launch the new guest ranch. Do you have any objections if I ask the Hayes family first?"

"Not a problem for me."

The thought of having Avery working full-time up at the ranch was the best thing he'd heard all week.

"Good." Chase nodded. "I wasn't sure whether working alongside Avery would be a problem if you stopped dating."

"It won't be."

Ry went up the stairs and headed for the bathroom. Chase didn't know that he had no intention of ever stopping dating Avery. He'd waited for her, and now he was fairly sure she liked him as much as he liked her. Despite his god-awful day, he found a smile. *She* gave him that. She gave him the courage to face anything, and if he was lucky enough to gain her love, he'd always be understood and loved for himself.

Sure, sometimes she understood him far too well for his comfort zone, but even that made him want to be better for her. To show her that he could be the man she wanted.

"Jeez, Rowdy Yates Morgan . . ." he muttered as he turned on the faucet. "You're besotted."

He stared at his reflection in the mirror, and slowly smiled.

Marley put her head around the office door.

"Hey, you busy?"

Avery jumped. She'd been sitting there staring into space, thinking about the events of the previous night up at the Morgans'. Several of the hotel staff had watched the show, and there had been a lot of chatter about it this morning. From what Avery could tell, the majority of the locals thought the family had been treated badly, and weren't very happy with their so-called hometown hero.

Worse were the rumors flying around about Ry's father, and whether he'd killed his own wife. She wanted to tell them to shut up and leave the poor man alone. Hadn't he been through enough already? She knew what it was like to suffer and rebuild your life, and she had nothing but admiration for what Billy had achieved. Most people who got that lost, never found themselves again or had the courage to admit their mistakes and make amends.

"What's up?" Belatedly she realized that Marley was beginning to look concerned.

"Mom and Dad want to speak to us."

"About what?"

"I dunno."

Avery grumbled as she pushed away from her desk and followed her sister next door. Her parents were both smiling, which immediately made her suspicious. Since Marley's return, they'd been looking haunted.

"Girls, we have a couple of things we want to share with you." Dad gestured at the chairs in front of his desk. "Take the weight off."

Mom went first. "There's been a big increase in reservations from tonight, so we'll be at capacity. I want you both at work for the next few days."

Marley nodded and opened her iPad. "Why all the sudden reservations? Is there something going on?"

Dad fiddled with the pens on his desk. "It's probably something to do with the story on the Morgans last night on TV."

Avery sat up. "I hope you're not intending to profit from that pile of crap, Dad."

"I'm merely a hotel owner offering people a place to sleep, dear. A guest's reason for staying with us is no concern of ours."

"Did you watch that thing?" Avery scowled at her parents. "It was *horrible*. Offering a place to stay to people who want to come and gawk at a long-forgotten tragedy doesn't make you a friend of the Morgans."

"It's okay, sis." Marley patted her knee. "Avery's upset because of Ry."

"Ry who?" Mom inquired.

"Ry Morgan. You know she's dating him, right?" Marley looked at her parents. "I know you said you don't inquire about what's going on in your own hotel, but I would think you might have met Ry Morgan creeping up and down the staff stairs recently. I know *I* certainly have."

"Thanks, Marley," Avery muttered. Sometimes her sister's honest streak sucked. "*Nice*."

"You're dating Ry?" Mom asked. "Why didn't you *tell* me?"

Avery gave her sister the death look. "Because it slipped my mind?"

"Then that brings us nicely to our next item for discussion. I had a phone call from Ruth Morgan yesterday, followed up with a job description for a full-time events coordinator up at the ranch."

Mom handed them both a piece of paper. "I printed it out for you. But isn't it great? The job would be *perfect* for you, Marley—just perfect!"

Avery stopped reading. "Hold up. If anyone gets this job it should be me. I'm already working with the Morgans."

"But—" Marley's excited expression faded. "It *would* be perfect for me. Chase is definitely looking for someone with the skill set I possess."

"But I'm pretty sure he meant to offer the job to me," Avery said.

"Then why didn't he say so?" Marley replied. "If he'd absolutely one hundred percent wanted you, he would have asked for you by name."

Avery squared up to her sister. "Maybe he doesn't know you exist."

"Of course he does. I told him what I was up to when I last saw him in town."

"Avery, dear," Dad said cautiously. "Is it possible

that the Morgans thought the job might be too much for you?"

"In what way?"

"Well, that you're more suited to a smaller environment that you are familiar with, and not around, um, horses?"

She glared at her father. "I have been doing fine with the horses! Ask anyone."

Mom hastened to intervene. "That's great, darling. But don't you think it would be fair to give your sister a chance?"

Avery knew damn well what they were trying to do, but she so wasn't buying into it.

"The job is meant for me."

"Did Ry tell you that himself?" Marley asked.

"No, he didn't, but—"

Marley folded her arms. "Then maybe he doesn't want you to do it either. It would mean you'd be stuck with each other all day long."

"Ry isn't in charge of who gets hired at the ranch. Chase is."

"But I thought you told me it was Ry's idea for you to coordinate the wedding, so if that's the case, why didn't he suggest you for the event coordinator position?"

Avery studied her sister, who had two red spots of color on her cheeks and her chin jutting out at an all-too-familiar confrontational angle.

"Marley . . ."

Dad cleared his throat and gave Avery the side eye. "If you want my opinion, I think Marley should take the job. There's nothing to worry about, Avery, you can carry on doing your thing here at the hotel. We'll take care of you."

She stood up. "It's my *job*. I'm applying for it."

Marley rose too. "So am I."

Avery stuck out her hand. "Then may the best sister win!"

Chapter Fourteen

"The phone's been ringing off the hook," Ruth said as she served the evening meal. "I gave up answering it after lunch, disconnected it, and hid it in the mudroom under a pile of towels."

Chase looked up from his pot roast and potatoes. "You could have just turned the ringer off, and let everything go to voice mail."

Ruth gave him a pitying look. "And had to listen to all those nosey parkers interfering in our business?"

"You could've just deleted the messages."

Ry almost smiled at his brother's impeccable logic, which didn't really work with Ruth.

"Most people I talked with thought we'd been treated badly, and that HW should be ashamed of himself." Ruth finally sat down and helped herself to some food. Roy passed her the salt and pepper and she thanked him. "I reminded them that TV producers make anything look suspicious these days. Look at what they do on those reality shows."

"She's right, you know." Roy poured himself more

iced tea. "No one who knows this family will believe that steaming pile of horse crap."

"Unfortunately that's a pretty small sample of the possible viewing audience," Chase commented. "I've had over two hundred calls and emails today, and my office has been inundated with reporters and calls as well."

"No one's called me," BB said with a wink at Maria. "They've got more sense. How about you, Ry? Did HW get in touch?"

"Nope." Ry continued to eat his corn bread, using it to soak up the rich gravy. "I didn't expect him to."

But at some level he had. The idea that his twin was in trouble and had chosen not to talk to him was . . . unsettling and unreal. Even now, if something went terribly wrong, he'd probably call HW. But did his twin even realize what he'd done?

The sound of a truck pulling up drifted in through the open window, and Ruth went to get up. Blue put his hand on her shoulder and eased her back down.

"That's probably Jenna. I'll go and say hi."

"And kiss her," Maria whispered as her father left the kitchen. "He's always doing that. It's *gross.*"

"Did you hear back from Avery about the job, Chase?" Ry changed the subject before they all started laughing.

"Nope. She was busy, so Ruth talked to her parents this morning. We'll probably hear something tonight or tomorrow."

BB came back in, his expression carefully blank. "It's not Jenna."

Ry blinked as HW came in behind his brother. He

looked like he hadn't slept for a week. His clothes were crumpled and he was unshaven.

"I couldn't get a flight. I had to drive. Sorry it took so long." HW nodded at them all, but he didn't sit down.

Chase slowly raised his gaze to his brother's face. "HW. Glad you could make it. Is there anything you want to say to us all?"

HW propped a shoulder against the doorjamb. "I didn't know Francesca was going to do that."

"You mean go back into the past and trash your family?" Chase shrugged. "You might have guessed what she'd do once you told her your life story."

"I didn't."

"Didn't what?"

"Tell her anything about Dad, or what happened to Mom. The only thing she knew about was Ry and me falling out."

"So how do you think she found out the rest?"

HW's fists slowly clenched. "She's a journalist. She must have decided to find out more all by herself."

"Unlikely, seeing as she hasn't done that for any of the other featured local heroes," Ry pointed out. "Why you?"

The searing gaze HW shot him gave Ry pause.

"I don't know! Maybe she picked up on something when she was here at the ranch—saw photographs, *something* . . ."

"So it's *our* fault? You brought them here, HW. If she did snoop around, it's totally your fault."

"As far as you're concerned, Ry, everything always is my fault, isn't it?"

Ry stood, his gaze locked on his brother's. Everyone

else faded away. "Because it usually is. You're so damned impulsive and—"

"Why are you so negative about me these days?" HW demanded. "Other people like me, but you? You're just so damned determined to undermine me that you suck all the joy out of my life."

"Then you should be happy I walked out, instead of crying to Francesca about what a big meanie I am."

HW shook his head. "Ry, just *listen* to yourself. Why did you hang around if you hated our life so much? Just to make me feel bad all the time?"

Something snapped and Ry literally saw red. "Because I'm supposed to protect you, goddamn it! That's what Mom said, and you know what she did to me when I didn't obey that order—you *know*!"

Ry only realized how hard he was shaking when he tried to unclench his fist.

"What did she do to you, Ry?"

His dad's quiet voice penetrated his furious haze. Ry struggled to breathe, his gaze still locked with HW's. "Nothing. She did . . . nothing."

"She hurt him. That last year after Rachel was born? She'd pinch him, and poke him, and threaten him, and blame him if anything went wrong." HW's voice was trembling. "She made him pay for every single little thing I did, and God knows I wasn't an angel."

"Shut up, HW."

His twin shook his head. "No, I won't. This needs to be said. Is that really why you stayed with me? Because she *said so*? That's sick, bro. That's . . . terrible."

Ry looked away. "That's not true."

HW came even closer until they were nose to nose.

"You still resent the hell out of me, don't you?"

All Ry's anger drained away, leaving him feeling sick and empty.

"For being the favorite child? Why the hell would I care, HW? I survived, didn't I? We were just kids."

"But—"

Ry straightened up. "And how about we get back to the matter at hand? How about you apologize for what you've put Ruth and Billy through instead of justifying and defending yourself?"

HW flinched as if Ry had slapped him. "Go screw yourself. I just told you I don't need your protection any longer, and I certainly don't need you telling me what to do. I was just *about* to apologize. Why the hell do you think I got here as fast as I could?"

Ry raised a skeptical eyebrow and HW slammed his fist in Ry's face. Pain exploded in his jaw and he rocked on his heels, trying to stay upright and not crumble into the pain.

"Yeah, nice." He rubbed his jaw. "Don't bother to apologize for that one either, bro. I'm out of here."

"HW! Leave it!" Ruth commanded as Ry pushed past his twin. "Let him be."

Ry stumbled down the steps and into the yard, climbed into his truck and was away before his mind caught up with him, and then he wished it hadn't. His face throbbed along to his ragged heartbeat and he just drove, aware of his cell buzzing in his pocket, but more than happy to obey the law and ignore it forever.

How the hell had it come to this? Brawling with his twin in front of his family? Losing his temper and stirring up shit that should've remained hidden? He'd have to go back at some point, and then there would be questions—questions he didn't have answers for.

He realized he was parked behind the hotel and had no clear notion of how he'd managed it. He went in through the kitchens, ignoring the startled faces of the staff until his arm was taken in a firm grip by Tucker, who led him into one of the offices.

"Were you in an accident? Do you need me to call 911?" Tucker asked, his concerned brown gaze just like his sister's.

"Where's Avery?"

"She's working in the restaurant."

"Can you tell her I'm here?"

Tucker opened the door. "I can do better than that. I'll take you to her room and let her know you're up there, okay?"

Ry nodded and meekly followed Tucker, who somehow managed to snag a bag of ice and a towel on the way back through the kitchen, which he offered to Ry.

"For your jaw."

"Thanks."

He left Ry sitting on Avery's bed. All Ry could think about was how good Tucker was at his job, and how much Chase might have to pay him to lure him away from the hotel to the guest ranch. But what would the Hayes parents do if the ranch stole two of their best employees?

"Ry?"

He didn't look up as Avery came in. She sank down in front of him and put her hand on his knee. Her nails were pink and had red hearts on them.

"Tucker said you were hurt."

He continued to study her nail polish. The hearts were random, and that was driving him nuts. And how the hell did you apply them when they were so small?

"You had your nails done."

She went still. "Yeah. Nancy did them for me. Do you like them?"

"The hearts aren't symmetrical."

"I know. You just shake up the nail polish and they come out on the brush when they feel like it. Nancy says it's good therapy for my over-organized mind." She paused. "Did someone hit you?"

"Yeah. HW."

She leaned over, picked up the bag of ice and the tea towel, and gently applied them to his jaw.

He winced and she kissed his nose.

"Did you get him back?"

He looked right into her eyes. "What makes you think I didn't hit him first?"

"Because HW's the firecracker, not you."

"I didn't touch him."

"Good."

He gingerly flexed his jaw. "I don't think it's broken."

"Even better."

For something to do, he pressed his hand over the now damp tea towel, releasing her fingers, and just focused on breathing her in. There was a subtle roar of conversation from the guests congregated in the bar beneath her room, and the occasional sound of a truck passing in the street.

Familiar sounds . . . comforting ones.

"Is it okay if I sit next to you on the bed?"

"Shit." He reached down to help her to her feet. There was no way she could've been comfortable on the floor with her weak hip. "Sorry."

She sat beside him, moving his hat out of the way. Her thigh was warm against his. At some point she'd kicked off her shoes to reveal pink socks with bunnies on them.

"Did you do your toes?"

"Didn't have time. The hotel's bursting at the seams. so we've all had to work full shifts."

"Sorry to drag you away."

She took his hand and squeezed his fingers. "That's okay."

Silence fell again and he marveled at not only her patience, but also her restraint. Most people would've been all over him for details, asking intrusive questions, and she just waited him out. Waited for him to work out what he needed to say, which was proving beyond him at the moment.

He wanted to make love to her—to forget everything but her scent and her welcome as he slid inside. He already knew what she'd say if he suggested that. She'd say he was avoiding stuff, and she'd be right.

He put the bag of ice and towel on the carpet and felt along his jaw. HW had caught him fair and square. Had he deserved it?

Probably.

Beside him, Avery stirred. "Do you want to get into bed so I can hold you?"

He swallowed hard. "Only if it's okay with you. I don't want—"

She gently touched his lips with her fingertip, silencing his protest. "I'm here, and I want to be with you. I just thought we might be more comfortable. You're shivering."

He heel-and-toed his boots off and got under the covers. She followed him, cuddling against his side while he put one arm around her shoulders. She hadn't bothered putting any more lights on, so there was only the faint pink glow of her bedside lamp. He bent his head and nuzzled her hair, inhaling not only the scent of her favorite shampoo but also whatever they'd been serving down in the hotel restaurant before he'd taken her away from her job.

"Do you need to get back?"

She placed her palm on his T-shirt right over his heart. "Nope. Tucker's covering for me."

He drew her even closer, allowed his head to fall back against the headboard, and closed his eyes. Images of his mom immediately overwhelmed him, so he opened them again. Eventually, he settled on someplace to start talking.

"HW said he didn't know what Francesca was going to do."

"It's possible."

"He insinuated that she'd gotten the idea after she'd been to the ranch—as if one of us had spoken out of turn."

"Well, that's HW all over. He's always been a creative thinker." She hesitated. "But at least he came back to face the music."

"Only because Chase told him to."

"Come on, Ry. If HW hadn't wanted to be found, he would have disappeared and only reemerged for the finals in Vegas."

He let that sink in.

"He didn't get much of a chance to explain himself."

"Before you two got into it?"

"He was saying stuff . . . about our mom, right there in front of everyone, talking about how she blamed me for everything, and made my life hell."

He breathed hard through his nose. "Talking about her telling me I was responsible for HW, who could do no wrong in her eyes. Saying I was the reason why she was mad all the time, and you know what? It didn't matter what I did, whether I tried to be perfect, whether I tried to make HW behave, or I looked after the baby when she couldn't be bothered. I was never good enough. I was always the bad seed."

"Ry . . ."

"And you know what else? How the *hell* could she say that?" Now that he'd started talking he couldn't seem to stop. His voice cracked. "HW and I are *identical*. What did she see that made her hate me, and love him?"

Avery made a distressed sound and wrapped her arms around him, drawing him against her shoulder, cutting off his words. With his mouth pressed against the curve of her throat, he shuddered and let go, felt the humiliating sting of his hot tears.

He had no idea how long she held him. Eventually he stirred, and she let him go. He couldn't look at her, didn't dare.

"HW said he was fed up with me looking out for him and stealing his joy. I lost it and called him out about how I was supposed to be the responsible one, the one who made things right for him because Mom said—" He sighed. "Yeah—so he called me out on that. Said I should've done what I wanted my whole life instead of following in his shadow making him feel guilty for being alive."

"I'm sure you never meant to do that. You love him."

She was offering him a lifeline—a way to claw back his self-respect and move on, but this time he wasn't in the right place to take it.

"I love him because he's my twin, but he's right. I also resented him for being the favorite. I didn't even realize how much until right now. It puts everything I've done for him in a new light, doesn't it?"

"Not everything."

"Maybe I stuck by him not out of love, but out of some perverse desire to make sure he failed."

She didn't say anything for a long while, and then she got out of the bed and stomped over to the door.

The bottom fell out of Ry's stomach, and he pushed the covers aside. "God, I'm sorry. Don't—"

She held up one finger. "Stay there, okay? I'll be back in a second."

Avery's heart was hammering as she went down to the kitchen and located her cell phone sitting on the windowsill. With fingers that trembled, she texted January.

Ry with me, tell Ruth not to worry

She exhaled at the instant reply.

Got it. x

She went into the pantry, grabbed the best brandy, two glasses, and two bottles of water, and went back up the stairs. Ry was out of bed, his back to her, staring out of the window. He hadn't actually looked at her since she'd gotten into bed with him.

He spoke without turning around. "Maybe I should go."

"Don't you dare." She carefully placed the brandy and glasses on her desk. "I just stole Dad's favorite brandy. He'll kill me if he finds out."

He finally turned. "I'll take it back when I leave."

Avery pointed at the chair. "Either sit down or get back into bed, Ry."

He made a hopeless gesture that almost broke her heart, and sat on the side of the bed, one hand rubbing the back of his neck as he stared down at his socks.

She poured them both a brandy and went to sit beside him.

"Here you go."

He took the glass and grimaced. "I don't like brandy."

"Neither do I, but I think we both need it." She swirled hers around in the large balloon-shaped glass and warmed it with her hands. "You've had a sucky kind of day."

There was a bruise forming on his jaw, and she wanted to kiss it better. She wanted to drive over to Morgan Ranch and slap HW silly for daring to upset her man.

"I'm sorry."

She sipped her brandy, appreciating the way the warmth spread through her body. "It's okay."

"It's not."

She hated the bleakness in his voice.

"All right—then how are you going to make things better?"

She kept her gaze on his strong, capable hands as he cupped the glass, gently swirling the brandy before taking a sip.

He sighed. "Find Mom, and have it out with her? If she hasn't bolted after all that crap on the TV."

"Oh wow, I didn't think about that. Do you think she would've watched the show?"

"If she did, and she knows we've been looking for her, then she might work out that things are about to go postal and leave."

"Or maybe it might encourage her to come forward."

"After twenty years? I don't think she wants anything to do with us."

Avery considered her reply. "Then, let's just hope she's not a TV watcher." She finished her brandy and waited until Ry did the same. "Better?"

He managed a faint smile. "Well, I'm not shaking or crying anymore, so I'd call that a win." He took the brandy glass out of her hand and set it on the bedside table beside his. "The thing is—at some point I've got to face them all at the ranch."

"What do you think they are going to do? Disown you for fighting with your twin?"

"No, they're used to that these days. It's more that they are going to want to talk about crap, about what HW said."

"Because they care about you."

"But it doesn't change anything, does it?" He finally looked her right in the eye. "You can't alter the past."

"True, but you do have to learn how to live with it." She hesitated, reluctant to sound like she was interfering in something so deeply personal. But he had come to her. She couldn't believe it, but it meant the world. "Isn't it better if you are all on the same page? It just means there are less misunderstandings as you move forward."

"You sound like Jenna. She spent years in family therapy and now she's starting to get into it with BB and the rest of us." He dragged an unsteady hand through his hair. "The thing is—I'm supposed to be the calm one, the one that nothing upsets—the peacemaker, you know? I *like* that. So now—with what HW told them, they're going to feel different about me."

"Why?"

"Because they'll think I'm . . . weak."

"For being unfairly picked on by your obviously depressed mother?" He didn't say anything. The vulnerability in his eyes made her want to weep and smash something at the same time. "They *love* you, Ry. They aren't going to judge you like that."

He let out his breath. "I don't suppose I have any choice in the matter, do I? I can't tell them how to act toward me."

She leaned in and kissed him. His lips tasted of brandy. "You don't have to go home right now, do you?"

"Haven't I dumped on you enough?"

She smiled into his eyes. "Nope. Stay the night. Everything will look better in the morning—*and* you can score a free breakfast at the buffet downstairs."

He kissed her very carefully. "Thank you, Avery."

"It's okay. I know how much you like your food."

"Not that—" He hesitated, and kissed her again. "You know what I mean. I'd love to stay."

She was so glad because she wanted to take care of him, to keep him safe and away from harm. If he'd tried to leave, she might have been forced to tie him to her bedpost. She smiled against his throat as he drew her into his arms with such tenderness that she felt like a precious object. Strange how he could still make her feel that way when he was the one who needed her tonight.

She stripped off his T-shirt to encourage him to get naked, and he helped her with her clothes until they were together under the covers. He reached over to turn out the lamp and she cuddled against his side. His hand moved down over her hip and settled on her butt, urging her even closer.

In the darkness he slowly exhaled and she rubbed her cheek against his chest.

"Okay?"

"Getting there."

From the relaxing of his tense muscles she really believed that he was.

Chapter Fifteen

Ry rode up to Roy's house and parked Dolittle outside the barn before heading into the kitchen.

"Hey, what are we doing today? More fences up at the ghost town?"

Roy was sitting at the table reading the local newspaper and eating some kind of breakfast burrito that was dripping greasy stuff onto the table. He looked over the top of the paper at Ry.

"Yup, fences it is. I'll be ready in a few."

Ry leaned casually against the countertop like he hadn't a care in the world. He'd decided to take the coward's way out and avoid the ranch house completely, so he'd snuck into the barn, saddled Dolittle and been away before the sun had fully risen. He figured Roy was the least involved in the whole mess, and would have the least to say. At least he hoped so. Roy could be blunt when he had something on his mind, and he'd been there when it had all gone down at the dinner table last night.

"Do you want me to check the supplies while you're finishing up?"

"Sure. Billy took a truckload of wire and fence posts up there yesterday, but we can always do with more." This time Roy didn't bother to lower the paper when he answered.

Ry was just about to leave when he finally took in the front page, which had a picture of HW on the front. Had Jada, the editor of the local rag, decided to go with the story, or had she been made to do so by her higher-ups? She was on the Morgantown Historical Society board, and was supposedly a friend of January's. He didn't pause to read the headline and went outside into the welcoming sunlight.

There was no getting away from what had happened. Like Avery said, he was just going to have to deal.

By the time Ry had saddled up the other two horses, Roy emerged from the house and made his leisurely way over to the barn.

"Good job, Ry. Let's go."

Ry mounted and held Dolittle in check until Roy was ready. He risked one casual question before they set off.

"Is HW still around?"

"Nope. Chase had him flown back to Vegas. He's supposed to be training out there."

"Okay." Ry looked straight ahead. "Is Dad going to help out with the fences today?"

"He might. It depends on BB and Maria's schedule. You know how he likes to be a good grandpa." Roy glanced at him. "Chase is home, BB is too, and Ruth's gonna have to be faced at some point."

Ry sighed. "Yeah, I know."

"Can't hide forever, son."

"Got it." Ry shortened his reins. "But maybe just for the rest of the day, okay?"

"Avery, we have to talk about this."

Marley came and sat on the corner of Avery's desk, blocking her escape unless she wanted to get really physical and karate-kick her sister out of the way.

"There's nothing to talk about. We'll both apply for the job and the best applicant will win."

"But I *need* this job. Why can't you understand that?"

"Marley, you have a degree, you can work anywhere in the world. Why on earth are you so fixated on getting a job on a ranch in the middle of nowhere? The place might not even succeed, and then where will you be?"

"But I want to stay here."

"Then work at the hotel." Avery patted her sister's hand. "If I had your qualifications I'd be applying for jobs in Hawaii, New York, and London . . ."

"You have experience, Ave. That counts for a lot more than a stupid degree. And it doesn't make sense. How can you get a degree rather than work, and then be told you have to have *experience?*"

"I *know* it's frustrating, but if you work here for a year or so you can then move *on* with that experience, and with your degree. Wasn't that the plan all along?"

"But Mom and Dad don't like me working here."

God, was Marley's lip actually trembling? Her sister really wasn't used to not getting what she wanted or not being the most successful member of the family. Avery tried again.

"They just need time to get used to all your excellent and necessary adjustments. You've got to remember that they've been doing things the way they like for twenty-five years."

"Which is why you fit in here so well. You don't like change either."

"I—" Avery considered that remark. "That's not true, Marley. I just haven't had much choice in the matter."

Marley sucked in a breath. "You *chose* to stay here. Once you'd gotten over your accident you could've left. You didn't, and now, just because I did those things, you want to make it difficult for me."

"If it was any other job for any other local family or business, I'd be more than happy to step down, but this is at *Morgan Ranch*. I'm the one who set up the office there, and I'm the one who is supposed to be taking that job."

Marley folded her arms across her chest. "What happens if you and Ry break up, and you still have to see him every day?"

"We're both mature people. If we break up, we'll be polite about it."

Actually, if Ry Morgan broke up with her she'd kill him, which meant she wouldn't have to worry about work or her family because she'd be locked up on death row.

"It's not healthy for a relationship to be twenty-four seven, Avery."

She rolled her eyes. "Yeah, like Mom and Dad's? They seem to have done okay."

"But I *want* that job." Avery half expected her sister

to stamp her feet and have a tantrum. "Couldn't you just—let me have it for a year, and then take it over when I move on?"

"No, Marley, I could not." She met her sister's pleading gaze. "Look, if Chase wants to hire you, fair and square? Then that's fine by me, but let him make the decision, okay? Don't let this come between us."

Marley slid off the desk. "He's going to choose me. I'm better qualified."

"And that's okay."

Marley headed for the door and then slowed to look over her shoulder. "If he doesn't pick me, how are you going to feel knowing you only got the job because of Ry?"

"That's not fair," Avery snapped. "How about I get the job because I'm the one who just spent the last month setting everything up? How about the fact that I get on with everyone up there?"

Marley gaped at her. "You're *shouting* at me. You never shout."

"Because I want you to drop it, okay? Maybe I'm sick and tired of always having to be the nice sister, the one who has no ambition. I *have* ambition, Marley. I was on course to become one of the best barrel racers in the country!"

She was standing and her knees were shaking as she focused in on her sister. Her parents appeared at the open door, Tucker behind them.

"Everything okay, girls?" Dad said brightly.

Avery glared at him. "Yes—as long as I let Marley get what she wants, as usual."

"Now who's being unfair!" Marley cried. "After

your accident you stopped wanting to succeed, you gave up! Nobody made you."

"Apart from the fact that I was physically disabled? Of course it changed me, but I've got to get past it."

"And taking *my* job in *my* field is the way you're going to proceed?"

"It's my field, too!" Avery was really yelling now. "I've worked at this place since I was a kid—paid and unpaid! I know more about how to run a hotel than you do in your little finger!"

Marley gasped and ran out of the office, her hand over her mouth.

"That wasn't a very nice thing to say, Avery," Dad admonished her, and Mom nodded. "She—"

Avery interrupted him. "She needs to understand that she can't have everything she wants. And you two need to stop pushing her to apply for my damn job just because you want to get rid of her."

"There's no need to curse, dear," Mom murmured.

Avery sat down with a thump as her parents departed, no doubt to comfort poor widdle Marley. She wasn't sure where all her anger had come from—hadn't even realized she'd been holding it in there for years.

The door closed with a soft click, and Tucker took up the perch on the corner of her desk that Marley had recently vacated.

She ignored him and opened her laptop. "I suppose you think I should apologize to her as well."

"No. I think she needs to understand that everything won't automatically fall into her lap."

"Really?" She looked up. "I was beginning to think it was just me."

"Of course she does have her reasons for being like that. It was hard for her after your accident. Mom and Dad had very little time for anything apart from taking care of you, and she was pretty much ignored."

"Great. Now you're laying on the guilt."

"I'm just trying to say that maybe this family *needs* a shake-up—for our parents to see you've changed, and maybe to wonder why Marley, who's achieved everything she ever dreamed of, decided to come home and wants to stay put."

"I asked her about that, but she didn't answer the question. Do you think something happened at college?"

Tucker shrugged. "I don't know, but with her degree she could find a job anywhere in the world, and she didn't."

"Now I have sprinkles of guilt on my guilt." Avery groaned. "I suppose I should try and find out what's going on."

"She'll tell you when she's ready. Remember, you don't have to fix everyone." Tucker vacated his perch. "And, by the way, I think you'll do a fantastic job up at the ranch."

She blew him a kiss. "Always the diplomat. I bet you'll be saying exactly the same thing to Marley in a few minutes."

"I doubt it. She needs more experience dealing with people." He shuddered. "She tends to order the guests and staff around, and no one likes that."

"She's young. She'll work it out."

Tucker left and Avery stopped pretending to check her email. God, why had she gotten so cross over something so minor? Or maybe it wasn't a small thing after all. Was she finally coming out of her shell and wanting more? She'd stayed in the same job for years. Even her room was the same as when she'd been a teenager. Had she gotten stuck somewhere?

Ry and Marley's return to Morgantown had made her think about what she wanted, and how little she'd done with her life since the accident. She shouldn't be shouting at either of them.

She should be thanking them.

Ruth glanced up from her cookbook as Ry entered the kitchen.

"You took your time."

He took a deep breath. "Yeah. About that—"

She pointed at a chair and he obediently sat down. Taking off her reading glasses, she came around the table and grabbed his chin, angling his head to study his jaw.

"Not broken?"

"Nope. Just sore."

"Good." She released her grip, reminding him of how she used to take hold of him by the ear when he was a kid.

"HW went back to Las Vegas."

"Roy told me."

"He told me to tell you he's sorry he hit you."

"Okay."

She held his gaze. "But I'm not sorry he did. There was some truth in what he said, wasn't there?"

"Yeah." She held his gaze, hers calm but expectant, until he felt obliged to keep going. "I suppose at some level I did resent him."

"And?"

"And what? Despite what he said, I didn't spend my whole time with him grumbling and complaining. We had our disagreements just like any brothers, but we stuck together. We had each other's backs."

"I'm sure he knows that."

"Didn't sound like it."

"Ry, your twin is under a lot of pressure at the moment, what with the finals and your mom reappearing, and the TV show . . ."

"I know. I'll call him and apologize, *okay*?"

"Now you sound like a teenager." She shook her head. "I'm so sorry, Ry."

"Because I'm acting like a teen? Don't be, you're right."

She cupped his bruised jaw. "For not seeing what was happening when you and HW were just kids."

"As I said, we survived, and there's nothing we can do about it now." He placed his hand over hers. "You gave me *so much* when I was a kid. I don't ever want you to feel guilty about a thing."

Her eyes filled with tears. "You're a good boy, Rowdy Yates Morgan."

"Don't cry, okay? I can't handle that." He tried to smile. It occurred to him that this was why he hadn't wanted to come home. Not that *he'd* be upset, but that everyone else would. "I prefer it when you get mad and tell me off."

"Oh, don't worry. I'm sure you'll do something fairly soon to earn my wrath."

"I can guarantee it." He kissed her lined cheek. "Any food needing to be eaten?"

She swatted him lightly on the head. "Dinner's in half an hour. Come back then."

Ry went up the stairs smiling to himself, only to pause when he found Billy waiting for him outside his bedroom door. With a sigh, he went in and left the door open behind him.

"Come on in, Dad. Let me have it."

Billy sat on the bed. Ry walked over to the window and parked himself on the edge of his desk as his dad started speaking.

"Your mom did make only one birthday cake. She said it was for both of you, but somehow she'd made it in HW's favorite color, flavor, and theme, and your name had somehow gotten smudged and fallen off the top of the frosting. It wasn't until I confronted her about it that I really understood how hard she was coming down on you." He shook his head. "I was . . . horrified. You were identical twins. There was no way in hell one of you was supposedly superior to the other."

Ry didn't say anything, but he nodded for his father to go on.

"I think it was at that point I realized she was seriously ill and needed help. I didn't get a chance to put any plan into action before she became violent and ended up running away." He looked up at Ry. "I know saying sorry doesn't change anything, but I'm saying it anyway."

"There's no need."

"Sure there is. We let you down, son."

He shrugged. What else could he do? There was no way he was going to discuss what had happened. At least everyone now knew why he was reluctant to make contact with his mom, and no one was blaming him, which was something of a relief.

Billy stood up. "If you want to talk about anything, you know where I am."

"Thanks, Dad."

"Hell, don't thank me for being a crap parent."

"You always did your best. Even back then I kind of knew you were the only one who believed there was something seriously wrong with Mom. I knew that if things got really bad I could always come to you."

Billy nodded once and then left. Thankfully without crying, but Ry sensed it had been close. He took a deep, shuddering breath and checked the time. Only his two brothers to deal with now, and neither of them were the emotional type. Compared to his dad and his grandmother, they were going to be a piece of cake.

Chapter Sixteen

"I didn't expect to get two applications for the event coordinator job." Chase sipped his coffee and frowned at his laptop screen.

Ruth smacked his shoulder as she put a jug of cream on the table. "And I don't expect you to be using your computer at the breakfast table. Where are your manners? I know I taught you better."

"Sorry, Ruth." Chase closed the lid.

Ry looked up from his bowl of oatmeal. "I thought you were offering the job to Avery."

"So did I. But I left it up to Ruth to ring the Hayes family."

"I called them." Ruth added the cream to her coffee. "Just like you asked me to."

"So why have both Avery and her sister applied for the same job?"

"*Marley* applied?" Ry asked.

"Yeah, she's actually better qualified than Avery, to be honest." Chase frowned. "Do you think this is Avery's way of suggesting she doesn't want the job?"

"By getting her sister to apply for it? Why would she do that?"

Even as he asked the question, Ry knew exactly why. She'd either think she wasn't good enough, or assume Marley would be better. Marley might even have insisted on being given the opportunity.

"What do you want me to do?" Chase looked at him. "On paper Marley has all the right things going for her, but Avery's already set everything up, and she works really well with all of us."

"It's not my decision, Chase. You need to do what you think is right. I don't want Avery thinking I influenced you."

"Maybe she's going to dump you, Ry, so she doesn't want to be up here anymore," BB suggested. "That could be super awkward."

Ry made an impolite gesture with his finger that he hoped Ruth couldn't see. "I don't think that's it."

BB regarded him over his coffee mug. "You like her, don't you?"

"I always did."

"Hey, that's right. You were sweet on her all the way through school—until she went and kissed HW at the prom."

"While he was pretending to be me."

BB winced. "Ouch. Sometimes I can see why he drives you nuts." He looked around the table. "Speaking of HW. Has anyone heard from him?"

"Nope." Chase surreptitiously checked his phone. January was away visiting her mom, and he was constantly texting her. "I know he arrived in one piece, because my pilot let me know when he exited the plane in Vegas."

"He's still coming back for the wedding, isn't he?" Ruth asked.

"If Ry's okay with it."

"Why wouldn't I be? It's your wedding. You can invite anyone you like." Ry stared at his oldest brother. "HW's an ass, but he's still part of this family."

"True." Chase looked at BB and Billy. "If being an ass ruled you out, there would be no one sitting at this table."

Ruth gave him a look. "Speak for yourself."

"Point taken. You are above reproach. I was talking about the guys." Chase's gaze dropped to his cell again, and he started to read.

Ry was just about to get up and put his bowl in the dishwasher when Chase cleared his throat.

"I've had a message to call my security firm. It's probably got something to do with Mom." He fixed Ry with his piercing blue stare. "Do you want us to pursue this, Ry?"

"You mean finding Mom?"

"Yeah. We talked it over last night and we wanted you to have the final say. Even HW agreed that was the right thing to do."

Ry sat down again and contemplated his joined hands. Part of him wanted to tell Chase to stop, but was that what he really wanted?

"Can I think about it?"

"Sure—as long as you don't take too long." Chase made a face. "Time is money, and in this case I'm being screwed by the hour by the investigators."

Ry stood and pushed in his chair. "Then I'll let you know as soon as I can."

"By lunchtime would be good."

"Will do." Ry checked he had the keys to his

truck, and went out. He was supposed to be meeting Roy up at Morgansville to complete the last section of fencing and the final gate. Instead he took out his cell and texted Avery.

> Are you around?
>
> I'm working a double shift. What's up?
>
> Do you get a break?
>
> I can take one—what time?
>
> 20 minutes at Yvonne's?
>
> Get me a strawberry tart and a latte. I'll see you there x

If he hustled, he could get there in ten, grab a table, and put in her order so it was ready when she arrived.

He texted Roy to say he'd be late, and then drove down the long driveway to the county road, which would take him directly into Morgantown. As he approached the final gate he squinted as the glare intensified, to find several TV trucks and a few reporters milling around.

His heart sank as they saw him, tried to wave him down, and pointed cameras at his truck. He slid his sunglasses down over his nose and glanced at Dog, who had somehow managed to get into the truck with him.

"Smile, buddy. We're going to get our picture taken whether we like it or not."

He drove about half a mile, pulled over, and took out his phone.

"Chase? We've got a problem at the back gate."

His brother groaned. "What now?"

"Paparazzi."

"You're *kidding* me."

"Nope. Gotta go." He didn't have time to get into it with Chase when he was rushing to meet Avery. And, anyway, his big brother was a match for anyone and had the financial resources to keep them all safe.

Well, Ry assumed he did.

He parked in front of Yvonne's café, leaving Dog in the truck bed, and went in, inhaling the comforting scents of coffee and chocolate like a drug. If she would just sell bacon, his life would be complete. Yvonne waved at him from the counter.

"Hey, are you wanting coffee, or is this about the wedding?"

"Coffee for me, a latte for Avery, and two strawberry tarts, please."

"For here or to go?"

"Here. If I can find a table." The place was packed with a mixture of locals and tourists, which was hardly surprising as Yvonne was a superb baker.

She pointed to a small table right beside the kitchen, which had a reserved tag on it. "Use this one. It's reserved for my friends."

"Thanks." He took a seat and consulted the time as Yvonne took more orders and disappeared past him to the kitchen.

"Ry?"

He looked up to see Marley Hayes smiling anxiously down at him. She wore a blue Hayes Historic Hotel T-shirt, a tight black pencil skirt, and high heels. Her brown hair was drawn back into some kind of fancy knot on the back of her head and her makeup was perfect.

He went to stand, but she slipped into the seat opposite him.

"I won't take more than a minute of your time, but I just wanted to know whether Chase has made a decision about who gets the events coordinator job."

"He only got your applications yesterday," Ry said cautiously. "I don't think he's done anything other than read them yet."

"Okay, that makes sense. He didn't mind that I applied for the job, did he?"

"Well—"

"Because I am qualified."

Ry looked her right in the eye. "Marley, what's going on here? What Chase does in relation to the running of the ranch is up to him. I don't make the decisions. I'm just a hired hand."

"Like anyone would believe that. You're a *Morgan*. Of course Chase listens to you, and as you happen to be dating my sister? I'm sure he listens to you a lot."

"I've got no intention of interfering with Chase's hiring process, okay?"

"Even though you suggested Avery as the wedding planner?"

"I did that because I felt sorry for her, and I thought her confidence needed a boost. It—"

He looked up, expecting Yvonne with the coffee, and instead found Avery listening in, and she sure as hell wasn't smiling.

"Hey." He stood up and kissed her averted cheek. "I've already ordered."

"Hey. Ry, did you come to let me know when we're going out horseback riding this week?" He blinked at her, and she kept talking. "You know, to see around the ranch so I'm more familiar with the place."

Marley did a double take. "You're getting on a *horse*?"

"Yes, I told you I was okay around horses now, didn't I?"

"If you're going out to look at the ranch, I should get to come as well." Marley swung around to stare at Ry. "That's fair, isn't it?"

"I—"

"It's fine by me," Avery said airily. "Just give us the day and the time, Ry, and we'll be there."

Ry just about collected his thoughts. "I can do Friday afternoon—if that works for you?"

Marley checked her phone. "We're both off for a four-hour block, so that could definitely work."

"Then I'll see you both at the ranch."

"Thanks, Ry." Marley reclaimed her bag of croissants and quickly vacated the seat. "Bye, sis. I'm going back to work now. I'll see you in a while."

Avery didn't say anything, but she did at least take the vacated seat. Ry slowly sank down to face her. He had the sense to know the riding was a diversionary tactic, and was keen to get back to the matter at hand.

"I don't know what Marley was trying to achieve by chatting to me," he said cautiously. "All I could tell her was that Chase received the applications and would be dealing with the matter himself."

She raised her eyebrows. "Fine."

Fine was never good. He tried again. "Chase asked me whether I knew you were both applying for the job, but I had no idea."

"Because you probably assumed the job offer was meant for me."

"Exactly."

"But from what you just said, Chase is considering us both."

He shrugged. "It's his decision, Avery. You wouldn't want me to get on his ass and play favorites, would you?"

She considered him for so long that he almost started to sweat. Luckily, Yvonne arrived with the coffee and fruit tarts and spent a moment talking wedding plans with Avery while he desperately wondered how to regroup. After she'd sipped her latte and taken a bite of her tart, he tried to change the subject.

"I called you because I wanted your opinion on something."

"What was that? Whether Marley should get the job?"

He put down his mug. "Avery . . ."

"Because she *is* better qualified than me, and you could probably recommend her without feeling sorry for her and thinking she needed a boost."

Damn, she had a good memory, as most women seemed to do when they were determined to have an argument.

"That was before we were involved. I wouldn't say that now."

"That you feel sorry for me?"

He groaned. "Okay, it was a stupid thing to say, but it's the truth. When I first came back here I hated seeing you so closed in, and I wanted to help you."

"Thanks."

"I don't feel like that now."

"Are you sure?"

He sat back in his seat. "What the heck is that supposed to mean?"

"That maybe with HW out of the picture you needed someone to . . . look after."

"And I picked *you*?"

She shrugged. "As you keep pointing out, I am practically a shut-in."

"You have no idea, do you?" He shook his head. "Yeah, that's it, Avery. I wanted to look after you."

"How come you say something horrible about me to my sister, of all people, and suddenly you're the one whose feelings are hurt?"

"Because you twist things around. If you really think that all I want is to look after you like you're my fricking horse, then go ahead. I thought we had much more going for us than that. Hell, I thought you were the one looking after me!"

His voice had risen, and several people were now staring their way. He took a deep breath. He didn't like all these emotions; he didn't like them at all. It made him feel out of control, and he hated that. He took a deep, steadying breath.

"Look, all I'm trying to say is that I don't feel sorry for you, and that I won't interfere if Chase decides he wants to interview both of you for the job. If that's a problem, tell me now, and tell me what you want me to do about it."

Avery dropped her gaze to the table and bit down hard on her lip. "I don't expect you to play favorites for me with Chase."

He nodded abruptly. "Okay."

"And I might be a bit touchy about the subject of people feeling sorry for me." She risked a glance upward. "*Very* touchy."

He sighed. "I get that. I shouldn't have said anything."

"Not to Marley. She's . . ." Avery hesitated. "She's used to getting what she wants, and she's determined to get this job."

"Why?"

"I don't know. Maybe to prove she's better than me, or something? You know what families are like. How competitive they can be."

"Do you want me to tell Chase to give you the job?"

Avery sighed. He was so straightforward. This was just what Marley had insisted would happen. "No. I want to win it on merit."

"And you will." He picked up his mug and sipped at his coffee. "And I'm sorry for being an idiot."

"I'm sorry for being hypersensitive." She took a gulp of her latte. "Now what did you want to ask me?"

"We're done arguing?"

"Well, I am if you are." She finished her strawberry tart.

"That's kind of refreshing."

"The tart?"

"No, the fact that we're going to get over this bump and keep moving on." He reached for her hand, which was sticky with syrup, and kissed her fingers. "I appreciate that."

She smiled at him. "We're finding our own way to keep communicating. Jenna will be so proud. Now what *did* you want to talk about?"

"Chase asked me if I was okay to continue the search for my mom. That they'd all decided the choice should be mine."

"And?" she prompted.

"My first reaction was to tell him to let it go, and then I started thinking. If I don't face her as she is now, I'll never be able to see her clearly. I'll always be that scared little kid."

She squeezed his hand. "That makes perfect sense."

"It makes no sense, but thanks for the support." He managed to smile. "I've got to go through with this, and part of me, the *kid* part, doesn't want to risk it."

"Also totally understandable." She paused. "But what if you meet her, and she hasn't changed?"

"Then maybe she can tell me what the hell I did to make her hate me. If she can't even do that, then I'll know she's the problem, not me. I'd rather know the worst and move on than live with the nightmares."

She surprised him by bringing his hand to her lips and kissing his knuckles. "This is exactly why I like you so much."

"Even when I say stupid shit in front of your sister?"

She smiled into his eyes. "Even then." Her cell buzzed and she groaned. "The hotel is heaving. I have to get back in five."

"Sure, but before you go? What's this about riding the range?"

She rolled her eyes. "Marley was doubting me. I had to show her that I'm perfectly capable of working around the horses at the ranch."

"You are. You don't need to get on the back of one just to prove that."

"But I want to."

Ry considered her resolute expression. "You sure about that?"

"No, I'm terrified, but I've got to try." She swallowed hard. "I know it's not quite the same, but it's a bit like you having to keep searching for your mom. You don't want to do it either, but you know it's necessary."

"So we're both going to have to be brave?"

She nodded.

"Then I'm in if you are."

"And Marley." She made a face.

"She can ride, right?"

"Sure she can. All the Hayes family rides." Her cell buzzed again. "Oh man. I've gotta go. Marley's such a nag."

She rose and he stood as well, leaning in to cup her chin and kiss her sweet, coffee-flavored lips.

"Mmm." He kissed her again, just for luck. "I'll see you Friday, if I don't see you before."

"Okay."

"And no pushing Marley down the stairs so you can't both come out and ride."

She fluttered her eyelashes at him. "As if I would do something like that."

"I come from a big family. I know what it's like."

"You pushed your brothers down the stairs?"

"I tied HW to a tree once and left him by the creek. Not that he didn't deserve it, but I was determined he wasn't going to get all the coconut cream pie Ruth was making."

She chuckled, and the sound made him want to scoop her up in his arms and carry her off somewhere more private, like the back of his truck, or her bedroom, or . . .

Behind him Yvonne cleared her throat.

"Can I get by, please? Coffee to grind, cakes to bake."

"Sorry." He drew Avery against his side. "We should go."

"You damn well should." Yvonne gave him a look as she squeezed past. "Cluttering up my shop with all that Morgan testosterone. What is it about you guys that's made all my girlfriends go gaga?"

He winked. "I'd tell you, but then I'd have to kill you."

"That line would sound so much better if it came from Blue, the scary Marine," Yvonne groaned.

Avery dug her elbow in his ribs. "Come on, cowboy. Let's go. We can't afford to keep Yvonne out of her kitchen. How would we survive without her baking?"

"Truc." Yvonne blew them both a kiss as she sashayed past. "Go on, you lovebirds. I'll see you next Friday for the catering meeting up at the ranch, Avery."

Ry paid the bill and followed Avery out into the sunshine. Dog saw him coming and sat up, ears flapping like sails.

Avery paused to pet him. "I didn't know you had a dog."

"He's one of Ruth's strays. People drop them off on ranch land all the time. He kind of adopted me."

"What's his name?"

"Dog."

She looked up at him. "That's it?"

He shrugged. "He seems to like it."

"You have no imagination, do you?"

He leaned against the side of the truck. "Now, you know that's not true, honey."

She actually blushed. "I'm not talking about . . . that."

"Glad to hear it, because no man wants to hear he's boring in the sack."

"Or woman."

He smiled into her eyes. "I never said you were boring. You make me hard just standing here."

"I do not." Her gaze dropped to his jeans. "Oh, good Lord. You . . . and I have to get back to work."

"So do I." He grimaced. "Let's hope everything's settled down before I have to get on the back of a horse."

She stood on tiptoe to kiss him. "Later, Ry."

He and Dog watched her walk down the street toward the hotel, her ponytail bobbing as the sun caught flashes of copper in her brown hair.

Lovebirds . . .

Ry unlocked the truck and waited for Dog to jump out of the back and join him in the cab. Did he love her? Was it even possible after such a short time? Love was kind of a terrifying concept to him. Shaking his head, he started the engine and backed out of his spot. Dog had nothing to say about the subject, so Ry filed the revolutionary idea in his head to be investigated at a later date.

Before he forgot, he took out his cell and called Chase.

"Hey, I'm okay to go ahead with the mom thing."

"Good. By the time you get back to the ranch there should be some security in place. I've given them your picture and vehicle information, so they should let you right through. If they aren't in place, I don't need to tell you to keep driving and make no comment, do I? The quicker we shut this down the better."

"Got it."

"Then I'll see you in a few."

Chapter Seventeen

"I'll ride Nolly; Chase is okay with that. Avery can take Dolittle, and Marley . . ." Ry looked around the barn. "How long is it since you've been on a horse?"

Avery forced her gaze to her sister, who was looking superchic in her skinny jeans and fancy red sweater. For some reason Friday had come along way too quickly this week for her liking.

"About a year."

Ry looked at Roy. "What do you think? Marigold?"

"Yeah. Sounds good to me. She's steady as a rock." Roy moved past Avery. "I'll get her out and saddle her up."

"Thanks, Roy." Ry opened Dolittle's stall. "Okay, stand back, ladies, and I'll see if I can wake him up."

Avery went out toward the hitching posts and open air. She was okay until the horses started moving in confined spaces. It reminded her of being trapped under her horse and almost suffocating in the mud of the arena floor.

"You doing okay, Avery?" Roy asked as she went by him.

"I'm good."

To her surprise he gently took her elbow and drew her to a stop. "You'll be fine. Dolittle's not going to do anything stupid, and Ry will take care of you." He paused. "And if he doesn't, you come and find me."

Which would be tricky if her body was smashed into a million pieces, but she appreciated the thought. "Will do. Thanks, Roy."

He nodded and went into the tack room.

She hesitated outside. "Do you want a hand with anything?"

"Sure. Come and help an old man out."

She'd forgotten how heavy the saddles were, and her left leg buckled as she attempted to lift one from its perch. Yeah, what a great way to start the day, failing to even have the strength to saddle her horse, let alone mount up.

"I've got that. Get Dolittle's bridle."

Ry came up behind her and took the saddle out of her hands with such effortless ease that she was torn between admiration and humiliation. He wasn't as broad shouldered as Chase and Blue, but his lanky frame was strong. She also knew from her up close and personal inspection of his body that he didn't have an inch of fat on him anywhere.

She trailed out after him, watching as he flipped the saddle on top of the blanket Roy had put on Dolittle. The horse barely bothered to open his eyes when Ry eased the bit into his mouth, buckled up the bridle, and then the cinch.

Nolly's behavior was another matter. He danced around, tossing his head and flicking his tail like a prima donna as Ry tried to get him ready. Avery kept close to the fence while Ry said some choice words to settle Nolly down.

"Knock it off, blockhead." He grabbed Nolly by the halter. "Chase said he'd stopped him playing tricks. I can't say I've noticed any improvement."

He managed to get the bridle on, and then gave Nolly a gentle knee in the belly as the horse did his usual thing and attempted to stop him tightening the cinch by inflating his gut.

"You okay, Avery?"

She turned away from Ry to smile at Marley, who had come up beside her. "Yeah, you?"

"Are you sure? You look a bit green." Marley hesitated. "If you don't want to do this—it's not a problem."

"I'm fine." She nodded at Roy. "I think he's done with Marigold. You should go and make friends."

Avery concentrated on watching Ry, who made everything look easy around a horse. The quietness of his voice, the sure way he handled each animal and persuaded them to listen to him and behave, was soothing her fears.

He looked up and caught her staring at him. She tensed, wondering whether he'd start in on her like Marley had.

"We're almost ready to go. Want a leg up?" He lowered his voice and pointed over at the barn wall. "I got the mounting block out for you if you need it."

"Great, so everyone will know I'm a complete wuss."

He frowned. "No one would think that. Are you still okay about this?"

Actually, she wanted to run away screaming, but she forced herself to nod.

He strolled over, took her hand, and kissed her on the nose. "You've got this."

"I so have not."

He leaned in and kissed her softly and thoroughly on the mouth. "Yeah, you do."

She was still blinking up at him when he lifted her in his arms and gently set her on Dolittle's back. It was like scaling a mountain. She grabbed the horn with both hands as a wave of nausea enveloped her.

"You're good. Hold on, and I'll get you settled."

His calm voice got through to her and she managed to breathe in and out, in and out, which seemed extremely hard.

"I wish it was just you and me going." Ry continued to talk as he adjusted her stirrups and slid her booted feet into them. "Because we could go skinny-dipping in the lake, and make love under the pines."

"In October?" She squeaked, but, hey, she was talking.

His golden gaze heated as he caressed her jean-covered thigh with long, work-roughened fingers. "We could keep each other warm."

"After we'd frozen to death in the creek?"

God, was she actually sitting on the back of a horse having an almost flirtatious conversation with her boyfriend? No wonder the horses loved him. He was obviously magic with humans as well.

"You gonna wear your gloves?"

She looked down at where her white-knuckled fingers were gripping the horn.

"If I want to put them on I'd have to let go."

He curved an arm around her back. "Do them one at a time. I'll help you."

Finally, he handed her the reins, and she took them in one shaking fist.

"You got this, and Dolittle's pretty much bomb-proof." His approving smile made her feel like she'd won the finals in Vegas. "I'm going to check Marley's okay, and mount up on Nolly. Roy's coming, too. He'll be right behind you."

Avery let out her breath and stared out between Dolittle's ears. He stood steady as a rock. Unlike most horses, he seemed unaware that he carried a bumbling mass of nerves on his back. The heat from his body seeped through Avery's jeans, warming her as she automatically gathered the reins and waited for the signal to move.

She was . . . *okay.*

Dolittle was nothing like her barrel-racing mare. He was more like her first pony, who had needed a lot of incentives to break into a trot, let alone a lope. The sky was a clear blue, and the air so sharp it almost hurt to breathe. Her world view sitting on the back of a horse was so achingly familiar that she wanted to stay there forever. She'd almost forgotten how much of her life prior to the accident had been spent on horseback. She'd *tried* to forget.

"Avery?"

Ry had reached the gate into the pasture, his body swaying easily in the saddle to counteract the squir-relly hops Nolly was performing as he crab-walked sideways up to the opening.

"I'm coming."

She clicked to Dolittle.

Nothing happened.

She squeezed with her knees, and with a grumbling snort he moved off, each step as reluctant as the last, but in the general direction she wanted him to go. Avery reminded herself about the necessity of breathing again, and settled into the saddle, too nervous about everything to notice the scenery anymore or even where they were going.

After a long while, she relaxed her death grip on the horn and flexed her left hand, shaking out the impending cramp. They were moving slowly but surely up the valley alongside the creek. If she remembered correctly, they were heading out toward the northerly part of the ranch where the old silver mine, and the ghost town of Morgansville, were situated. The air already seemed colder and thinner, and she was glad she'd worn her down jacket.

Marley shivered. "Why is it so cold and barren up here?"

Ry slowed down to ride alongside her. "A combination of being in the foothills of the Sierras, and the deforestation caused by the mining."

"The trees still haven't grown back?"

"Nothing to grow in. When the settlers and miners took out the huge sequoias, the topsoil blew away, leaving the dust."

"So why haven't you guys done something about it?"

"Because it's part of the history of the ranch."

"But you could plant a pine forest, or . . ."

"And swallow up the mine and the ghost town in the middle of it?" Ry shook his head. "It wouldn't work." His gaze scanned the barren landscape. "This *is* history. This shows what idiots humans are when they chase after silver and gold."

Avery smiled at the conviction of his words. Ry

loved his home and respected the past. What more could a woman want?

Oh God, was she getting all sappy about him now? Hard not to when he looked like a god on a horse, and spoke such beautiful words. And made love to her as if she was the most precious thing in his universe . . .

"All right there, Avery?"

She jumped as Roy circled back toward her, and she realized she'd stopped moving.

"Sorry, I was just staring at the view."

Roy snorted. "If you consider Ry Morgan the view, then I believe you. But he's a good boy. You could stare at a lot worse."

"Do you think he'll stay here?"

"At the ranch? I think so. He seems to fit in real good."

Ry paused to open another gate, and Marley was already riding through it. He looked back down the trail and waved them on.

"We should go."

"Yup. Too cold to be standing around chatting." Roy clicked to his horse and moved off, and Dolittle followed. "We just finished putting all this fencing in last week."

"To protect the mine and ghost town from the cattle, right?"

"That and the tourists. We've got no actual plans of the mine workings, so if anyone falls in they're a goner."

"That's good to know." Avery smiled. "Not that I plan on exploring down there anytime soon, but if I'm working at the ranch it's important to know why we need to keep people away."

"You can tell them till you're blue in the face. They still go and do stupid stuff." Roy shook his head. "I'm surprised no one has been killed." He slowly chewed his gum. "Mind you, even if they were, we might not know unless the body turned up."

"Yeah, right." Avery tried not to let her imagination take her too far down Roy's horror movie path. He'd certainly succeeded in making her forget she was on the back of a horse. "Let's hope the bodies stay where they are."

Ry was waiting for her by the gate, his face half in shadow beneath the brim of his Stetson.

"What's Roy blathering on about?"

"You don't want to know." She eased Dolittle past Nolly, who tried to nip but missed her horse's ear by a mile. "Let's just say you don't want to get on the wrong side of him."

"I already knew that. We're not going to stop until we reach Morganville, is that okay? Marley thinks she can make it that far."

"She looks pretty good on a horse." Avery tried to be fair. "I don't think she wanted to ride much because she didn't want to have to compete with me. You know what families are like."

"Makes sense." He left Roy to sort out the gate, and continued on beside her.

"So why did you join the rodeo circuit?"

"Good question." He rode on in silence for a few beats, and she wondered if that was all the reply she was going to get. "It seemed like a cool thing to do when I was eighteen, and I was good at it. But after a few years I realized I didn't have the desire to put in all the work necessary to be *great*. And I hated all the moving around—the lack of permanency, and the uncertainty."

"I wish I'd had the chance to find out if I would've liked that life," she admitted. "After the accident, I couldn't believe I wouldn't somehow get better, be *fixed*, you know?" She glanced over at him. "That's what's supposed to happen. You get hurt, you recover, and you go back. But my hip and thigh were broken in so many places the surgeon said it was like piecing together a smashed china cup."

"What happened?"

She rarely talked about her accident anymore, but for some reason she felt safe telling Ry. "It was raining and the ground was all churned up. We came into the first barrel too fast. Mellie lost her footing, and I ended up underneath her, facedown in the mud. She rolled over me as she got back on her feet."

"*Shit.*"

"Yeah. Luckily I blacked out before I could decide whether drowning or suffocating was the worse way to go." She broke off and stared ahead at the barren, scrubby track. "Sorry. I hate it when I whine. I thought I'd trained myself out of it."

"You can whine at me anytime you like."

The sincerity in his voice carried across the quietness and wrapped itself like a warm fist around her heart.

"Thanks, but it's not my most attractive feature."

"Why not?" He shrugged, the movement graceful. "It's okay to be angry when life throws you a curveball."

"You hate getting angry."

"Yeah, but that's me."

"And if I tell you the same thing, that it's okay? Will you believe me?"

He didn't answer, his gaze fixed ahead on Marley, who had reined in her horse and was waiting for them by the next gate.

"Ry . . . ?"

"I hear what you're saying, Avery."

"But you don't think it applies to you. It's okay to be angry with your mom even though she wasn't well."

"I know. I'm working on it."

She snorted and he flashed her a quick grin.

"I'm not convincing you?"

"That's what I used to say to Mom when I was supposed to be doing my homework."

"Damn, I thought I was the first one to ever use that phrase. I got it from Jenna." His smile dimmed. "Seriously, I'm trying to get my head around it. If we find Mom, then maybe I can set my mind at rest once and for all."

"And if you don't?"

"Then I'll be coming to see you, and doing a bit of whining of my own."

Ry loved it up by the ghost town. It really was as if time stood still there. Rather than just falling into gradual disrepair, the whole town had uprooted itself one summer and the entire population moved down the valley to what was now Morgantown. Until Chase's fiancée, January, had come on the scene and read his great-great-grandfather's diary, no one had known exactly why.

They were standing on what had once been Main

Street, between the upright shells of the mainly wooden buildings. The horses were tied up in the parking lot behind them, right next to where the original Morgan family livery business had operated. The sky was a cloudless pale blue, and wind weaved through the deserted buildings, sending clouds of fine dust dancing and swirling like mini tornadoes.

The strangest thing was the silence, as if the town were just holding its breath, waiting for the people to reappear and start living again.

"So why did everyone leave?" Marley was already asking the inevitable question.

Ry reached for Avery's hand and drew her against his side. "January thinks it has something to do with the mine and the stamping process. She figures the creek dried up and there wasn't enough power to run the mill, so they moved everything down the slope and built a new mill and a new town."

"Seems a bit extreme," Marley commented.

"The silver was running out, and most of the original mining families were moving on or turning to other trades. That's certainly when my family decided they'd make more money feeding and supplying the miners than risking their lives down a mine."

"Sensible folk, those Morgans," Avery said.

"They reopened their livery stable in Morgantown, and bought the land for the ranch." He shivered. "I'm glad they moved downstream. This place gets cold."

"And it's pretty darn scary at night," Avery added. He looked down at her. "You came up here?"

"For goodness' sake, Ry, *everyone* came up here."

Avery rolled her eyes. "Well, all the kids who lived around here did. It was something of a local tradition."

"Even though it's on private land?"

"That just made it more fun. Me and Tucker intended to spend the night." She shuddered. "We didn't stay long. It felt spooky as hell."

"Even Chase thinks there are ghosts up here, and he's the biggest nerd I've ever met." Ry turned to his quiet companion. "What do you think, Roy?"

"Ghosts," Roy said. "Definitely."

"Why didn't they break down the houses and reuse the wood?" Marley was still intent on getting answers. "Why did they just leave it all hanging?"

Ry answered her. "January thinks they left the outer shells of the buildings intact in case they had to move back up here. They had no guarantee that moving down the hill would work. I suppose after a while, when things got more stable, they just moved on and forgot about the place."

"And the land was sold off to the Morgans and fenced in," Roy added.

"True." Ry grinned at Avery. "Not that anyone who grew up in Morgantown seems to have cared much about that minor detail."

Avery turned a slow circle. "It's eerie. I keep expecting someone to come out of one of the houses."

"Yeah, I know." Ry took her hand. "Our family owned the third house on the right as well as the livery stables. It still feels . . . lived in."

"Ghosts." Avery shuddered delicately.

"Just family to me."

Roy stamped his feet. "It's getting cold. We should take these ladies home. There's a storm coming in."

Marley raised an eyebrow. "How can you tell? Did you read the clouds or something?"

"Nope." Roy showed her his cell. "I just checked the weather app."

Ry hid a smile as they walked back to the parking lot. It was so quiet he could hear Avery's breathing. She nudged his side.

"I just noticed there aren't any birds."

"No trees."

"I'd forgotten that."

He kept hold of her hand. "How are you doing?"

"With the whole horse thing?"

He nodded.

"So far so good."

He gave her a leg up into the saddle. This time she took the reins and slid her toes in the stirrups by herself. He wrapped his fingers around her calf.

"Take it easy on the way back. No circus tricks."

"Don't worry. I know what I'm capable of."

She sounded . . . confident. The last thing he wanted was to jinx anything. He'd tell her how proud of her he was when they were safely back in the barn.

He mounted Nolly, checked that Marley was good to go, and took the path that led back around the abandoned mine, and down the slope on the opposite side of the creek, which would eventually take them home. He'd had his doubts about Avery's plan to ride again, but it seemed to be working. Nothing like a bit of sibling rivalry to get a person doing stupid shit. He could attest to that.

Checking to see that Roy was close to Avery, Ry caught up with her sister, who was obviously dying to move faster. Since she hadn't been on a horse for a year, she might end up being glad they'd only moved at a walk.

"You doing okay?"

"I'm enjoying it." Marley glanced across at him. Like all the Hayes family she rode well, with a natural grace that spoke of years of familiarity with horses. "Did you know that your family's original livery stable in Morgantown is now part of our hotel?"

"Yeah? I suppose it makes sense."

"Dad found some of the original records. The livery stable was attached to a saloon, which eventually became a hotel."

"You should tell January. She loves all that stuff."

"I think Dad's scheduled to speak at the next meeting of the historical society. He's totally thrilled."

"Cool."

"Avery's doing okay, isn't she?" Marley sighed. "I was worried about her before we set off. She looked like she was going to puke."

"Not surprising, really."

"I suppose you think I should be mad she's doing okay because I don't want her to get this job."

"It's not my business to comment on your relationship with your sister."

Marley flicked him a glance. "Wow, you really are diplomatic, aren't you?"

"I try to be. I certainly know better than to get in between two sisters."

She chuckled. "Somebody in a big family has to calm everyone down. We usually leave that to Tucker."

"He's a good guy."

"So are you." She hesitated. "Avery and I fight sometimes, but I still love her."

He didn't say anything to that.

"She's had it tough for a few years, but I'm really glad she found you again."

"Yeah?"

"You've made her reach out, and do stuff."

Ry took a moment to tighten his reins as Nolly again attempted to kick off into a lope. "I'd love to take the credit for that, but she's done it herself."

"Well, let's just say you've given her an incentive." He grinned. "Hell, I thought that was *you*."

She reached out and bumped fists with him. "Team Avery, right?"

"Sure, but don't the hell tell *her* that."

As they approached the barn, the light faded behind the Sierras to a sun-streaked lavender, turning the trees and bushes into gray ghosts against the towering rocks.

BB's truck pulled up in the yard, and he got out, turning to wave at the incoming riders. Within seconds, he opened Maria's door and she spilled out of the cab, one hand carrying a party bag and the other wrapped around two balloons.

"Ry, look! I got balloons!"

She jumped up and down and one of the balloons gently detached itself and floated his way on the evening breeze. Nolly saw it coming and immediately panicked, backing into Marigold, who reared up. As Roy reached out to help Marley, Ry struggled to regain control of Nolly, and caught a glimpse of Dolittle's wide-eyed terror.

"*Shit.*" He turned Nolly's head in such a tight circle that the horse was practically chewing his own ass, but at least he'd stopped kicking out. "Avery, hang on!"

"I've got him. Go." BB grabbed Nolly's bridle, freeing Ry to jump off and run over to where Dolittle was bunny hopping around the paddock. Avery was still on board, but she was barely hanging on, and the reins were flapping, scaring Dolittle even more.

Ry lowered his head and slammed his weight into the horse's shoulder. He wrapped his arm around Dolittle's neck, grabbed the reins, and turned him in a close circle.

"It's okay, boy. Stand easy, it's okay."

He slid his other arm around Avery's waist, holding her steady as Dolittle did one more kick and then settled down, his sides heaving. He nuzzled Ry's head, knocking off his hat and slathering him in drool, as if he was apologizing.

"Well, we finally found out what scares you," Ry murmured. "No kids' birthday parties for you, dude."

He took a firmer grip on the reins and looped them over the saddle horn, making sure Dolittle was settled before turning his attention to Avery.

"You okay, honey?"

"Get me off this horse, right now."

Her face was paper white. He took a deep breath. "No can do. You'll have to ride him for a few seconds more."

"Get me *off*, Ry."

"Look, you know as well as I do that we have to get things back to normal as fast as possible, which means you stay on his back for the next sixty seconds until we tie him up at the hitching post and rub him down."

"I don't *want*—"

"I know, but you're going to have to." He glanced up at her and steeled himself. "I don't want to ruin a good horse, Avery."

"You promised me that you'd never force me to do anything with a horse."

"And I meant it."

"So *let me goddamn down*."

He held her gaze. Her icy calm had deserted her and she was literally seething with rage. "In one minute you can get down yourself. Can you just do that for me?"

She glared at him, her hands clenched into fists, her teeth chattering. "I'll do it for the horse, *okay*? You lied to me. We're *so* done."

Her words hit him like a punch to the heart. He clicked to Dolittle, who obediently started moving like nothing had happened, which was just what Ry had wanted. He walked alongside the horse to the hitching post, talking to him, and quickly took off the bridle, replacing it with the halter and rope. The faster he tried to go, the harder his fingers shook as his mind caught up with his reactions and replayed all the things that could have gone wrong.

Surely, Avery hadn't meant they were done as a couple, had she? Wasn't she just upset, and not thinking clearly? Once he sorted out the horse issues, he'd get hold of her and talk it through. She'd like that. Women always wanted to discuss stuff.

"Everyone all right?" BB joined them, leading Nolly. "I'm sorry, guys. Maria's in tears because of what happened."

"Not her fault," Roy said. "Horses are big scared chickens, and we're all okay."

"You sure about that?" BB looked at Ry, and then up at Avery. "Do you want a hand down, Avery?"

Ry kept his attention on untangling the reins and hanging the bridle over the fence while BB helped Avery dismount. Marley immediately came rushing over to hug her sister.

"Oh my God, I thought you were going to fall!"

Avery said something incoherent and buried her face in her sister's shoulder. Ry tried not to notice that she hadn't even looked at him, or come to him for comfort. He took off the saddle and walked it back into the tack room, the bridle over his shoulder. When he returned for the blanket, Avery and Marley were nowhere in sight.

He halted and looked carefully around. "Did they *go*?"

BB grimaced. "Yeah. Avery was pretty upset. Marley said she was going to drive her home. I asked if she wanted to wait to let you know she was leaving, but she said she had nothing she needed to say to you."

"Figures."

"You did the right thing, bro."

"I sure as hell did not, because she couldn't wait to get away from me."

"I heard what you said to her about staying on the horse. That was good advice. When she calms down, she'll get it."

"Yeah? She told me she was done, and I don't think she was just talking about horseback riding." He slapped his hat against his thigh. "*Shit*. What the hell else was I supposed to do?"

BB patted him on the back. "She probably meant it at the time, but you'll bring her around. You're a Morgan."

"A guy she doesn't trust anymore who lives on a ranch surrounded by horses." Ry shook his head as he took the saddle pad, and marched back toward the tack room. "She'll never let me near her again."

"Avery . . ."

She took another sip of her hot chocolate, and made sure the fleece blanket was still wrapped tightly around her shoulders. She couldn't seem to stop shivering.

"*Avery.*"

"What?"

"Mom wants to know if you need her to fetch the doctor." Marley looked up from her phone.

"No, I'm fine. Just shaken up, but you don't have to tell her that bit." She scowled at her sister. "Or else she'll be breaking down the door and taking me to the clinic whether I want to go or not."

Her bedroom door opened. Avery jumped and prepared to defend herself from a concerned parental attack.

"Hey, what's up?" Nancy scowled at her. "You were supposed to be hanging out at the bar with Ry tonight. Where were you?"

Avery shuddered. "Ry who?"

Nancy took the seat beside Marley and elbowed her in the side. She wore black jeans and a black T-shirt. Her fair hair was now dyed almost white. "What happened to her?"

"We went riding. It was all good until a balloon

spooked the horses. Dolittle got a bit panicked, and tried to throw Avery."

Nancy looked Avery up and down. "You stayed on, right?"

"Like a pro bull rider. Free hand waving and everything."

"That's awesome."

Avery put down her mug. "What? It was *horrible*. I kept getting all these flashbacks to my accident, and I panicked like a complete fool."

"But you didn't let go, fall off, or get hurt."

"So what?"

"So that's progress, right?" Nancy raised an eyebrow. "Doesn't that prove that you can get on a horse—even one that gets scared—and come out in one piece? That's *awesome*." When Avery didn't speak, Nancy turned to Marley. "Am I missing something here?"

"She's mad because Ry made her stay on Dolittle and ride him to the barn." Marley shrugged. "I know, I don't get it either."

"He *promised* me he'd never make me do anything on a horse that I didn't want to do."

Nancy just looked at her. "But if you'd gotten off all upset, you probably would never get back on again. Calming Dolittle down and making you stick together like a team was the right thing for both of you."

Avery glared at her friend and her sister, who were both nodding like two wise women.

"Who said I was ever getting back on a horse?"

"You will if you want to work at that ranch." Marley uncurled her legs and got up. "I'll go and fend off the parents, okay?"

"Thanks, sis," Avery managed to mumble.

Nancy stretched out on the couch. "I can't stay long. I'm on my break."

"You can go anytime you like. Traitor."

"*Now* who's in a snit because they know they're wrong?"

"I am not wrong. I—" Avery paused. "Why is everyone *picking* on me?"

"Because you overreacted, and don't whine. If that had been your brother Mark on that horse? You would've done exactly what Ry did."

Avery rubbed her cheek against the soft underside of her blanket. "I suppose next you'll say I should be apologizing to him."

"Damn straight, girlfriend." Nancy pointed a finger at her. "You know it, and you're just grumpy because you hate being wrong."

"Not that you are ever like that," Avery muttered.

"Stop changing the subject." Nancy's cell buzzed and she checked it. "Damn, Jay's wondering what I've been doing in the bathroom for twenty minutes and does he need to break the door down."

Avery blinked. "He thinks you're in the bathroom?"

"I climbed out the window." Nancy shrugged "I'd better go. He was a Navy SEAL. He'd take that door out in a second. Later, Ave."

After Nancy left, Avery continued to huddle in her blanket as she reluctantly played back the events of the day. Eventually, in the peace of her own room, she realized two important things. One was that she *had* managed to stay on the horse. That was a big deal, and something to be proud of. Two was that she'd definitely overreacted and needed to talk to Ry.

If he'd let her. His shuttered expression after she told him to get lost had almost made her cry. He didn't let people in very often, and now she'd basically ordered him to leave her alone. He'd do it, too—taking on the guilt for what had been an unfortunate accident, even when it wasn't his fault.

She checked the time and yawned so hard she practically dislocated her jaw. It was too late to talk to him now, and she had to get to bed because of her early shift in the morning. When Dolittle bucked she'd almost wrenched her arm out of its socket. Luckily she had some good painkillers stored away, which would help with that, and her hip and leg were fine. She suspected the other kind of pain—the one centered around her heart from being a frightened, self-centered jerk—wasn't going to be so easy to fix or forget.

Chapter Eighteen

"So. I'm thinking we'll hold a pre-wedding supper up at the hot springs a week before the wedding—which means it will be coming up fairly soon. Just immediate family, fiancées and girlfriends, and Roy, of course." January looked around the table as she spoke.

Ruth grabbed a notebook and started making notes. "We can bring picnic food, and have a barbecue. How does that sound?"

"Awesome." January grinned at Ruth, and clutched Chase's hand. "If that's okay with you, Chase."

"Fine by me. You know I have some great memories of the hot springs." He winked at January, who went beet red.

They were so unbearably in love that Ry sometimes felt like rolling his eyes just like Maria did. It had been three days since he'd heard from Avery. True, she'd previously told him she was working through the whole weekend, so he hadn't expected to see much of her anyway. But they usually kept in touch by texting, or long stupid phone calls late at night. And it was now Monday evening, and she hadn't texted him yet.

Should he text her?

He wanted to, but—

Ruth leaned over and poked him hard in the ribs. "Ry? Are you listening to a word I'm saying?"

"Sorry, what's up?"

"He's brooding about Avery—whom, by the way, I saw in town today looking just *fine* in Yvonne's."

Ry stared at BB. "Thanks for the update."

BB shrugged, his blue eyes glinting with amusement at his brother's expense. "Well, I thought you'd like to know if you're too wussy to go down and see for yourself."

"I'm giving her some space, okay?"

"So she can really make up her mind to dump you?" BB grinned. "Man, you want to keep your woman, you've got to fight for her."

"I didn't notice you riding in on a white horse to save Jenna."

BB winked. "I didn't need to. Because I wasn't stupid enough to let her go for long enough to get away from me."

Chase cleared his throat. "That's not what I heard."

"Me neither," January chimed in. "In *fact*—"

Ruth banged on the table with her spoon. "Can we get back to the matter at hand? I'll work up a menu with January, and you boys can organize the rest of it, okay?"

"Yes, ma'am." BB saluted. "At least now you have an excuse to go see Avery, Ry. You can ask her to come to the party."

"I don't need an excuse."

Chase looked up. "Actually, I was going to ask you whether it would be okay to have both the Hayes girls up here for interviews this week."

Ry stood up. "It's got nothing to do with me."

"Do you still think Avery will be interested after what happened with Dolittle?"

"I don't know. Seeing as it was your dumbass horse that caused all the problems, ask her yourself!"

"It wasn't Nolly's fault. He's just excitable." Chase frowned. "You sure you don't want to ask Avery? It gives you a legitimate reason to call her."

Ry shoved his chair in with some force. "I don't need an excuse to speak to her. I didn't do anything *wrong*. It was all her idea! She chose to get on that damned horse."

"So you're waiting for her to apologize?" BB snorted. "Good luck, bro."

Ry swung around. "You—"

BB held up his hands. "I'm not fighting with you, okay? Number one, I could take you down *way* too easily, and number two, Ruth would kill me."

"None of you are fighting, and BB, leave Ry alone or I'll—"

Ry was already out the door before he heard what Ruth thought she could do to a big bad Marine. Not that he doubted her. She'd already earned his respect, and BB was no fool. He'd shut up, now that Ry had gone. He walked down to the barn and through to Dolittle's stall. To his relief the horse hadn't suffered any ill effects since the balloon had gone up, and was back to his lazy, amiable self.

Ry rested his chin on his folded arms and stared into the stall. Dolittle didn't stir. It was quiet in the barn, apart from the usual sounds of horses and the other smaller creatures that hung out there. Maria had adopted a bunch of kittens that were growing up to be excellent rat catchers, and had joined the already substantial feral cat collective that hung out at the barn.

He pulled out his cell and stared at the blank screen. Nothing from HW and nothing from Avery. But was BB right? Should he be waiting on them? Learning to be a strong and independent person didn't mean he had to lose the ability to admit when he'd screwed up.

His thumbs moved over the keys.

How's training going?

That was nice and neutral for HW. Now for Avery . . .

Are you okay?

Lame, but it was the best he could come up with at the moment. He waited a moment, but neither of them replied. He was just about to wander down to the tack room and fix one of the bridles, when Chase came into the barn.

"Hey." Chase came to look in at Dolittle as well. "He seems okay."

"Yeah."

"If Avery was in Yvonne's today, it probably means that she's okay, too."

"Yeah."

Chase sighed. "I've got some news."

"About Mom?"

"About the guy she married. He's willing to talk to us if we go up to Humboldt."

"When?"

"Sometime this week."

"Fine by me."

"Cool. I'll let you know the final arrangements as soon as I've set them up."

Ry nodded. Chase didn't go away.

"You really like Avery, don't you?" Chase let the question hang, but there was no way in hell Ry was going to get into a conversation about that. "I can see why. She's smart, funny, and brave."

"She's all that," Ry reluctantly agreed.

"So sometimes, if it's the right woman, even when it's not your fault you have to be prepared to grovel."

"Like you did?"

"Hell." Chase shoved a hand through his thick black hair. "I still do. January's a saint to put up with me."

"True." Ry hesitated. "But what the hell am I supposed to say?"

"Sometimes it's not about what you *think* you have to say, but simply being there and listening to what the other person wants to say to *you*."

"That sounds like something Dad or Jenna would come up with."

Chase shrugged. "Maybe their wisdom is rubbing off on me. It's about time."

Ry stared out across the barn and studied the endless blue sky. Maybe it was time for him to take a risk, and be proactive. He liked that word. He liked it a lot.

"I'm going to Vegas."

"To see HW?"

"Yeah."

"Well, that's a start." Chase slapped his shoulder. "Do you need a plane ticket?"

Ry pretended to pout. "No private jet?"

"That was a one-off, but my admin can probably wrangle you first class. But in return you have to promise to bring him back with you for the party."

"If I can, I will. Even if he won't come, I'll be back."

"Good man." Chase winked at him. "What about Avery?"

"I'll go into town and see her right now."

"Then I'd better get those tickets sorted so you can keep on going to the airport."

"Avery, Ry's in the lobby asking to speak to you," Marley called up the stairs. "Shall I tell him you're coming down, or are you still sulking, I mean, avoiding him?"

Avery clutched the bedspread to her chest. Was she ready to face him yet? Was she willing to turn into one of those people who could never let anything go?

"Tell him I'll just be a minute, and make sure he knows I don't have much time to chat."

"Will do."

Avery replaced the clean comforter in the linen closet and took a deep breath. The fact that he'd come to the hotel when he probably knew she was working wasn't a good sign. He *probably* thought it would only take a minute to break up with her—or for her to dump him.

Making sure her T-shirt was free of dust and lint,

she went down the main staircase and immediately spotted Ry standing just inside the door. He wore his Stetson, a brown leather jacket, and faded jeans, and was drawing plenty of admiring glances from everyone who streamed past him. As she drank in his long, lean, relaxed body, she let out a sigh of pure lust.

He looked up and caught her eye, immediately removing his hat as he came toward her.

"Avery."

She waited, but he just continued to watch her.

"I don't have a lot of time to talk, Ry. We're superbusy and understaffed." Good, she sounded friendly but distant, polite but dignified. Nancy would be so proud.

"So Tucker told me." He hesitated. "I won't be at the ranch for a couple of days."

"Okay."

"I just wanted you to know that I wasn't ignoring you or anything."

She just looked at him.

He swallowed hard and fiddled with the brim of his hat. Maybe making him do all the talking was punishment enough.

"And I wanted to wish you good luck with your interview."

She debated turning around and letting their conversation stand, but curiosity overcame her.

"Where are you going?"

"To see HW."

"Cool."

He half smiled, and she noticed he still had a bruise on his jaw. "I'm not sure about that. But I owe him an apology."

What about me? She pressed her lips together so hard it hurt.

He cleared his throat. "Are you okay?"

"I'm fine, and about that—"

He held up his hand. "I know, I suck. Can we talk about it when I get back? I can't get my head around trying to put out two fires at the same time."

"And sorting out HW takes priority?"

He studied her face. "Hell, have I screwed up again? I thought I was doing the right thing—giving you time to think—not pressuring you into making rash decisions."

"Like dumping you?"

His breathing hitched. "Yeah. Like that."

She raised her chin and channeled Lady Mary from *Downton.* "I have no intention of dumping you in the middle of a hotel lobby. I will wait until you get back, and we can have a civilized conversation about it then, all right?"

"Fine by me. I've gotta plane to catch." He bent his head and kissed her on the lips. "Take care, honey, and hang in there."

She stood still, watching him walk away, her fingers pressed to her lips. What had just happened? He'd come to see her, which was both unexpected and kind of amazing, and he'd indicated that he was the one who sucked, which wasn't true. But then she should've known he'd take the responsibility onto himself. She wished she'd taken the opportunity to apologize, but he'd caught her unprepared. She hadn't had time to prepare her I-forgive-you speech.

"Okay, sis?"

Tucker came up beside her and she jumped.

"I'm good."

"Everything okay with Ry? Marley said—"

"Marley has a big mouth." She met his gaze. "Everything is fine. I've got to get back to work."

It didn't occur to Ry until he was disembarking from the plane that he didn't have an address for HW in Vegas. He checked his cell and found no reply to his text. Shouldering his backpack, he texted HW again.

> I'm in Vegas. Either come by and pick me up at the airport, or give me your address.

While he waited for a reply, he got some coffee and pretended not to notice the slot machines dotted around the airport lounges. You literally could gamble the moment you got off the plane. He didn't need to chance his luck in a casino. He was rolling for much higher stakes than that. His phone buzzed.

> I'll pick u up.

Ry let out a relieved sighed. OK. I'll be out front.

About ten minutes later a battered truck pulled up alongside him, and the window went down.

"Get in, bro."

Ry picked up his backpack and got into the truck, glancing quickly at his twin as they pulled away from the curb. "Thanks for coming to get me."

"I was in town. Chase called and said you were coming."

"He did? That was nice of him."

HW snorted. "I thought he was giving me the opportunity to avoid you."

"Possibly," Ry conceded. "But he really wants you to come to his pre-wedding barbecue thing up at the hot springs on Friday."

"So he said."

Ry lapsed into silence as the weirdness of Vegas sped by. They were heading out into the desert. The farther they drove the more ridiculously out of place the city looked, like it had been dropped onto the sand from space.

"Where are you staying?"

"Out on a ranch near Lake Mead—a friend of BB's from the Marines."

"Cool."

HW slowed down for a red light. "I'm sorry I punched you."

"I had it coming."

"Maybe, but I still shouldn't have done that in Ruth's kitchen." He sighed. "I felt like a complete shit afterward."

"So did I."

HW cleared his throat. "I don't think you stayed with me just because of Mom."

"I know." Ry stared straight ahead. "And I don't think you're an irresponsible jerk—well, not all the time."

"Then, we're good?"

Ry considered his answer as they turned off the highway and onto a smaller complex of narrow roads. "You didn't have to tell them all that crap about Mom."

"They needed to hear it. And if she's alive? Maybe she needs to hear it, too."

"There's no point. You can't change the past."

"But you can apologize for your part in it, and move on."

Ry turned to study his twin's stern profile. "I always forget what a Dudley Do-Right you are at your center."

"So are you."

"Yeah, but I'm the quiet one, and you're supposed to be the rebel."

"Maybe that needs to change as well." HW drew the truck to a stop and punched in a code to open a five-barred gate. He turned to fully face Ry and didn't move off. "Look, not having you around for a few weeks? It's made me think. I took you for granted, bro."

Ry shrugged. "I let you."

"I also realized you were right about some of those assholes I was hanging out with."

"Whoop-de-do."

The gate slowly opened and they went through.

"So can you stay for a couple of days, and then I'll come back with you for the party?"

Ry smiled. Sorting shit out with his twin was way easier than dealing with Avery. Maybe that was why he'd jumped at the easier option and left her hanging . . . "I'll check in with Roy and Chase, but it sounds like a good plan."

Chapter Nineteen

"Did you hear anything from Chase?" Marley came into the office before Avery got the chance to hide under her desk.

"Nope, you?"

Marley gave her the death glare. "Why would I be asking you if I'd heard myself? Did you talk to Ry?"

"No. He's in Vegas with his twin."

Marley sighed. "Then when will we find out?"

"Marley, Chase is getting married in a couple of weeks, and he runs a multimillion-dollar company out of San Francisco. I'm pretty sure we aren't a priority at the moment."

Her cell buzzed and she took it out of her pocket. Her stomach flipped as she saw it was from Ry.

Party on Friday?

She texted back. At the ranch?

Yeah. Come with me?
U Sure?
Only if u want to.

Avery frowned at her phone.

"What's wrong?" Marley asked.

"Ry's asked me to a party up at the ranch."

"And?"

"I don't know why he wants me to go."

"Because you're his girlfriend? Duh."

Avery narrowed her eyes at her sister. "You're sounding more and more like Nancy every day."

"Really? Cool. I love Nancy. Of course you should go. Maybe he wants to make up for the horse fiasco thing."

"I thought we'd all agreed that was my fault."

"Which it was—which is why you go to the party, apologize to Ry, and then everything will be all right again."

Avery groaned. "Like relationships ever happen like that."

"Be positive. That man adores you."

She sat up straight. "You think so?"

"Yes, God knows why, but he does, so go with it, sis, and make him yours." Marley headed for the door. "Because if you don't, some other lucky girl is going to scoop him up, and if it can't be me—and I'd never ever date one of your castoffs—I'd rather it was you than anyone else."

"Wow, thanks."

"You're welcome. Now go get him, and don't forget to find out who got the job while you're there."

"You have such a one-track mind!" Avery shouted after her sister, who made some snorting kind of noise as she disappeared from view.

She texted back to Ry.

OK, that sounds good. What time?

6 at the house? I'm flying back with HW today.

Sounds good. She hesitated, her finger hovering over the *x* and then pressed Send without it. When she saw him she'd much rather give him the kiss up close and personal. She could only hope she'd get the chance.

Avery parked her car beside Ry's truck and retrieved her backpack from the passenger seat. She made her way up the steps through the screen door and toward the kitchen.

"Hey."

She stepped neatly to one side as Chase went by her, carrying a load of boxes.

He winked at her and carried on walking. "Ry's inside getting his orders from Ruth."

"Then I'll go and help as well."

She went into the kitchen, where the table was stacked high with coolers ready to be moved out.

"Hi, Ruth," she called out. "What can I do?"

"You can carry some of the boxes out to Roy's truck." Ruth was taking something that smelled like honey out of the oven. "Ry can give you a hand."

"Hey." He smiled down at her and she grinned back like a loon. "What's up?"

"Nothing much. How are you?"

"I'm good."

Ruth cleared her throat loudly. "Now you've gotten the hard part over, can you stop before you get to the canoodling, and help me out?"

"Sure." Ry dropped a kiss on his grandmother's head. "Just being polite."

"Roy's waiting for those coolers so he can go on up to the site and get the fires started."

"Then we'll take them out to him." Ry pointed out a couple of boxes to Avery. "Start with those."

It was nice not having anyone question her ability to help out. She stacked the boxes on top of each other, guessing from the lack of weight that she had plasticware and cups, and headed outside. Ry had propped the screen door open, which made everything a lot easier.

After a couple more trips the table was clear and Roy's truck was full. He started the engine and leaned out of the window.

"You want a ride, young Avery?"

She glanced over at Ry. "No, it's okay. I'll wait."

"You sure?"

Ry shifted his feet and stuck a hand in the back pocket of his jeans. "You can go with him if you like, Avery. It's not a problem."

She looked from him to Roy, and back again. "Is there something I'm missing here?"

"Nope. I can take my truck," Ry hastened to reassure her.

"He was going to ride over, but he's right, he can take his truck." Roy nodded. "Tell Ruth I'll be back to pick her up in a few."

Avery stayed where she was as Roy's truck disappeared down the road, brake lights flashing red in the gloom.

"I'll just check in with Ruth and get my keys," Ry said.

Avery took a deep breath and started walking down toward the barn. Sure, her heart was beating way too fast and she was regretting every step, but it felt right. It might be the best way to show Ry exactly how she felt about him.

"Hey, where're you going?"

She wasn't sure if she had enough saliva in her mouth to actually shout back, so she just kept moving. He caught up with her and gently drew her to a stop right outside the barn.

"Avery?"

She raised her head and looked him right in the eye. "I think I'd rather ride up there. It's not that far, is it?"

He went still and just stared down at her, his expression inscrutable.

"You . . . want to *ride*?"

"Yes. Can I take Dolittle?"

He blinked at her. "Sure. I'll . . ." He waved a hand in the general direction of the barn. "I'll ride one of the other horses."

"Not Nolly, though."

"No, Chase has already taken him out."

"Good." She walked into the barn and down to the last stall. "I'll get Dolittle if you grab the saddle and other stuff."

He studied her face for another full minute. "Okay. He's already got his halter on."

To his credit he turned his back and walked away, leaving her to enjoy the stupendous stupidity of her own choices without an audience. Muttering a prayer, she went into Dolittle's stall. He was fast asleep. It took her a while to wake him up and persuade him it was a good idea to move.

She stared him right in the eye. "Look, doofus, you'd better behave, okay? I need to look like a strong, competent woman right now, so do me proud."

Dolittle sighed, rolled his eyes, and snuffled at her hair. She led him out to the yard, where Ry had already deposited the saddle and bridle and was now leading out another horse.

"This is S'more."

She glanced over at the white-and-brown quarter horse. "Great name."

"Maria chose it. She's got her eye on riding this horse one day. So I need to make sure he's up to the job."

He left her to saddle and bridle Dolittle while he worked on his own horse, whistling as he did it. She was all fingers and thumbs, but she managed everything and attached her backpack to the saddle.

"You ready?" he asked. "Want a boost up?"

"I'll use the mounting block." There was no point in being stupid, and she didn't want him to touch her right now because then he'd know how hard she was trembling. "Can you line Dolittle up for me?"

"Sure."

She waited for him to take the reins, and managed to mount without looking like a fool or a newb. Gathering the reins in one hand, she forced herself to relax her tense shoulders.

"I'll have to follow you, Ry. I have no idea where we're going."

He came up alongside her on S'more and gave

her a quick once-over that she pretended not to notice. "It really isn't far."

"Cool."

His smile was warm enough to calm all her jittery nerves. "Then let's go."

It was a nice slow ride, and she actually enjoyed it. Something about the tranquility of the land as it sank into blackness called out to her, calming her nerves, making her realize that her little problems were totally minor in the big scheme of the universe.

"See the lights?" Ry pointed ahead. "HW, BB, and Chase were up here earlier, making the place fit for a party."

"It's pretty." She looked down on the entrance to the hot springs and the grove of trees that were now festooned with strings of lights that swayed gently in the night air. "I haven't been here for years."

"Me neither. Did you bring your bikini?"

"I don't own one. Too many scars. I did bring my swimsuit and shorts."

"I'm not much of a swimmer myself, but I figure I can stay afloat."

"Didn't you surf when you stayed on the coast?"

"No time." He brought his fingers to his lips and whistled loud enough to wake the dead. "Incoming!"

BB waved. "Come down this way. We've made a temporary shelter for the horses."

Avery followed Ry to the sheltered spot under the pine trees. Nolly whickered a greeting as the other horses drew to a stop.

"I've got you." BB reached up and brought Avery to the ground in one smooth motion. "No mounting block out here."

"Thanks." She retrieved her backpack. "Where's Jenna?"

"She'll be coming later. She's just finishing up afternoon surgery. Maria's already in the caves with January and HW."

"Cool." She reached for Dolittle's reins, but BB got there first.

"I'll take care of him. You go and enjoy yourself."

"Thanks." She smiled at him. "It looks like it's going to be a great party."

Ry threw S'more's reins at BB, his gaze on Avery's retreating form. "Help me out, bro?"

"Sure, go get her."

Ry ran after Avery. "Hey, wait up."

She turned back toward him. "What's wrong?"

He took her hand and stepped them both off the path and underneath the trees. Walking her backward, he eased her up against a handy trunk and framed her face with his hands.

"I thought you weren't ever going near me or a horse again."

Even in the filtered green light he could see that she was blushing.

"I changed my mind."

"And why is that?"

"Because if I want to work up here full-time, I can't be scared of horses."

"You still want to work here?"

"Sure I do."

He smoothed his thumb over her jawline. "What about me?"

"I'll work alongside you, if I have to."

"And?"

"And what?" She blinked at him, all innocence.

"You forgive me?"

She shrugged. "Nothing to forgive, really. You were right to make me stay on that horse, even though I hated you for doing it."

"You don't hate me now?"

"No! Why do you think I got back on your stupid horse?" She sighed. "Wow, men really are dense sometimes. I was sending you a *message*."

He fought a smile, and she frowned at him.

"What?"

"You're beautiful when you're angry." He silenced her spluttering reply by kissing her so thoroughly that she couldn't do anything except kiss him back. When he finally drew away, he tucked a strand of her hair behind her ear. She looked so flushed and rumpled and . . . he never wanted to let her go. "We're good now?"

"I suppose we are."

"You don't sound too happy about it."

"I'm just mortified by how easily I fold when you look at me."

"Goes both ways."

"Really?" She held his gaze. "That's kind of wonderful, but scary at the same time."

"Tell me about it." He kissed her again, took her hand, and started back up the path to the hot springs. "I'd rather take you somewhere more private, but Chase would have my ass if we didn't stay at the party and January got upset."

"I know."

At the top of the path where the ground evened out, Roy had set out the barbecue, built a campfire, and was directing HW as to how he wanted the tables laid out.

"Hey," Ry called out to his twin, who turned to smile at him.

"What's up?" HW spotted Avery and nodded. "Avery, how's it going?"

Roy came up to them, his truck keys jangling in his hand. "Can you help HW while I go and fetch Ruth?"

"Sure."

Ry walked over to the tables and helped HW line them up, while Avery looked through the boxes for the place mats and plastic utensils. HW was already more relaxed. They'd spent three days together on the Nevada ranch, working with the horses and perfecting HW's technique for the finals. Ry had enjoyed it immensely, and for the first time his twin had really listened to what he had to say. True, they'd had some disagreements, but that was to be expected. There had been none of that underlying tension that had bedeviled all their recent fights.

January came out of the entrance to the hot springs, Maria by her side.

"Good, you're here." She grinned at Avery. "Jenna just texted me to say she's on her way."

"And Ruth and Roy will be back soon," Ry added.

January looked thoughtful. "I don't think either of them are planning on getting into the water, so we could start without them."

"Roy said he's going to get the barbecue going, and I doubt Ruth will leave him alone with that."

"True." He and Avery spoke at the same time.

Ry looked down at her. "So do you want to go and take a soak in the natural hot tub before we eat?"

"I'd love to."

"Then you go ahead and we'll join you later." January nodded. "I'm just going to fetch Chase and tell BB Jenna's ETA." She patted Maria's shoulder. "Do you want to come with me, or go back in the water?"

"I'll come with you," Maria said. "Jenna's bringing Grandpa, so I'll wait for him."

"I suppose that just leaves you and me, Avery?" Ry winked at her.

"And me," HW piped up.

Ry gave his brother the side-eye. "You could make yourself scarce for a few minutes, bro, couldn't you?"

"Nah."

Ry narrowed his eyes. "Go. Away."

HW consulted his watch. "It's cold out here. Ten minutes max, and then I'm coming in after you."

Ry led Avery inside the cave. "Best to take off your boots right now. It gets slippery in there."

"Great," she muttered.

"It's okay. I'll hold your hand." Ry sat down to pull off his boots and socks and also shucked his jeans. "I've got my board shorts on, so I'm almost ready to go."

"What about when you have to put your jeans back on? Did you bring spare boxers?"

"Nope. I'll be fine."

She winced. "On the back of a horse?"

"As long as I do some careful . . . arranging, I don't see a problem."

"Rather you than me."

He sat down and helped her pull off her socks. "It also means I'll be undressed quicker when we finally make it back to bed."

"I love the way you always see the positive in

things. Let's just hope I don't get too impatient and yank down that zipper of yours too fast."

"Hey." He winced and put a protective hand over his groin. "There's a separate space at the back of the caves the girls always used to get changed. I'll show you where it is."

He loved the caves, with their frosted roofs and sulphury smell, but they could be tricky to navigate. He took his time weaving through the varying sized holes filled with steaming water, making sure Avery was following carefully. It was rather like being in a sauna as the air temperature was way warmer than outside.

Someone had lit a load of candles and spread them throughout the caves, which made everything a lot easier to spot, and turned the space into an enchanted grotto.

"This would make a fantastic spot for a wedding," Avery mused.

"Yeah? I hadn't thought of that. You should mention it to Chase."

"I will." She almost slipped, and he steadied her with one arm wrapped around her waist. "Maybe put some mats down first though. Wouldn't want the bride suffering a concussion."

He paused by the wall jutting out into the main cave. "You can change back here."

"Okay, I'll just be a minute."

She disappeared from view.

After half a minute Ry glanced back toward the entrance, and then made up his mind.

"I'm coming in."

"Ry! I'm not—"

Sweet Jesus, Avery was half-naked, and that suited him just fine. He gathered her into his arms and kissed his way down her throat to her naked breasts, one hand cupping her ass as she wiggled against him. His fingers found the edge of her panties and slipped beneath the lace to caress her most secret flesh.

"God, you're wet for me." He breathed the words against her skin as she bucked against his hand, his thumb searching and finding her, dipping deep as he groaned her name.

"Ry . . ." Her fingers tightened in his hair as she took her pleasure from him in long, sweet waves that made him so hard he wanted—

A cheerful whistle echoed through the caverns.

"Dude. Time's up! Last one in the pool's a loser."

Ry reluctantly released Avery. "That man has no soul. Remind me to interrupt him when he gets a girlfriend. If he ever does with that attitude and ugly face."

Avery pushed him gently away. "Go. I'll be out in a minute."

"Like this?"

She glanced down at his tented board shorts. "Oh. Is there a cold pool you could jump in first?"

He was still smiling as he backed out of her space and went to find his brother, who was sitting on the edge of the largest pool, his back to the changing area. Ry went to sit beside him.

"Thanks for nothing."

"You're welcome. Glad to help you mind your morals."

"Says who?"

"Ruth, for one."

"Yeah, right."

"Maybe I'm just envious that you've found some-one."

Ry let that hang in the steamy air as he considered what to say. "You should be."

"She's a keeper?"

"I think she is."

"Dude . . . What is it with all you guys?" HW shook his head. "Must be something in the water out here."

"Could be."

"You've only been back a few weeks."

"And I'm planning on staying here forever."

"Even if I win big in Vegas, you won't come back and travel with me?"

Ry kicked at the water with his foot. "You told me it was time for me to be myself. I'm not good enough to compete at your level. I'd rather be here, mending fences, dealing with the horses and the incoming guests, hanging out with Avery . . ."

"You mean it, don't you?"

"Yeah, I do." Ry met his twin's golden gaze. "You okay with that?"

"Don't suppose I've got any choice." HW's smile was wry. "But I'm not going away completely. Some-one's got to keep you in line."

"I thought that was my job."

"Things change, bro, *people* change." HW contem-plated the steaming pool. "Whether we want them to or not."

"Wow, how profound. You should write a book."

HW shoved him hard in the chest, and Ry shoved him back, and they both fell sideways into the water, still entangled. When they resurfaced Avery was sitting on the edge of the pool, shaking her head.

"You two . . ."

Ry grinned at her. "We're just playing."

"Yeah." HW reared over Ry and shoved him back down so hard his feet touched the bottom of the pool and he had to kick off to reach the surface.

Spluttering and wheezing, he dashed at the water in his eyes only to see HW grab Avery from her seat and hear her shriek as she was dunked into the pool. Her head disappeared beneath the surface. Terror gripped him and he yanked hard on HW's arm.

"Let her go!"

The last thing he saw was HW's startled face before he dove down, wrapping his arms around Avery and propelling her up to the surface of the water.

She pushed at his chest. "Ry? What's wrong? I was fine, HW didn't . . ."

He managed to find his way out of the water and sank down beside the wall, head in hands, his whole body shaking. Within seconds, HW was on one side of him and Avery the other.

"She was okay, Ry." HW's voice was incredibly gentle. "I wasn't going to hurt her or anything."

He dimly heard Avery's voice. "But why would he even *think* that?"

"Our mom . . ." HW sighed. "That last night, she—"

"She was supposed to be giving Rachel a bath," Ry interrupted as it all came back to him. "And she tried to drown her."

"We both tried to stop her." HW sounded so much like him they spoke with one voice. "When I got Rachel away, Mom tried to drown Ry instead."

Ry flinched as Avery wrapped her arms around him and held him tight. She didn't say anything. Hell, what was there to say? He'd suppressed that doozy of a memory for so long, extracting it made him feel empty.

"Are you guys okay?"

Ry jerked his gaze toward the entrance of the cave, where January's voice came from.

"Let's get back in the pool." He glared at HW and Avery. "Let's keep this between ourselves, okay? I don't want to ruin January's party."

After a shared glance, HW and Avery hauled him to his feet.

"I'll go check in with January," HW said. "You two stay here."

Ry slid into the heated waters and closed his eyes as Avery joined him. For a long while they just floated together, breathing in the minerals, returning to a womb-like state that felt surprisingly safe.

"Sorry I scared you," he managed to murmur.

"It's all good." She nipped his ear and held him even tighter.

"It's not, but I want it to be." He opened his eyes and found hers waiting for him. "I need to get this thing with my mom dealt with, and then . . ." He held her gaze. "Depending on whether I survive that, I want to be with you."

"Sounds good to me."

He slid a hand into her wet hair. "I mean *seriously* with you, like in love with you. But I can't say the words until I know what kind of man will be left for you *to* love."

She blinked at him, her wet eyelashes all clumped

together, making her look like one of Maria's old dolls.

"You have to wait to decide whether you're in *love*?"

"Come on, Avery, you know that's not what I meant."

"You think I'll change my mind about you because of what happens with your mom?"

"Yeah."

"Then you're an idiot."

. She dunked him under the water. By the time he resurfaced she was climbing awkwardly out of the pool.

"Hey!"

"I'm going to dry off, and then I'll help Ruth with the food."

"But what about—"

She was already gone. Ry sighed and floated on his back, staring up at the crystalline white rock ceiling. After a while his heart rate settled down and he somehow found a smile. She hadn't told him to go to hell, and she hadn't insisted she wasn't in love with him.

He'd call that a win.

Avery put her shorts and T-shirt over her wet swimsuit, and walked as briskly as she could to the front of the cave, where she could already smell barbecue cooking on the grill. Her steps slowed and she paused to gaze out on the busy scene in front of her.

Just before she'd shoved his head under the water, had Ry Morgan actually said he *loved* her? And had she just told him he was an idiot?

"Nice, Avery," she muttered to herself. "Good job."

HW came over, his expression concerned. "You okay? How's Ry doing?"

"He's his usual fatheaded self."

"Good." HW grinned. "Nice to see you totally get him." He leaned in toward her, one hand braced against the side of the cave opening. "Seriously, he's okay?"

"Yes. Considering what he just remembered." Avery sighed. "God, HW, I'm trying to feel sorry for your mom, but she was way out of line."

He nodded. "I read up about this a lot, and there's a kind of postnatal depression that is basically psychotic. I guess that's the kind she had." He hesitated. "Maybe Mom got some help. I damn well hope so."

Avery studied HW's familiar features. Sometimes he was nothing like Ry, and then other times . . . they were eerily similar.

"Will you tell Ruth and the others about this?"

"Not today. Don't want to spoil the party. We didn't tell them at the time either. I'll leave it up to Ry to make the decision." He kissed her cheek. "You sure you're talking to the right twin now?"

"Seeing as you're up close, and you do nothing for me in the knee-trembling department, I'm pretty sure you're not Ry."

She squeaked as a pair of arms came around her from behind.

"Back off, loser. This is my woman," Ry growled close to her ear.

"Oh please." HW gave him the finger. "Keep the caveman impressions for someone who cares."

"Jealous, huh?"

HW's smile died. "So jealous I could choke on it." He turned and walked back to where Roy was busy flipping burgers and hot dogs on the grill.

Avery turned in Ry's arms to stare up at his face, but he was watching HW.

She asked, "Is he really okay?"

"Yeah. He's just . . . getting his shit together."

Avery sniffed. "About time one of you did."

He rubbed his nose against hers. "Hey, I know what I want. Didn't you hear me back then?"

From the heat rushing to her cheeks she knew she was blushing. "I heard you."

"And?"

"I'll talk to you after you've sorted out this issue with your mom."

He angled his head to study her, his golden eyes gleaming in the candlelight. "Nothing else you want to say to me?"

"If that's another leading question, you've already got the best answer I can give you right now."

His slow smile was worth waiting for. "Liar."

She raised her chin. "And what is that supposed to mean?"

He took her hand and placed it over his heart. "You are totally, one hundred percent into me."

Avery rolled her eyes. There was no way she was playing that game. "You Morgan boys are *so* conceited."

"That's because we're pretty awesome."

"And *so* modest."

He shrugged, his smile deepening. "You can fake it all you like, Avery, but we both know you're in this just as deep as I am."

Was he really attempting to sweet-talk her into

telling him she loved him back? It was somewhere between infuriating and cute. A girl had some standards, and she needed to talk to Nancy before she decided exactly how and when she might let him know the truth.

She batted her eyelashes at him. "Is that Ruth coming up the hill? I'd better go and help her unload the truck."

She slipped away, leaving him standing at the mouth of the caves. Ry Morgan might *think* he had everything worked out, but it was fun to yank his chain just a little bit.

Chapter Twenty

Ry took the seat next to Chase in the lawyer's office, and BB and HW filed in beside him. It was a bright, sunny day in Humboldt, but Ry didn't really care. While Andrew was making small talk with Chase, he was too busy trying to keep his shit together to worry about such stupid topics as the weather.

"I don't think Professor Ford will be much longer."

Even as the lawyer spoke there was a knock on the door. The admin ushered in a tall, thin man with fading white hair, who almost took a step back when all four brothers rose simultaneously to their feet. His gaze fixed on Ry and HW, and then moved back to the lawyer.

"Good morning, Andrew."

"Professor, thanks so much for joining us. These are the Morgan brothers, Chase, Blue, Ry, and HW."

He nodded at them and took a seat. "I understand you wished to speak to me about a matter regarding my wife, Annie."

"That's correct." As already agreed, Chase took up the conversation. "I'm not sure exactly what Andrew has told you, but we believe your wife was once married to our father, William Morgan."

"I know that Annie was married before. She told me that, and obviously she had Rachel with her when we met." His gaze returned to Ry and HW. "You both look rather like Annie and Rachel."

Chase handed over a small photograph of Annie with all four of the boys. "This is one of the last pictures taken of our mother at the family ranch."

Professor Ford studied it for a long while. "It certainly looks like her."

"Did she ever tell you why she left her first husband?"

The professor sighed and removed his reading glasses. "From what I understood, she was deeply ashamed of what happened back then, and convinced herself that the best thing she could do was leave before she seriously hurt someone. I understood that she was suffering from an extreme form of postnatal depression after Rachel's birth."

"Did she tell you she had more children?"

"No."

Ry looked out the window. It sounded like she hadn't really changed at all . . .

"Do you think she might be willing to at least meet us?" Chase sat forward. "Or just email, or . . ."

"That's not possible." Professor Ford frowned. "I apologize if I didn't make that clear immediately. She died two years ago of cancer of the liver."

Ry sucked in a breath as all the air in the room seemed to disappear.

"What?" BB was the first to recover. "She's *dead*?"

"Yes, it was mere months between her being diagnosed and her death." He cleared his throat. "Rachel and I were both with her at the end. She died peacefully."

Chase sat back. "That's . . . sad to hear. We all hoped to get a chance to reconnect with her, you know?"

God, and Chase did sound sad, as did BB. Ry wasn't sure how he felt. The relief that he wouldn't have to face her coupled with the idea that she no longer existed and couldn't provide any explanation for her behavior was blowing his mind. HW snuck an arm around Ry's shoulders.

"Just before she died, Annie did try to tell me that she hadn't revealed everything about her former life. She was greatly troubled by the harm she might have caused. If she'd been more specific, I would have tracked you down and offered you the opportunity to say good-bye to her."

She'd never say good-bye now . . .

"Does Rachel know anything about her real family?" Chase asked.

The professor's smile was pained. "For all intents and purposes I've been her father, and she had all the advantages of growing up in a real family."

Chase quickly corrected himself. "I apologize. I meant, does she know anything about her biological family's history?"

"I don't think so. She was just a baby when Annie left her first marriage, and around three when I first met her mother."

Chase nodded. "Do you think you might tell

Rachel about us? Just the facts." He placed a folder on the lawyer's desk midway between them. "I've compiled all the relevant information here—including health concerns for her biological paternal line."

Professor Ford took the folder. "Thanks." He hesitated. "Is he still alive?"

"Our father, you mean?" Chase nodded. "Yeah."

"Annie was worried about him, I remember that. She felt she'd let him down terribly. I'm glad to hear he's still in good health."

Ry literally had to bite his tongue not to share the hell his father had gone through since Annie had left him. That story was for another time—or maybe never. He glanced over his shoulder at the door. He just wanted to get out of there. Chase was still yakking.

"I included information about how to contact us if Rachel wants to do so. I give you my word that we won't attempt to talk to her without running it by you first."

"I appreciate that." The professor stood, his gaze lingering on Ry. "She never told me she had identical twins who looked just like her. It's quite amazing." He shook hands with Chase. "I promise I'll consider everything you've told me very carefully and make a decision about whether Rachel should be informed."

"We'd appreciate that."

The door closed behind the lawyer and Professor Ford, leaving the four brothers alone.

BB kicked the leg of the desk. "Well, that was a complete bust."

"Not really." Chase had his annoyingly bland voice on. "We established that Annie did survive, and went on to marry again. It's a pity she wasn't around to see us."

"Yeah, she managed to avoid taking responsibility for all her shit," Ry heard himself saying.

"That's not completely true, bro," HW said carefully. "It sounded like she had plenty of regrets."

"Like not remembering she had four kids she abandoned and a husband she drove to drink? Yeah. Nice."

"Ry . . ." That was Chase, of course.

He flung up a hand. "It's okay, I get it. She was depressed and she left."

"She *left* because she realized she might hurt someone, and she was right. She tried to drown her own *child*, Ry. That must have been terrifying. She *thought* she was doing the right thing."

Ry walked over to the window and stared out across the parking lot. He remembered the horror on her face when HW had fought her off and pulled him out of the tub, soaking wet and shivering. That's why he had ended up cleaning the bathroom by himself, because she'd turned tail and disappeared down the stairs, where she'd almost taken their father out with a knife.

HW came to stand beside him. "She must have left because of what happened that night, Ry. In her mind, leaving was the lesser of two evils, and maybe she was right." He squeezed Ry's shoulder. "She wasn't like that before Rachel was born, don't you remember?"

"I can't." His voice emerged sharp enough to cut glass. "All I can remember is her being angry."

"Maybe she'll come back to you, now she's at peace."

Ry considered that as he struggled to accept what would never be. "Maybe."

* * *

When they arrived back at the ranch, the lights were blazing and everyone was in the kitchen, waiting dinner for them. Ry had thought about leaving quietly and going to town to see Avery, but she was right there helping Ruth dish out the lasagna. He had no desire to hear the whole thing rehashed over the dinner table, but he guessed he had no choice.

Avery sat next to him, one hand on his thigh whenever she wasn't working on her food. She hadn't said much, but he could see the anxiety in her occasional glance his way. At least Chase had passed on a few of the important details in a phone call to Billy so he could brief Ruth.

Eventually, they were all drinking coffee or tea and Ruth looked over at Chase.

"So Annie is dead, then?"

"Apparently."

Ruth shook her head. "May she rest in peace, the poor girl."

"Amen," Roy murmured.

"And what about Rachel?"

"She doesn't know anything about us," Chase said. "I asked Professor Ford to consider informing her of our existence. He didn't seem that keen."

"She's an adult now, right?" January asked.

"She must be *twenty*." Billy studied his scarred, joined hands. "I can't believe that."

"But that means he can't stop you contacting her if you want to."

Chase let his gaze wander around the table. "I'd rather wait and see what he does with the information before I blunder in there and upset her."

"Agreed," BB said, and HW nodded.

"What do you think, Ry?"

He looked up to find everyone staring at him. "Fine by me."

"You sure?" Ruth reached for his hand. "It's going to be okay, darling boy. It really is."

He found a smile somewhere. "I know."

A while later he walked out onto the porch with Avery, and they settled into the swing BB had recently installed there. He kicked off from the floor and let them rock gently back and forth, soothed by the creak of the rope and the whisper of the wind coming down the mountain pass.

"So that's that," Ry finally said. "She's gone, and I'll never get to see her again."

Tucked against his side, Avery placed her palm on his chest. "Maybe it's for the best."

"I hate things being so . . . *unfinished*, you know?"

She looked up at him, her brown gaze clear. "But life isn't like that. You can't expect everything to be tied up in a neat bow."

"Why not? That's what Chase expects."

"He wanted to see your mom again, didn't he?"

"Sure."

"Then he didn't get what he wanted either, did he?"

"None of us did." Ry hesitated. "It's weird. All that fuss and anxiety and now nothing." He shifted his weight and rocked the swing again. "I wonder if Chase regrets starting the search at all."

Avery chuckled. "He might be cross at how much it cost, but I don't think he's the kind of guy to regret anything he sets his mind to solving, do you?"

"You make him sound so attractive."

"I'm not attracted to him in the slightest, and you know it. And January would kill me if I tangled with her man."

"She might," Ry acknowledged. "She's got a bit of a temper on her, despite all that sweetness." He glanced down at her. "Like someone else I could mention."

"Are you talking about me?"

"You know I am, but I'd rather see you all riled up than sitting around feeling sorry for yourself."

She sat bolt upright. "Ry Morgan—"

He stopped her talking by kissing her, and then kissing her again when she tried to splutter something else. Eventually, she kissed him back. It felt so right sitting there on the porch next to his woman, surrounded by his family and doing something he loved. All those things—*all of them* meant so much more than the ghost of a mother who had made some bad choices and lived to regret them. Hopefully time would help him forgive her, and let him remember how she'd been before . . .

He eased back a little and stared down at Avery's flushed face and parted lips.

"Avery . . ."

She scowled. "You really need to stop *doing* that kissing thing. It makes me forget all the important things I mean to say to you."

He grinned. "I'll do it again if you don't stop and listen."

"You are *so*—"

He kissed her nose. "Amazing, I know. And I love you. I think I always have." He smoothed her hair out of her eyes. "Ever since you were fourteen and you fell off your horse into our creek."

"Not when I kicked you in the shins?"

"There was that, too, but seeing you dripping wet, climbing back on that horse, stole my heart. You laughed, didn't make a fuss. and just kept moving."

Her smile was as wobbly as her voice. "Sometimes that's all you can do, right? Just get up and keep going."

"Some of us take longer to work that out than others. You had to deal with all that shit when you were eighteen, and here you are, still driving me nuts seven years later."

"You weren't here to drive nuts. I wish you had been."

He mock frowned at her. "That's beside the point. I realized the other day that every woman I've met since I left home hasn't stood a chance because they weren't you."

Her breathing hitched. "Oh, Ry, that's the nicest thing anyone has ever said to me."

"Nicer than *I love you?*"

"*Different* nice." She made a face. "Now I feel stupid saying it back to you because you're going to think I'm saying it because you did."

"What?" Ry held her gaze. "I'm a simple guy, Avery. If you mean them, I'd like to hear the words."

"Okay." She drew a deep breath and looked so serious he wanted to laugh. "I love you, Ry."

He bit back a smile and tried to look as solemn as she did. "Thank you."

She flopped back against his shoulder. "Man, that was hard."

"You should've practiced, like I did."

"You *practiced*? Like in the mirror?"

"Dude. I didn't want to make a complete fool of myself. Getting all mushy and confessing you're in love isn't in a man's comfort zone."

"I can't believe you said it first."

"Neither can I. HW will laugh his nuts off."

She snuggled up against him, and he held her tight as happiness flowed around him and through her.

"I'm glad you told me this now, Ry."

"Why's that?"

"Because I'm going to be so busy with the wedding preparations that I'm not going to see much of you for a couple of weeks."

Ry stilled the swing by digging the toe of his boot into the planking. "But if you stay up here, I'll get to see you every night."

"Good thinking, cowboy."

Behind them, the screen door opened and a beam of light spread like a golden carpet across the shadowed wooden planks.

"You guys doing okay out there? Swing holding up?" BB called out. "Ruth wants to know if you want a blanket, or are you coming in for hot chocolate?"

Avery shivered.

"We're coming in." Ry helped her out of the swing and, ignoring BB's wink, walked back into the house holding her hand. In one day he'd had to deal with his past, but he'd also made strides toward a much better future.

Chapter Twenty-One

"Everything is under control, January. Trust me."

Avery said the same words for the thousandth time, and really tried to mean them as she shut the door and went down the stairs. Dealing with Chase was even worse, seeing as he'd drawn up timesheets and protocols for every emergency under the sun, including an earthquake and a nuclear explosion. He'd also accessed her event database, and every time something on the schedule slipped, he was texting her to ask why.

She was used to dealing with hysterical and demanding brides, but if Chase didn't knock it off she was going to set Ry on him. Coming down the stairs, she paused to check the kitchen, where some of the staff were plating up the food that didn't need cooking. Ry's dad had been supervising them for a while but had gone up to get changed.

"Everyone okay?" she asked brightly. "Good."

No point in stopping in case anyone actually did have a problem. She had more important things to focus on right now, such as the non-appearance of the band, and the disappearance of half the floral arrangements.

Yvonne and her chef friend were busy in the industrial-size kitchen tent they'd erected in the pasture near the house. The Hayes staff, headed by Marley, had done all their cooking at the hotel and brought everything up to be dealt with by the chef. It was chaos in there, and Avery was keeping clear until she was called in to help.

Her cell buzzed with another text from Chase, and she said a very bad word.

Out behind the barn she found the man she was looking for.

"Ry!" He was moving toward her with his usual lack of urgency. "Come here!"

He raised an eyebrow and changed course. "What's up?"

"Number one, you should be changed by now, and number two, tell your brother Chase that if he doesn't stop calling me I'm going to take his cell phone and do something really unpleasant with it."

"I'm going to change right now. We had some problems moving Nolly away from all the people. He seems to think he should be a bridesmaid or something."

Avery sighed. "Darn, I wish I'd thought of that. It would've been hilarious."

"Except he'd eat all the flowers and crap on the carpet."

"I think he's already eaten half the flowers," Avery said darkly.

Ry patted her shoulder. "I'll talk to Chase. He's just a tad nervous."

"Just a *tad*? He's worse than *January*."

"He can't help it. He's a bit of a control freak."

She opened her eyes wide at him. "You *think?*"

Ry gave her a sympathetic hug. "How's everything else coming along?"

"Great, actually. We're all set."

"Cool." He kissed her cheek. "Don't get so caught up in organizing everything that you forget to enjoy the wedding yourself."

"I'll do my best."

Her cell buzzed again. She didn't even need to look down to see it was Chase. She might have growled.

Ry whistled. "If you keep clenching your teeth that hard you're asking for a lifetime of dental work."

"As is your oldest brother if he doesn't stop texting me."

"I'll get him calmed down, I promise." He blew her a kiss as he walked away. "Avery?"

"*What?*"

His gaze dropped to her scuffed cowboy boots and torn jeans. "You might want to think about getting changed yourself."

"Oh crap," she whispered, and stumbled back to the house.

Ry took up his station at the back of the seating area, and surveyed the seated guests. Avery had transformed the ranch into some kind of mythical fairyland, complete with hundreds of lights illuminating the trees, candles everywhere, and a flowery arch under which his brother Chase was currently pacing and checking his watch.

During an earlier struggle, Ry had taken Chase's cell away from him. He'd promised to return it after the ceremony. Avery had blown him a kiss when she'd passed by, and he handed it over to her, which had made him feel like a hero. Soft music wafted over him in the still air. Ry couldn't see where the live band had been hidden. It was definitely a classy wedding, but somehow it still fit with the ranch and their family.

BB was up front with Chase, wearing his fancy Marine uniform and attracting a lot of covert glances from the female guests. He only had eyes for Jenna, who was sitting behind him in the row reserved for close family. Maria was upstairs with January, getting changed into her bridesmaid outfit, which just left him, HW, Ruth, and Billy to get up the aisle. He checked the top button of his new shirt. Thank God Chase hadn't insisted on tuxes and had gone for a cowboy theme.

Someone touched his arm, and he turned to see Avery all dressed up, her hair piled in loose curls on the top of her head and her blue dress shimmering under the soft lights.

"Wow."

"Wow what?" She still had her earpiece on and looked busy.

"You are so beautiful."

She raised her chin and studied him right back. "Thank you. You don't look too bad yourself."

"Seeing as you picked out exactly what HW and I were going to wear, I suppose you would say that."

"Only to you." She cupped his chin. "HW looks *okay*, but—"

A snort behind him made Ry look over his

shoulder to see his twin, who was wearing almost exactly the same gear as he was. He winked at his brother.

"Well, they do say true love is blind."

"And I do love you," Avery added, and kissed his cheek.

HW groaned. "Don't tell me there's going to be another wedding around here. I've got to get through BB and Jenna's next."

Avery stepped out of Ry's arms. "And I've got to get everyone through this one first. Are you all ready? Billy, can you escort Ruth, and can you two boys follow them up the aisle?"

"Boys?" Ry questioned.

"You know what I mean." She made a shushing notion at him. "Move it."

He progressed down the aisle, seeing familiar faces from the town and a collection of hippie types from the commune where January had grown up. Apparently, she had several half siblings because the commune had been founded in the spirit of free love, whatever that meant. They'd all turned up for the wedding, which had made January very happy.

Chase turned to greet them when they arrived at the front, and accepted a kiss from his grandmother. Ry couldn't help noticing that his usually calm and confident brother was as pale as his white cotton shirt. He shook hands with Chase and then gave him a manly hug.

Ry patted his shoulder. "It's all good, Chase. Avery's got everything right on schedule."

"Actually, according to my calculations, she's running five minutes late."

Ry gave his bro the look, and Chase shut up.

They all filed into their front-row seats. He left the one on the end vacant for Avery, and hoped she'd make it. The music changed, and the volume increased. Ry craned his neck to look backward, where he could just see a white figure accompanied by Roy in his cowboy best, coming up the aisle.

January's dress wasn't huge, and it didn't have one of those long train things that he'd never seen the point of. It was lacy and delicate, and just right on her. He guessed Chase wasn't looking at the dress anyway, because January's brilliant smile was all he needed to see. When they reached the front, Roy kissed the bride and took his seat while Chase looked even more petrified.

HW nudged him. "Do you think he's gonna puke?"

"Maybe." Ry considered his normally unflappable brother, who seemed unable to form words as he stared at his bride. "Or pass out."

"Cool."

"Dearly beloved . . ."

Ry stood with the rest of the congregation and listened carefully to the local Morgantown preacher as he extolled the virtues of marriage and set about making Chase and January husband and wife.

Avery slipped into the seat beside him, her cheeks flushed, and he took her hand. It didn't take him long to imagine himself up there saying the words that would bind him to Avery for the rest of his life. He glanced down at her. Would she go for that? Today was not the day to ask, when she was so caught up ensuring this wedding went off without a hitch. But the idea scared him a lot less than he'd anticipated, and the benefits of having Avery sharing his life outweighed everything else.

The thought of having a family of his own still scared the crap out of him. How could he have kids when his memories of being a child were so painful? But he'd learned something important from Avery about taking those small steps to get back into something. He'd have to start with the whole relationship and marriage thing, have an honest conversation with Avery about his fears, and take it from there.

So he had a future, and a plan. Everything that had brought him to this point, good *and* bad, had somehow given him everything he had ever wanted. He swallowed hard, and Avery offered him her handkerchief, which he scorned. He had nothing to cry about anymore. He was one very happy, very lucky cowboy.

Avery kicked off her shoes and surveyed the dance floor, where the newly married couple was wrapped in each other's arms dancing—if you could call it that—to something romantic. She loved this part of the wedding. Now all she had to watch out for were the drunks and the criers, and her evening would be complete.

Chase had grabbed hold of her earlier and thanked her for everything she'd done to make the wedding a success. He'd followed up by offering her the job at the ranch, which had made her very happy indeed. Marley wasn't going to like it, but there was definitely something going on with her that she needed to sort out before committing herself to staying home for at least another year.

Avery smiled as Chase gave her a thumbs-up from the dance floor. He was so besotted with January that he'd forgotten to ask for his cell phone back. She would have to remember to hand it over to Ruth before she left. If she gave it to one of the other Morgan brothers, she doubted Chase would ever see it again.

"Would you like to dance?"

She turned to find HW grinning down at her.

"Sure, as long as you don't pretend to be Ry and kiss me."

"Busted." He traced a cross over his heart. "I promise I'll behave."

She allowed him to lead her out onto the dance floor and gather her close.

"Thank you, Avery."

"It did go rather well, didn't it?" Avery smiled up at him.

"Not for this—although you did a fantastic job—but for looking after Ry."

"He doesn't need looking after."

"Yeah, he does. I never thought about what he'd been through with Mom much. I was too busy trying to survive my part of it." He grimaced. "But he needs to be loved unconditionally for *himself*, and you get that."

"Well, duh. He's easy to love."

"Yeah, but I'm glad it's you he loves back." He kissed her forehead. "I know he's in safe hands."

"Certainly safer than yours."

"Dude, I'm his twin. I was born to drive him crazy."

Avery cupped his cheek. "Take care of yourself, too, won't you? Come back and see him. He misses you a lot more than you might realize."

"Let me get through the next few weeks and the finals and I'll get back to you on that, okay?"

"Sure."

For the first time, Avery had a sense that whatever had happened to Ry had also affected HW quite deeply. Typically, he wasn't ready to share how he felt, and he might never open up to her. She hoped with all her heart that he found his peace and someone to share his life with. Under that high-gloss exterior, he and Ry weren't that much different after all.

"Ry's spotted us. How long do you think it will take him to get over here and interrupt?" HW said. "*Damn*, he's fast."

He stepped back and kissed Avery's hand. "Thanks for the dance."

"You're welcome, and good luck in the finals. We'll be in the stands cheering you on."

She hadn't been to Las Vegas for the finals since her accident, hadn't wanted to risk seeing anyone she knew live out her dreams. Ry put his arm around her shoulders and hugged her tight. She had new dreams now, and a different life, with so much to look forward to. Ry had helped her manage those few faltering steps to jump off the cliff and find her own kind of freedom. She liked to think she would've done it all by herself eventually, but the extra little push certainly hadn't hurt.

And even better . . . he'd been there to catch her.

A lone figure dressed in jeans and carrying a backpack was walking down the slope from the ranch house, toward the dance floor. Ry and HW noticed at the same time Avery did.

"Who's that?" HW asked.

"No one I know," Ry replied. "Is it one of the catering staff?"

"They're all in uniform, and none of them should be heading home yet," Avery said. "Or I'll want to know why."

Ry reclaimed her hand as she started back up the slope, and she was glad of the support. A whole day on her feet had killed her hip. The figure went still as they approached, and waited for them. Light glinted on hair as blond as the twins'.

"May I help you with something?" Ry called out.

The woman turned toward them and shifted her backpack onto one shoulder, her bright blue eyes widening at the sight of them.

"I'm so sorry, I didn't realize there was a wedding going on or I wouldn't have come."

Beside her the twins had gone equally still.

"Dad's eyes," Ry muttered.

"Yeah . . ." HW replied. "And our hair."

The woman cleared her throat. "From looking at you two, I think I must be in the right place. My name's Rachel Ford." She searched their faces. "Or it might once have been Rachel Morgan."

RUTH'S POT ROAST FOR RY

Ingredients

One 4- to 5-pound chuck roast
2 Tbs olive oil (or one tablespoon each olive oil and butter)
2 onions
6–8 carrots
Salt (optional)
Pepper to taste
1 cup red wine (beef broth can be substituted)
2–3 cups beef stock
3 sprigs fresh thyme, or 1 tsp dried
3 sprigs fresh rosemary, or 1 tsp dried

Instructions

Choose a nicely marbled piece of meat. This will enhance the flavor of your pot roast like nothing else. Salt and pepper your chuck roast and preheat the oven to 275° F.

Heat a large pot or Dutch oven over medium-high heat. Then add the olive oil (or butter and olive oil).

Cut two onions in half and cut carrots into 2-inch slices. When the oil in the pot is very hot (but not smoking), add in the halved onions, browning them on one side and then the other. Remove the onions to a plate.

Throw the carrots into the same very hot pan and toss them around until slightly browned, about a minute or so.

Place the meat in the pan and sear it for about a minute on all sides until it is nice and brown all over. Remove the roast to a plate.

With the burner still on medium-high, use either red wine or beef broth to deglaze the pan, scraping the bottom with a whisk to get all the flavor up.

When the bottom of the pan is sufficiently deglazed, place the roast back into the pan and add enough beef stock to cover the meat halfway. Add in the onion and the carrots, as well as rosemary and thyme.

Put the lid on, then roast in a 275° F. oven for 4 hours.